The Diplomatic Corpse

Anne Marshall Zwack

ISIS
LARGE PRINT
Oxford

First published in Great Britain 2007
by
John Murray (publishers), an Hachette Livre UK Company

Published in Large Print 2008 by ISIS Publishing Ltd.,
7 Centremead, Osney Mead, Oxford OX2 0ES
by arrangement with
John Murray (publishers), an Hachette Livre UK Company

British Library Cataloguing in Publication Data
Zwack, Anne Marshall
    The diplomatic corpse. – Large print ed.
    1. Revenge – Fiction
    2. Diplomats' spouses – Fiction
    3. Adultery – Fiction
    4. Large type books
    I. Title
    813.6 [F]

ISBN 978–0–7531–7988–8 (hb)
ISBN 978–0–7531–7989–5 (pb)

Printed and bound in Great Britain by
T. J. International Ltd., Padstow, Cornwall

To the Hungarian husband

Acknowledgements

I would like to thank my daughter-in-law Leonor Correa da Silva Zwack, my stepdaughter Iris Zwack, my good friends Tanja Star-Busmann, Elisabetta Michahelles, Kirsten Hadik, Idanna Pucci, Katharina Alles, Sissi Ago, Magda Zalan, Patricia Perini, Francesca Sepe, Nicholas Ingham and the late Alex de Gelsey, all of whom gave me valuable help, as well as members of the Diplomatic Corps of Great Britain who wish to remain anonymous. I would also like to thank Nicholas Perren and my wonderful editor, Kate Parkin.

1
VIENNA

By five o'clock the funeral was over. Maggie had sat through the whole ceremony in a daze. Her big husband had suddenly seemed so small in his oak coffin in the nave of the English Church in Vienna. It was the same with embassy Christmas trees, she had found herself thinking; they always looked smaller when they were delivered, lying all trussed up on the floor of the atrium before they were hoisted, branches spread wide, to the ceiling. At the end she had stood in the receiving line, just as she had done for so many years, side by side with Jeremy, in the cities where they were posted. She had shaken everybody's hand and said all the right things, her mind a blank.

It was the second secretary and his wife, Eileen, who brought Maggie home in their little brown Ford. The embassy car that Maggie and Jeremy had always used was now chauffeuring the acting ambassador, "I'll do my best to hold the fort," Mackintosh had said pompously to the man from the Foreign Office who had flown over especially for the service. Hilary Mackintosh had insisted on holding her hand throughout the proceedings. It was a rather damp hand, but Maggie had felt it would have been ungracious to withdraw hers. Like everyone else, she was just being kind.

3

"Would you like a cup of tea?" Eileen asked brightly as they came into the residence hall.

Maggie looked around her, at a loss. She started to pick at the fingers of the black cotton gloves which she had worn for the funeral. She belonged to a generation that wore gloves to church.

"Perhaps she'd rather have a brandy?" suggested the second secretary from his position on the doormat, cracking his knuckles nervously.

"Well, maybe a sherry would be nice," Maggie said.

The second secretary was immediately galvanized. Drinks were a matter for which he felt physically and mentally equipped. Consoling widows in these special circumstances was a task for which he had never been primed. He came back promptly from the drinks cabinet with a little glass of amber liquid. "Amontillado?" he asked Maggie, who murmured her thanks.

"You are all being so kind," she said. Indeed, everybody was being very kind.

"Would you like us to stay with you?" asked Eileen dutifully from the middle of the room, her little patent-leather handbag clutched in both hands.

"No, no, please don't bother. I'll be fine. Really I will. You've all been so very kind."

"But what about supper? You really should eat to keep up your strength."

"Oh, but I'm not at all hungry at the moment. Esmeralda always leaves plenty of food in the freezer when she goes away on holiday. Don't worry about me!" Maggie was secretly relieved that the cook was on her yearly holiday in Portugal. Esmeralda's grief would have been tumultuous and trying. By the time she came back in a day or two, Maggie thought she herself would feel strong enough to face her. For the time being, she wanted very much to be alone. She would let everything sink in, in solitude.

The couple retreated to the hall and stood uncertainly in the brash light of the chandelier. Maggie found herself thinking how many chandeliers had illuminated her life with Jeremy. It seemed to be an essential feature of embassy life wherever they were: Vienna, Budapest, Rome, Paris . . . all lit by a succession of sparkling crystals, a brightly lit world that allowed for no shadows or secret corners.

"Well, if you're quite sure . . ." said the second secretary, his hand on the doorknob.

"Take care, now," said Eileen.

The door closed with a tactful click behind them and Maggie was alone at last.

She took the glass of amontillado over to her usual chair. She had sat in this chair for three and a half years now, ever since Jeremy's posting to Vienna. On the other side of the hearth was the high-backed wing chair covered in moss-coloured velvet in which Jeremy had always sat when he came home from the embassy, his whisky and soda on a little coaster on the occasional table beside him. The chair was still dented with the hollows left by his stately frame. The standard lamp was unlit and shadows lurked in the velvet corners where her husband of twenty-five years had faced her every evening, his face a mask of mild disdain.

5

Jeremy had been an eminently able civil servant and he possessed in full measure all the attributes of the conventional diplomat. Vienna had been his first posting as an ambassador but there had been the strong possibility that in six months or so he would be sent to Washington as the final accolade to a distinguished career. He had been tall, elegant, his prematurely silver hair impeccably parted above a lofty forehead, his glass always held in the slightly effeminate hands with their soft palms, the light from the inevitable chandeliers glinting on his signet ring. A career diplomat, he looked and behaved much as one imagined an ambassador should. He always knew the right thing to say and never spoke out of turn. He knew that the worst thing for an ambassador was to make waves or exhibit signs of a flamboyant personality. Maggie had followed circumspectly in his wake, toeing the line and observing the rules, and Jeremy had been, in his undemonstrative way, proud of his pretty little wife dutifully shaking hands in the receiving line.

Now Maggie sat sipping her drink and the sherry warmed the parts of her that were frozen, except for her heart. Her feet hurt in the good shoes she had worn for the funeral. Her feet had always troubled her: she had acquired bunions from the pointed shoes she had worn as a teenager. She realized, with something akin to relief, that she was now free to kick them off without Jeremy raising his eyebrows from the moss-coloured velvet chair. Jeremy had always frowned on informality. Maggie was allowed slippers only in the bedroom. She kicked off her shoes and wiggled her toes. She looked at her watch. It was just after six. The evening yawned in front of her. In all these years there had always been something happening, a function nearly every evening: a National Day, a choir practice for the carol singers, the vernissage of a painter exhibiting at the British Council, the British Women's Club meeting to discuss the charity bazaar. In addition, Jeremy often had other commitments where her presence was not required. The evenings when she and her husband could eat quietly together at home in the residence were few. "Evening off, old thing," he would intone from the depths of the moss-covered velvet and she would have Esmeralda cook up some lamb chops and the cauliflower au gratin he liked, and they would share a bottle of Bordeaux. Jeremy liked his wine and had become quite a connoisseur during their various postings in wine-making countries all over Europe.

Darkness was falling outside. Maggie looked hard at the shadows gathering in the chair opposite her and began to wish she had not so glibly sent Eileen away. It was not Jeremy's presence that she missed; it was his absence that was so appalling. She thought of her mother, who had become a widow when Maggie was a little girl. "I felt as though a bomb had dropped," she had told her years later. Maggie had always been fascinated by a scrapbook her mother had kept during the war. There was one newspaper cutting in particular, showing a housing block in London that had been bombed. Bereft of its facade, with beds and cupboards and sideboards all jumbled higgledy-piggledy, it was exposed to the elements and to public view. Maggie's mother told her that there had been purple flowers growing up out of the rubble. That's how she felt too, she thought; the wall between her and the world had been brutally wrenched away, one whole flank now prey to the cruellest of draughts. Meanwhile, she kept waiting for the grief that didn't come. "I don't understand it, I can't feel anything at all," she had told Hilary Mackintosh earlier. "That's because you're in shock," the wife of the acting ambassador had said, giving her gloved hand a damp squeeze.

Maggie got up and walked over to Jeremy's desk in her stockinged feet. She really ought to call his sister in New Zealand. Isobel was only his half-sister and considerably older than Jeremy, and had had very little contact with him over the years, but it was only right that she should be informed. She tried to calculate what time it would be in New Zealand. Something like the same time only either yesterday or tomorrow. She looked at the neat piles of papers on Jeremy's desk, the visiting cards stacked on his blotter, his precise jottings on the pad near the telephone. His finicky neatness had always irritated Maggie, but now she suddenly felt a surge of unutterable tenderness as her gaze fell on his old-fashioned fountain pen resting in its accustomed groove. For the first time since Jeremy died she found herself in floods of tears; they poured down her cheeks like a monsoon rain, uncheckable and wetter than she could ever remember tears being. Hers had been the moistening of the eyes, the tickling of the nose, the quickly rectified downward turn of the lips, the stifled dry sob, never this watery onslaught that now caught her by surprise.

She sat down at the desk and stared through the rain at the jotting pad. Wet blots started spattering the few notes Jeremy had made in the days before he died. "Tell Z to take car to service" was one. "Greeks" was another. Today was the Greek National Day. In normal circumstances, Jeremy and Maggie would have been driven to the Greek residence, she in the uncomfortable shoes she had just kicked off by her chair, and stood in line until it was their turn to shake hands with the Greek ambassador and his plump little wife and their first secretary and the military attaché. Then they would have drunk a flute of pseudo champagne and eaten a little morsel wrapped in vine leaves and nodded at the Greek Orthodox cleric in his tall black hat, and briefly chatted with a few other fellow ambassadors before discreetly taking their leave. She idly wondered why he would have noted down "Florist". It was always his secretary who ordered the prim little flower arrangements they occasionally sent to thank or to condole. She began to look for his telephone book.

Mopping at the tears coursing down her face and neck with the pocket handkerchief she always kept tucked in her sleeve, she pulled out the little drawers one by one until she found it, the same worn black-leather book Jeremy had been using for as long as she could remember. His sister's name was under I for Isobel. He would call her every year at Christmas and there had been quite a few calls when their father had been terminally ill. She took a deep breath and carefully dialled the number. It took a while for the Viennese telephone to understand the enormity of the distance it was required to breach and then a foreign ringing sound could be heard a long way away. It rang for a long time. Maggie started to fear she was, perhaps, calling in the middle of the night.

"Hello," said a wavering voice at last.

"Isobel, is that you?"

"Yes, who is it?"

"Isobel, it's Maggie."

"Maggie, my goodness, where are you? You sound as though you were in the next room!"

"I'm in Vienna. Look, I'm sorry, but I have bad news."

There was a pause. "Jeremy?" asked the voice at the other end of the world.

"Yes. I'm afraid he died on Thursday."

Another pause. "Poor Jeremy. Was he ill?"

"Not that we knew of. He died of a heart attack at his desk."

"Who would have thought Jeremy would die before me?" said Isobel in a wondering voice. "Are you all right, my dear?"

"Oh, yes," said Maggie with a brittle matter-of-factness she didn't feel. "The funeral was today."

"Well, I'll have to rewrite my will," said Isobel. "I was going to leave everything to Jeremy. You know I don't have any other relatives left."

"Well, don't worry about that now. Just look after yourself. I think," said Maggie, her voice beginning to tremble, "I'll ring off now."

10

"Yes, yes, of course you must. Goodbye, my dear. Let me know if there is anything I can do." The line went dead and the silence was filled with the hollow sound of wind and waves.

Maggie picked up the telephone book and held the familiar covers in her hands for a while. She heaved a sigh. The crying had felt good and she felt almost refreshed. Finally, she had managed to do the right thing. Widows wept for their husbands, after all. She remembered how distraught the wife of the Spanish cultural attaché had been when her husband was knocked down by a tram. And she and Jeremy had been such a devoted couple; everybody said so. She blew her nose lengthily and noisily. There was nobody to hear. The silence in the room was overpowering. The only sound was a faint rushing noise coming from the fridge in the little kitchen. As she replaced the telephone book in the drawer she noticed a number of Moleskine notebooks neatly stacked at the back which she didn't remember seeing before. She was about to close the drawer when on impulse she picked up the top notebook and flicked through the pages. A diary! Of course. Jeremy had always been jotting down his thoughts. "One day I'll make you famous," he once told her jokingly. "I'll write my memoirs and you'll be the next Lady Diana Cooper!" She began to read.

4 OCTOBER. Mackintosh leaves for Montenegro. Shirley is off work until Monday. Met Eisenberger at the American embassy. Seems to think there

might be a chance of an IBM deal. Spent 450
schillings on new pyjamas for Venice.

When was he thinking of going to Venice, she
wondered. She couldn't remember the subject coming
up. She flicked over a couple of pages. As memoirs
these would not find many publishers.

8 OCTOBER. Called Mausie. Not free until next
week.

Who on earth was Mausie? Didn't Mausie mean
mouse?

12 OCTOBER. Met Mausie at the Sacher. Tafelspitz
and a good Gewürztraminer. Mausie had shrimp.
** The ministry asking for financial report. Call
Mackintosh.

What were the two asterisks for? Could Mausie be a
nickname for someone in the Viennese foreign
ministry? None of them looked particularly like a
rodent, as far as she could remember. More porcine
faces lined their dining-room table whenever she and
Jeremy entertained. The minister himself, with his
hairy nostrils and prominent teeth, looked rather more
like a wild boar than a mouse, but maybe that was the
name for him in the British secret service. They were
always hiding behind initials and passwords and
nicknames.

15 OCTOBER. Mausie joins me at the Wildrösslstüberl on the Danube. Our favourite trout. Grüner Veltliner so-so. Lovely afternoon.*

This time only one asterisk followed the entry. Clearly Mausie must be someone from MI5. That would explain why Jeremy had never mentioned him.

20 OCTOBER. Mausie in blue. Usual place. Mausie had deep-fried octopus but complained they were chewier than usual. Splurged on champagne for once.*

One asterisk. Obviously, this was in code.

22 OCTOBER. Went to the little Beisl near the Stephans Platz. Mausie loved the scarf but peeved about the pickled herrings. Both had a tankard of beer.

These fish were obviously weapon deployments or something. Jeremy had been much involved in disarmament lately.

23 OCTOBER.

Maggie's birthday, which Jeremy had missed, away for a few days in Brussels on a conference.

Picked Mausie up at her apartment and drove to the Attersee. Rained the whole time. Mausie ate rainbow trout every evening and was in splendid form. This Kracher makes very good wines.***

Three asterisks! *Her* apartment? Mausie is a female agent? And why wasn't Jeremy in Brussels?

With the icy sloth of a melting glacier, a hint of doubt began to insinuate its way into Maggie's consciousness. Then, the trusting complacency of twenty-five years abruptly crumbled like a biscuit under an unheeding heel. She felt the hand holding the notebook start to tremble uncontrollably and her tongue, suddenly large and unwieldy, sticking to the roof of her mouth.

It was to be a long night. Maggie unplugged the telephone, then took all the little notebooks out of the drawer and rearranged them in chronological order, year by year. She started at the beginning, three and a half years ago, and worked her way through fifty-five notebooks until the day before Jeremy died. Mausie was first mentioned quite early on. Sandwiched between memoranda about social occasions and instructions to Mackintosh and to Zoltan, his chauffeur, Jeremy had noted down every rendezvous with the insatiable fish-eating Mausie. The entries were inevitably followed by a string of asterisks, the significance of which slowly permeated the ingenuous fluff of Maggie's mind. She realized with a shock that she could not remember their last asterisk. Could it have been after the New Year's Eve party at the Peruvian residence? Soon after he met her, Mausie's birthday is celebrated with lobster —

lobster! An unheard of luxury in her life with Jeremy — and he even comments on how sexy she is as she licks the butter off her fingers!

Rage started mounting in Maggie and, together with the amontillado, it made her head feel bulbous and glowing like a Belisha beacon. She glared at her reflection in the mirror above the mantelpiece and found herself fighting with an irrepressible urge to shatter its unclouded surface with one of the fire irons. But it was government property; everything was government property, even she and Jeremy had belonged to the government for all these years . . .

At one point Jeremy and Mausie appear to be in Rome. That must have been when Maggie's mother was dying and she was staying with her sister, Sue, in Herefordshire. In her time of need, he had been cavorting in Rome? This was something that really cut to the bone. Mausie is being taken to the restaurant which had been their favourite when Jeremy was posted in Italy. Maggie wondered if the waiters had changed since then, because surely they would have remembered her and noticed that Jeremy was not dining with his wife. Giuseppe, for instance. Surely he would have raised an eyebrow? How many other people had seen him with Mausie, she wondered. Did the office know? It was hard to keep things like this secret in an embassy. Had there been nudges and pitying glances behind her back? Why is it that a cuckolded spouse is always somewhat of a figure of fun? And then here they are buying shoes at Ferragamo! While she had had to economize on the uncomfortable pair she wore to National Days and her husband's funeral.

A meeting with Mausie is noted down in Jeremy's journal at least once a week. In between there are telephone calls, of which he records cryptic passages. Mausie has been to a concert, she has been sent flowers. Ha, the florist! And tuberoses to boot. She has met someone from the embassy at her gym class. She has cut her hair in a fetching way. They have seen a film together in the afternoon. Well, that was something Mausie was welcome to: Maggie and Jeremy had not shared the same taste in films. Maggie preferred the more romantic, while he favoured gory battle scenes and science-fiction fantasies. Except this film is shown at a vintage movie theatre and sounds French Nouvelle Vague — how strange.

During their first winter in Vienna, Jeremy even goes skiing with Mausie for a week in Kitzbühel! That must have been when he said he was in London for consultations. She remembered now. Even at the time she had queried that a week seemed a long time and he had said he would take advantage of the trip to visit his father. For once Mausie seems to favour fondue over fish and they drink their wine hot and spicy, as *glühwein*, in the mountain huts. Neither Maggie nor Jeremy were expert skiers; they had had little opportunity. But no doubt Mausie, being Austrian, was born on skis and looked tanned and gorgeous in tight-fitting ski pants posing on the snow-clad slopes. Oh, the unfairness of it all!

16

Maggie had never felt inadequate before. She had felt competent to behave decorously as Jeremy's wife in public and comfortably ensconced in her private role; and, from the rare compliments he tossed her way, she had always been confident that she was doing all the right things. Now she was confronted with the fact that she had evidently been found wanting. Mausie clearly had had much to offer that she had not. Perhaps she had been taking her husband for granted. Perhaps she had let herself go a little lately as she slid into middle age. She no longer had the svelte figure of the young girl who had married Jeremy, dazzled by his elegance, his erudition, his glowing future career. Maybe it was true what they said in magazines: that one should wear lacy underwear and use expensive face creams. Her Marks & Spencer underthings and nightly smearing of Nivea were obviously lacking in charisma. She could always go on a diet now that official embassy dining was a thing of the past. On the other hand, what was the point, if Jeremy was no longer there to see the difference?

If only Jeremy wasn't dead. She could have interrogated him, reproached him, flung her resentment in his face. If he had been there in front of her now she could have stamped on the toes of his shiny lace-up shoes, she could have climbed up on a footstool and ruffled the immaculate silver hair, she could have smashed the mild disdain off his face with one of his golfing trophies.

Maggie at last fell asleep on the sofa, exhausted and not a little drunk. Her last thought as she closed her eyes was that, unlike her husband, Mausie was presumably still alive . . .

That night, Maggie dreamed that she was taking part in a joust. At the opposite end of the field was Mausie, mounted on a killer whale. Jeremy's chauffeur, Zoltan, was helping Maggie onto her charger, which was the largest horse she had ever seen, and she felt quite dizzy when she looked down from the saddle at the green grass far below. Jeremy was seated in the grandstand, but Maggie couldn't help noticing that he didn't look his usual self at all. Bloated and oval, her late husband looked uncannily like Humpty Dumpty. Mausie had crimson plumes in her helmet and the sunshine was glancing off her breastplate.

"Hilary," cried Maggie in anguish to the wife of the acting ambassador, who was hovering near by holding a towel, "I don't have a breastplate!"

"Yes, you do," said Hilary soothingly. "You're just in shock."

A bell rang and the two jousters faced each other. Suddenly Jeremy stood up and fell out of the grandstand, smashing into pieces. Maggie woke up. The bell was still ringing for the joust to begin. It took her a full minute to realize that it was the doorbell that had been ringing insistently for some time. She stumbled up and quickly smoothed her hair in the gilded mirror above the fireplace.

"*Wer ist da?*" she asked in the basic German she had picked up in the last three and a half years.

"Modome, it's Zoltan," came the gruff answer from the other side of the residence door. "I tried to call but your telephone isn't working." Zoltan stood on the doormat looking hangdog and solemn, his moustache even more drooping than usual. He seemed at a loss for the right thing to say. In one hand he carried a stiff little bouquet of orange zinnias. It was so Hungarian to bring flowers, Maggie thought. Zoltan stuck out his hand formally and bowed slightly, with an almost imperceptible clicking of heels. "Kiss the hand," he said gravely.

He was clearly deeply affected by the loss not only of the ambassador, but inevitably of his job as a chauffeur as well. He had followed Jeremy from their first posting on the Continent, in Budapest. At first he had not been officially employed by the embassy as Jeremy's status had not warranted a chauffeur of his own. Jeremy had hired him as a private proposition when he developed problems with his vision, especially at night, and could no longer drive a car. Back in those days, it had not been easy to obtain a permit for Zoltan to leave Hungary when Jeremy was posted to Rome. Jeremy had sometimes wondered if Zoltan had not been let out of the country in order that he could act as a spy on embassy activities in Western Europe. But, somehow, over the years Zoltan had managed to dispel any such suspicions and make himself invaluable. He learned the short cuts in every city in Europe within days, was infinitely resourceful and could fix and mend everything and anything that came his way. Other members of the embassy came to rely on his multifarious expertise. Whenever a problem arose beyond his ken he had a stock phrase, wherever they were: "I have a friend." He was the soul of discretion but also an unfailing source of information and reliable gossip, which could be of vital interest to a diplomat navigating his way in a new embassy in a country that was not his own. By the time Jeremy was sent to Paris as minister, Zoltan had become a bona fide employee of the British Foreign Service.

"What will happen to you, Zoltan?" Maggie asked.

Zoltan's eyes rolled upwards towards the ceiling. "Nobody has said anything yet," he said, "but I don't think they'll need me any more."

"What will you do?"

"I could go home to Hungary, I suppose. Things are much better there now."

Maggie made them both a coffee in the little kitchenette she and Jeremy had had installed in their private apartment so they did not to have to go two flights down to the main kitchen. In all the years they had spent together, Zoltan had never refused a coffee, which he drank strong and black while smoking a smelly cigarette.

"I brought boxes from the embassy," he said after the last puff, as he stubbed out the damp tip in the ashtray. "Shirley thought you'd rather not empty all the ambassador's drawers yourself. There were some clothes as well. Shall I bring them up?"

While Zoltan was in the garage, Maggie went into the shower. She stood under the gushing water, revelling, despite herself, in its warmth and invigorating pressure. Wrapped in her towel, she stared at herself in the mirror. She looked awful, she thought; her eyes swollen, her skin pasty. On the other hand, that was probably how a widow was supposed to look. She had to admit, however, that grieving had given way to something more like rage and there was nothing widow-like about the fierce glint in her blue eyes as she quickly dressed and brushed her hair. The doorbell rang again. She took a last look at herself in the mirror, squared her jaw and defiantly applied her reddest lipstick. Maggie was now ready to face Zoltan and the world.

There were six large cardboard boxes containing what seemed to be files and notebooks and dictionaries and pen-holders and the collection of silver frames featuring Jeremy's many encounters with the famous and powerful of this world. Zoltan reverently laid a loden coat over the back of a chair and put a spare pair of shiny lace-up shoes underneath. Jeremy's rolled umbrella he propped against the door jamb. In his hand he also carried a shopping bag.

"I'll go through all that later," said Maggie, suddenly feeling crushed and oddly breathless at the realization that the owner of all this paraphernalia was quite simply no longer there, furled away for ever as neatly as his Briggs' umbrella. There was a chilling sense, bordering on panic, that here she was, alone, with no one to buffer her from the world outside.

She had lived for the last twenty-five years in the shadow of a person who had perhaps existed only in her mind. But however much of a blackguard he had turned out to be, his tall elegant figure had loomed large between her and the aggravations and fears of everyday life. In all these years she had rarely had to drive a car, post a letter, iron a shirt, pay a bill or make a decision more important than what she was going to wear or serve at dinner. The embassy staff took care of everything. Hers was not to wonder why; the Foreign Office assumed the task of dictating all the big decisions and a lot of the small ones in her life. She could not even change the slip-covers on an armchair without asking their permission. She had lived wherever they had sent her, in the houses they had chosen, waited on by staff hired by someone else. Freedom of any kind was by now totally foreign to her nature. The few choices open to them in their private lives had been Jeremy's to make. Only now was she alone, truly alone for the first time; she was free to take decisions. She felt as though she was standing on tiptoe on the edge of a precipice and dared not look down.

Zoltan was on his knees plugging in the telephone on the desk. When it started ringing right away, they both jumped.

"Thank goodness! I thought your telephone wasn't working!" It was Shirley, who had been Jeremy's personal assistant. "Lots of people have been trying to get through. Mrs Mackintosh was particularly concerned."

"I'm sorry," said Maggie. "I unplugged it in the night."

"I thought you might like Zoltan to drive you around for the next few days," Shirley continued. "I thought perhaps you might want to go to the bank and things like that. Tie up a few loose ends."

"How long can I stay here?" asked Maggie, suddenly aware that some sort of action would be required of her.

"Oh, don't bother about that," said Shirley briskly. "They won't have another ambassador for ages, I'm sure. It was all so unexpected. I'm sure you can stay as long as you like. As soon as Esmeralda gets back she can start helping you pack up and we can send people over from the embassy too, to lend a hand."

The bank sounded like a good idea. Maggie had only a couple of hundred schillings in her purse. Zoltan ceremoniously held open the front door and then followed her into the lift down to the garage. They had allotted her the number two embassy car, the dark red Rover. Really everybody was being so kind. She must call Michael Mackintosh when she got back and thank him.

Maggie had always travelled in the back of the car with Jeremy, but today, by a sort of tacit agreement, it seemed natural to climb into the front seat next to Zoltan.

"Who was it who found Jeremy?" she asked suddenly as they drove into the centre of Vienna.

Zoltan made an elaborate show of adjusting the heating buttons and directing the hot air to their feet. "Shirley," he said at last. "It was in the office."

"I thought someone said it was the cleaning lady," Maggie ventured.

"Shirley and the cleaning lady together," said Zoltan with a note of finality. He changed gears loudly. "They say the weather is changing for the worse," he said. Zoltan, Maggie had discovered over the years, delighted in bearing bad news. His weather forecasts were invariably dire.

The people at the bank were very kind and assiduous with offers of coffee and biscuits and mineral water and a new desk diary for the coming year. The preliminaries out of the way, it soon became apparent that, on top of the small inheritance from his father, which he had invested and which yielded good dividends, Jeremy had accumulated quite a sizeable capital over the years. He had had the foresight to invest it in both of their names. He had transferred part of his account and stock portfolio to this private bank in Vienna as, he explained to her, it was unwise to have all one's eggs in one basket.

The penny-pinching she had been encouraged to pursue during their many postings had evidently paid off. She owned shares, she discovered, and the cautious investments in which Jeremy had engaged had shown a gratifying profit. The extravagances involved in wining and dining Mausie had not made significant inroads into the number of noughts at the bottom of the line of figures. With that in mind, Maggie asked if she could cash a cheque there and then and, not without qualms, signed her name under a sum of a magnitude she would never have dared to withdraw from their joint account before Jeremy's demise. She had no idea at the moment what she intended to spend it on. She could hardly concentrate on the measured tones of the bank manager gently showing her bewildering sheaves of papers. Between Maggie and the page a female form kept insinuating itself, acquiring new features all the time. Blonde and blue-eyed, the face had high cheekbones and glossy lips, she licked her fingertips with a clink of bangles, ankles crossed and slim feet in shoes with tapering toes.

"Thank you, it's so kind of you to take so much trouble," Maggie murmured and left with a bulging wallet and her share portfolio under her arm.

They went shopping at Meinl's, Zoltan pushing the trolley. Maggie suddenly realized that she was terribly hungry and everything looked so tempting at the cheese counter, with the oozing Brie and the flaky Parmesan, and at the delicatessen, with its Parma ham and different kinds of olives and sun-dried tomatoes and all sorts of exotic things she had never bought before. She paused at the fish counter, where a lobster was valiantly trying to climb out of its box and heaps of chewy octopuses wallowed in black ink, only to stride resolutely past. They piled everything into the back of the Rover.

"Where to now, Modome?" asked Zoltan.

Maggie couldn't think of what to do next. She was so unused to free time, unused to not having to check her watch, to meet Jeremy at a "preordained venue", as places were always referred to in the embassy. She looked questioningly at Zoltan. The streets of Vienna suddenly seemed full of pretty blonde girls with blue eyes and glossy lips, tripping down the pavements in pointed-toed shoes. Maggie looked down at the uncompromising flat pumps she had donned that morning. "I think I'd like to go shopping," she said.

Walking down the Kärtnerstrasse and looking in the shop windows, Maggie slowly shed the lingering feeling of guilt that for once she was not usefully employed and began to feel on holiday. She celebrated with a *Melange* and a *Topfenstrudel* at one of the pavement cafes. She made her way into every shoe shop on the street, becoming braver and braver as she went and more and more reckless as she tried on more and more outrageously priced shoes. "I think I'll keep them on," Maggie told the suave young sales assistant, as she made her final choice. Who was it who wore red shoes, she wondered, the image jogging her memory. Why, Marie Antoinette, of course, when she mounted the scaffold. She made her way as fast as she could on her new heels back to Zoltan and the car, stricken with remorse that he had been waiting for so long. He was dozing in the front seat, a sports paper on his knee, his moustache fluttering with every sonorous breath. He woke up with a start.

"I'm so sorry to have kept you waiting," she said and then, sheepishly triumphant, she wiggled her toes in the soft red leather that smelled gratifyingly new. "I bought some new shoes." This was information Maggie would not normally have shared with Zoltan, but it was too exhilarating to keep to herself.

Zoltan looked down at Maggie's feet in silence as she climbed into the seat beside him.

"Perhaps they're a bit much?" Maggie queried, instantly doubtful as she calculated that with the price of her new red shoes she could have bought an aeroplane ticket to Paris. *Aller*, she thought, pointing her left foot, and *Retour*, extending her right. "Oh, dear," she said.

"Not at all, Modome," said Zoltan as he eased the car away from the kerb. "I think they are very nice shoes."

Zoltan helped her with her packages up to the door of her apartment and then took his leave, muttering about something he had to do at the embassy. Maggie unpacked all her provisions and ate the whole slice of Brie standing up in the kitchen. She went into the larder, brought out a bottle of Bordeaux and poured some into a tumbler. These were all things that Jeremy would have found in appallingly bad form. She took a large gulp from the glass and carried it into the drawing room, glancing at herself in the looking glass over the fireplace. It was amazing what a pair of frivolous new shoes could do for the morale. Maggie felt buoyed up by the rage fomenting within. Little incidents, insignificant at the time, now came back to bruise her like the blow of a blunt instrument, little lies and subterfuges and nagging coincidences. Whole episodes in her life with Jeremy suddenly took on a new light. She took another gulp of Bordeaux.

Another blank afternoon stretched in front of her. Maggie looked around the room. It was a pretty room; she had always had a knack of making their various residences pleasant to live in and Jeremy had often praised her for what he called her "flair". They had argued only about the pictures, which Jeremy insisted on hanging far too high up on the wall. Maggie flicked the message button on the telephone. A number of people had called with condolences and offers of assistance. There were two calls from her sister, Sue. She decided she couldn't face talking to any of them now. She could hear the cleaning lady, Mrs Lebowski, hoovering the reception rooms downstairs. Sooner or later she would have to descend and accept her formal condolences and listen to the litany of misfortunes which were a leitmotiv in Mrs Lebowski's daily life. She supposed she could start gathering her personal odds and ends from the occasional tables. She really ought to call Michael Mackintosh.

It was Shirley who answered the telephone. Her voice took on the reverential tone she had been adopting around Maggie ever since Jeremy died. "Oh, how *are* you?" she wanted to know.

"Thank you, quite well in the circumstances," Maggie replied in her little-woman-soldiering-on voice. "I wanted to thank Mr Mackintosh for being so kind and lending me the car and Zoltan for the next few days. It'll be a godsend."

"I'm afraid Mr Mackintosh is out at the moment," said Shirley. "I'll be sure to tell him you called."

"You've been such a help too," said Maggie. "It must have been a terrible shock for you to find Jeremy like that . . ."

"Oh, but I'd already left," said Shirley. "It was just after eight o'clock."

"But nobody told me until nine!"

"Well, they had to call the doctor and try to resuscitate him, maybe that's why."

"Who's they?"

"Zoltan found him. I thought you knew."

Maggie felt the now familiar ice sliding downwards like fingers kneading her heart, and her tongue began to thicken once again. "Oh, yes, of course, how silly of me. It's all been such a terrible muddle."

"Yes, of course it has," said Shirley soothingly. "Now you take care of yourself. Let us know if there is anything you need."

"Was it Dr Benton who came?" Maggie asked.

"I believe so," but Shirley sounded vague.

"Well, thank you again for everything." Maggie put down the receiver and reached in the drawer for Jeremy's telephone book. There were two telephone calls she urgently wanted to make.

The first was to Dr Benton. His secretary passed her on to him straight away. "Maggie," his voice was warm and comforting, "I've been thinking about you a lot."

"I'd just like to know a little more about how Jeremy died," said Maggie.

"Well," said Dr Benton slowly, "it was pretty instantaneous, you know. I don't think he had time to realize what was happening."

"I was just wondering why nobody told me immediately."

"Well, I suppose everybody was in a panic." Dr Benton cleared his throat. "Calling an ambulance takes time."

"Yes, of course, that must have been why. Everybody was in a panic." Maggie's head was beginning to pound.

"Let me know if you need anything," said Dr Benton.

"Thank you," said Maggie automatically, "you've all been very kind."

The second call was to Zoltan.

"We need to talk," Maggie told him, "right now!"

Maggie stuffed Jeremy's boxes into the spare room and hung his loden coat in the hall cupboard. She left the umbrella where it was. The carrier bag was still on the sofa where Zoltan had left it. Inside was a pair of brand-new pyjamas in a lilac and grey stripe. Venice, she thought with fury.

"Modome, it's me, Zoltan," he said, wiping his feet with elaborate care as he came in.

"Zoltan," said Maggie, trying hard to keep her voice steady, "I think the time has come for a moment of truth."

"Truth?" Zoltan's eyes rolled in panic and he looked over his shoulder, only to find the passage barred by an alarmingly determined Maggie, standing six inches taller in her new red shoes.

"Where, would you kindly tell me, did you find my husband?"

"I told you, he was found in the office. Shirley and —"

"Zoltan! I know all about Mausie."

"Mausie. You do. I see." Zoltan swayed from one leg to the other, the picture of misery. "Well, then, you know."

"Know what?"

"About where the ambassador died." Zoltan looked as though he was about to cry.

"Because he died with Mausie?"

"Well, you could say that, yes."

"In bed with Mausie?"

"They would have been in the bedroom, yes."

"And Mausie called you?"

"Mrs Morgenstern called me, yes, that's correct."

"And you called Dr Benton?"

"Yes."

"And Dr Benton called the ambulance?"

"Yes."

"And you all met at Mrs Morgenstern's apartment?"

"Yes."

"And you all went to the hospital?"

"No, Mrs Morgenstern stayed behind."

"And then you called Mr Mackintosh?"

"Yes."

"And Mr Mackintosh called me?"

"Yes, that's what Mr Mackintosh would have done, yes."

For a moment Maggie relented. "I'll make you a coffee," she said.

Zoltan sipped his coffee in silence and lit up his smelly cigarette. Maggie waited until he had stubbed it out. He unfailingly screwed it down into the ashtray and made it turn a couple of circles before he was convinced that it was effectively extinguished.

"Zoltan, I have a proposition to make you," she said. "You are going to help me get my own back on Mausie. I am going to employ you at your usual salary for as long as it takes."

Zoltan's moustache visibly bristled in alarm. "I can't break the law, Modome, I can't. I have only a temporary permit and if —"

"I shall not be asking you to break the law."

Zoltan looked relieved.

"Only a little bit."

Zoltan lit another cigarette.

"You are going to show me where Mausie lives."

"I think it's going to rain," said Zoltan weakly.

They drove down the Rennweg and took a right turn into a street opposite the Belvedere. Zoltan came to a halt outside a tall facade with a big wooden front door, but he left the engine running. "Modome," he pleaded, "I really don't think you should go up there. Mrs Morgenstern —"

"Don't worry. I'm not going to make a scene. Which are her windows?"

Zoltan pointed at a row of handsome windows along the second floor. Thick draperies could be glimpsed scalloped above the windows.

"Did the ambassador have a key?"

Zoltan looked even more alarmed. "Yes, I suppose he would have done. I wouldn't know."

"And where would those keys be?"

"They must be with the things I brought back from the embassy."

"Then we'd better go back and look for them."

Maggie strode out of the lift with Zoltan lagging behind. She went straight to the spare bedroom and emptied one of the boxes onto the bed: small change and pens and drawing pins and ink cartridges spread out over the bedspread as well as a number of bunches of keys. Maggie recognized those for their own front door. She pointed to the other key rings and looked at Zoltan.

"These are the office keys," he said, picking up a batch hanging from a miniature gold golf ball Maggie had given Jeremy for his birthday. Another bunch appeared to be attached to a silver dolphin.

"And those?" she asked.

Zoltan's Adam's apple jerked convulsively.

"Those must be Mrs Morgenstern's." Maggie swept them into her handbag.

"But, Modome, you can't just walk in there and —"

"Don't worry," she said, "I have no intention of embarrassing you. I want you to find out exactly when Mrs Morgenstern is going to be away for a while. Only then will we use these keys."

That night it was a long time before Maggie fell asleep. She tossed and turned, images crowding her mind as she plotted her revenge on the iniquitous Mausie. She concocted scenarios where she would confront Mausie on her own turf. Mausie would come home to find Maggie ensconced in an armchair, her ankles neatly crossed. Maggie would be wearing the green dress that Jeremy had always liked, which would look even better now with her new red shoes. Maybe she would be a little slimmer by then. "What are you doing in my house?" Mausie would ask, to which she would reply: "What were you doing in my husband's bed?"

Time and time again, Maggie would pulverize the unfortunate woman with the diamond edge of a number of cutting repartees. In one scene, she bumped into Mausie at the opera. Maggie never went to the opera because Jeremy had always said it was too expensive, but on this occasion she was even attending a premiere. Somebody introduced them. "Oh, do you know Mausie Morgenstern?" Maggie graciously inclined her head and turned towards the male figure escorting Mausie. "Someone else's husband, I presume?"

As the night wore on, when her sleepy thoughts merged into a sort of dreamy oblivion, the encounters with Mausie degenerated somewhat. The two women met casually on the Kärtnerstrasse. Maggie was looking very glamorous in a fur hat. No, she wasn't. She didn't have a fur hat and anyway she didn't believe in fur. "Oh, look," she said to her companion — who could it be? Maybe the wife of the Peruvian ambassador — "there's my husband's little whore." "I am not a little whore," an outraged Mausie would say. "Oh, no, I know you aren't." Then came Maggie's punchline: "You're a big whore!" As sleep finally overcame her, she was battering Mausie's scalp with the heel of a bright red Ferragamo shoe.

Mausie was always beautiful in these reveries; for some reason it made the betrayal less hurtful than if she had been a plain and plump little woman. However, Maggie was dimly aware that none of these enactments was in the least realistic and it was not until she at last fell fast asleep that the perfect solution came to her in a dream.

Maggie woke late next morning. Her hand strayed, as it had every morning during her marriage to Jeremy, towards his side of the bed. Wherever they had slept, whether in the early days in Washington or later in London, Rome, Paris, Vienna or Budapest, Maggie had always lain on Jeremy's right side. The chill between the sheets brought Maggie brusquely into the present. Ever since Jeremy died there had been those few seconds' limbo upon awakening when life was reassuringly the same as it had always been, before reality hit her with a sickening suddenness. Once again, she withdrew hurriedly from the edge of the precipice. She was alone; tentatively, she let out a loud fart and lay there marvelling at her sheer audacity. All by herself on the right side of the bed, she relished the novelty of the thought that this was a day when nobody expected anything of her: no lunches, no meetings, no Esmeralda to contend with. She was free to do whatever she wanted. Freedom, she decided, might not be such a frightening prospect after all. As she made herself a cup of tea in the little kitchen, she started to work out the details of the impending nemesis of the unsuspecting Mausie.

When Jeremy was alive, the mornings had been her favourite time. He was an early riser and climbed out of bed at the first shrill summons of the alarm clock. Maggie would lie propped on the pillows with her cup of tea and listen to the sound of splashing and whistling from the tub. Unlike Maggie, Jeremy had always preferred wallowing in hot water to brisk showers. He favoured old-fashioned music-hall songs like "The Man Who Broke the Bank at Monte Carlo" or "Mad Dogs and Englishmen". Lately, she realized, with a stab of fury, he had been humming a Viennese *Fiakerlied*. Then came the loud wet suction noise of a large body emerging from the suds and Jeremy could be glimpsed through the open door of the bathroom, a towel around his waist, lathering shaving cream onto his pink cheeks. Jeremy had never used an electric razor; the one she had given him for Christmas a few years ago was still in its box. Sometimes he would make an appearance, shaving brush in hand, if a thought had occurred to him: "You won't forget my dinner jacket is at the cleaner's, will you, my dear?" He would leave, impeccably suited, his highly polished shoes clonking on the parquet floor, his sober tie matching his socks, the fragrance of his favourite Floris soap wafting in his wake. "See you this evening, then," he would say, as he had every morning for the last twenty-five years.

How reassuring rituals were, Maggie thought, as she sipped her tea. Jeremy had thought that Earl Grey tea bags were common and drank only a special blend of his own specially shipped from Fortnum's to wherever they were posted. Maggie had never liked surprises or sudden changes in routine. For her, sameness and the status quo spelled contentment, days melting into days without untoward jolts or hiccups in their progress; she had never questioned the firmness of the surface on which she walked. She had thought that life would go on like this for ever and she had been convinced that Jeremy also felt the same way. It was evident she had seriously miscalculated and he was no longer there to ask. It was maddeningly too late now.

Zoltan was at her door punctually at nine. She noticed he no longer wore the dark suit and navy-blue tie that had been his uniform as Jeremy's chauffeur. Today he looked more like a gloomy cowboy in a checked shirt and brand-new jeans that had been hemmed as though he were planning on a growth spurt or feared that they might shrink drastically in the wash. His feet were enclosed in pale grey loafers with a woven motif over the insteps, the unmistakably Eastern European touch. He was stroking his moustache with the long fingernail of his little finger, something that had always irritated Jeremy. "What does he need such a long fingernail for? To dig the wax out of his ears or as a screwdriver?"

Zoltan stubbed out his cigarette. "Mrs Morgenstern went on holiday for two weeks as of today."

"How do you know?"

"She called and said that she still had the ambassador's briefcase. She wanted me to come and collect it."

"So you went round to pick it up?"

"Yes, yesterday evening."

"How did she look?" Maggie couldn't resist asking.

"Much the same as ever," was Zoltan's non-committal reply.

"Pretty and elegantly dressed?"

"Yes, I suppose so. She looked tired."

"Ah." Maggie would have liked to ask more but desisted. "Is there anybody else in the apartment?"

"Only Fatima, but Mrs Morgenstern said she was giving her a holiday. That's why I had to go and pick up the briefcase yesterday, before they both left."

Fatima! So that's where Esmeralda's cousin had ended up. Jeremy had asked Esmeralda if she knew of anyone who could come and do for a colleague of his. Maggie felt the now-familiar hot rush of rage. If Fatima worked for Mausie, then Esmeralda knew everything. Once again, this conspiracy of silence was like a suffocating cushion surrounding her.

"We are going out to buy fish, Zoltan," said Maggie with a dangerous glint in her eye, "lots of fish."

Maggie had always loved markets, everywhere they had been posted, unlike Jeremy, who had preferred the hygienic efficiency of the major supermarkets. She loved chatting with the people behind the stalls, especially those who had come in from the country and wore headscarves and had red hands smelling of carbolic soap. She loved the sounds, the sense of excitement, the banter and camaraderie of the vendors, loud and theatrical in their gestures and tone, the off-colour jokes she didn't fully understand. They made her feel one of them, not an ambassador's wife protected by a screen of protocol from real life. The Naschmarkt was one of her particular favourites, with its rows of low-roofed stalls and people stamping their feet in the early morning chill, their breath ballooning out in front of them. She walked slowly up and down, feasting her eyes on the fish laid out on slabs. She had brought a very large basket with her, but it clearly would not be big enough. Maggie proceeded to be more wantonly extravagant than she had ever been in her entire life. Formerly, she had always weighed the pros and cons of every purchase and, even when sorely tempted, the cons had inevitably had the upper hand. Indeed, Jeremy had always complimented her on her parsimoniousness.

Piles of shellfish and octopus, their tendrils slithering out from the paper, were weighed and packaged up together with rainbow-scaled mackerel and trout, two giant lobsters which she chose from the deep freeze so that they would not try scrambling out of her basket, and knobbly string sacks of mussels and clams. She could feel Zoltan's disapproval rising like steam off his bony shoulders weighed down by her shopping bags. At the end of the last counter a very large carp caught her eye. It looked as though, rather than being hooked by a fisherman, it had died of natural causes, its eyes veiled by cataracts and a sort of growth sprouting from the corners of its mouth. "*Und das auch,*" she told the fishmonger in his striped apron. They didn't have a large enough bag for the carp and, like a baby in her arms, Maggie stiffly carried it to the car, with a silently mutinous Zoltan following a few steps behind. They filled the boot of the car with their purchases.

"Would you please drive me to Mrs Morgenstern's?" said Maggie firmly.

There were so many questions that Maggie would have liked to ask Zoltan, but years of training held her back. Jeremy had frowned on any fraternizing with the staff and his own conversations with Zoltan had focused exclusively on the traffic and the weather. Maggie decided to start off the conversation on a safe footing. "It looks as though it might clear up," she said, looking innocently at the looming clouds.

"They have forecast rain for the whole weekend," was Zoltan's wooden reply.

Maggie took a deep breath. "You must know this route very well," she hazarded, feeling very daring.

"I know my way around, yes."

"I mean, you must have come here very often?"

"Quite often, yes."

"You must have got pretty bored waiting all that time in the car."

"I didn't have to wait. The ambassador always sent me away."

"I see." There was a long pause. "And then he rang you to ask you to come and fetch him when —" Maggie suddenly felt a little queasy — "it was over?"

"Yes."

There was another long pause. They sat side by side waiting for the traffic lights to change.

"But sometimes you took them both to a restaurant?" Maggie felt as though she were on a downhill slope, but at this point she might as well slide to the bottom.

"Sometimes we were joined by Mrs Morgenstern, yes."

Mausie had sat in her seat in the car! Her place, on Jeremy's right side. Maggie rolled down the window and let the breeze cool her cheeks. Zoltan was parking with elaborate care. As she slowly got out of the car, Maggie realized that she and Zoltan had tentatively crossed a demarcation line.

In the tall vaulted entrance hall Maggie felt a quiver of misgiving. It was the same feeling of excitement and dread that she had as a little girl when she was about to do something very naughty. She looked over her shoulder at Zoltan stoically walking in her wake.

"Second floor," he said tonelessly, two bags of fish dangling from his arms. He pushed the lift button with his chin.

At Mausie's front door, which had very shiny brass knockers and plates, Maggie handed Zoltan the keys. Three different keys fitted three different locks and it took a full five minutes of turning and tinkering until they could make their way inside. The apartment was very much as Maggie had imagined it: pale grey wall-to-wall carpets, pastel-coloured walls, Biedermeier furniture and oil paintings lit by little sausage-shaped lights on top of the frames. Zoltan flicked on the lights and a number of chandeliers leapt into life. There was a grand piano in one corner of the salon draped in a silky shawl and covered in a large personal retrospective of photographs in highly polished silver frames. Presumably, that was Mausie as a baby, Mausie on a pony, Mausie at her debutante ball and Mausie on her wedding day.

There was only one recent photograph of Mausie, who was indeed blonde and willowy and looked forty-something. She was seated on one of the damask-covered armchairs in the salon, her slim ankles crossed, and an older man was leaning over the back of the chair with one hand on her shoulder.

"Her husband?" Maggie asked Zoltan, who was discreetly loitering in the background.

"She was a widow," he said glumly.

Maggie turned away from the piano. She had to admit that Mausie was not only blonde and beautiful, but she also had a nice face. But then nice women didn't go to bed with other people's husbands, did they? She started unpacking her shopping basket.

Zoltan dutifully went to look for a stepladder and stood at Maggie's elbow as she went about her mission. After a while, she could feel that he too was entering into the spirit of the thing. They threw open Mausie's closets to be confronted by rows of elegantly pointed shoes. Maggie put a seaweed-encrusted mussel in the toe of each one. The shrimps she distributed among Mausie's many pockets, while the baby mullet were fitted into the cups of Mausie's frilly bras and scattered around her flimsy lingerie.

They went into the kitchen. Maggie had to admit that it was a very pretty room, more like a sitting room, with a parquet floor and a little armchair in the corner with a computer on the table in front of it. No doubt Mausie also knew how to master the rebellious mouse, cut and paste and surf the internet. There was an apron hanging on the door, printed with a scene from the ceiling of the Sistine chapel. Rome, thought a wrathful Maggie. Inside one of the cupboards she found dainty coffee cups in neat rows while an uncompromisingly British teapot was standing next to a tin of Fortnum's tea.

"Zoltan, where did we put those little crabs?" Maggie asked.

One speckled crab went into the teapot, one into the tea and a third into the sugar bowl while the others she stuffed into the white plastic kettle. That should put Mausie off afternoon tea for life, she thought.

The bathroom held little of interest. It too was pretty, with mosaic tiles and embroidered borders on the hand towels, but there was little of a personal nature; Mausie had taken that with her, Maggie realized. She opened the mirror cabinets and studied the pill boxes and make-up on the shelves: lots of vitamins and homeopathic powders. She opened each box and inserted a striped clam among the pills. The creams were clearly expensive — there the magazines were right — but they nearly all had to be squeezed out of tubes and could not be tampered with. There was one large pot of cream *pour le corps*, however, and Maggie pushed the largest clam she could find below its pink surface.

The lobsters she left to defrost on the dining-room table, propped against the silver candelabra. She wondered idly if fish also produced maggots as they decomposed, or was that only meat? Zoltan didn't know, or rather he had never heard the English word "maggot". It was his idea to hang the octopuses from the chandeliers. It took the two of them a while as, slimy and unwieldy, the polyps more than once plopped wetly onto the carpet and had to be strung up again. One of them fell onto the toe of Zoltan's grey shoe and she saw him go rigid, his face flushing pink, but, well-schooled in self-effacement, he stifled his disgust. Maggie thought for a moment that she was going to get the giggles, but one look at Zoltan's face and she changed her mind. One of the larger octopuses, its tendrils entwined in the crystal droplets, became partly disentangled and remained suspended in mid-air, its eyes bulging grotesquely.

They were left with the question of the carp. Zoltan, like all true denizens of a land-locked country, could not bear the very idea of shellfish, which walked, he assured Maggie, "backwards on the plate", but on the other hand he thought very highly of carp. "What a waste," he said reprovingly. "Do you know what a good fish soup you could make with that?"

Maggie walked purposefully into the bedroom. There was, just as she had imagined it, a large double bed with a gold-framed baroque headrest upholstered in pale blue silk. She snorted and turned back the covers. So it was here that her husband had died.

"Modome," murmured Zoltan nervously behind her, holding the carp at arm's length.

"Put it in the bed," ordered Maggie.

Zoltan gingerly slid the large fish between the white-linen monogrammed sheets. Maggie grabbed a dainty little pillow and stuffed it under the carp's head, standing back to admire her handiwork. She tucked in the sheets and laughed out loud. The poor fish looked so ridiculous framed in lacy frills, like something out of *Alice in Wonderland*.

Maggie turned her attention to a little desk in the corner of the bedroom. It was a charming piece of furniture in rosewood with a matching chair upholstered in floral petit point. There were two rows of little cubbyholes with lilac envelopes and various letters stacked in them. Maggie itched to riffle through these for ultimate proof of Jeremy's perfidy, but she could feel Zoltan's censorious eyes staring at her back. Propped against a Victorian inkwell was an old snapshot of Jeremy looking younger and thinner than Mausie had ever known him. It must have been taken during the Budapest days. Maggie suddenly felt an overwhelming urge to sit down on the demure little petit-point chair and have a good cry. She heard a coughing noise behind her; Zoltan was proffering the last of their shopping bags.

"We still have the trout," he said.

Maggie put a trout or a mackerel in each cubbyhole, facing outwards like horses looking over the doors of their stables. There was one last crab at the very bottom of the shopping bag. She gingerly fished it out and put it on the blotting pad, inserting Jeremy's photograph between its scissor claws. "There!" she said triumphantly.

She could have sworn that beneath Zoltan's moustache she had glimpsed something resembling a smile.

"Shall I turn up the heating?" he asked.

Maggie beamed. "Zoltan, you're a genius," she said. She decided not to ask how he knew where the switch was. "I think we should go out to lunch to celebrate."

Zoltan looked momentarily taken aback. "Are you sure that's allowed?" he asked dubiously.

"I'm not an ambassador's wife any more, Zoltan. We can do whatever we want."

Maggie took Zoltan to Königsbacher, a restaurant she and Jeremy had favoured, but which was not mentioned in his diary, perhaps because fish was not featured on the menu. To his delight, Zoltan found veal goulash, on the other hand, was highly recommended. They had beer in very large mugs and Zoltan's moustache was soon decked with white foam. He lit one of his smelly cigarettes and leaned back in his chair. There was no doubt now that he was smiling.

"Oh, Modome," he said, smoke unfurling from his nostrils, "I can just see Mrs Morgenstern's face when she comes back!"

Maggie was feeling mellow too. "You know, Zoltan," she said, "I really don't think you need to call me Madame any more."

After lunch, Maggie sent Zoltan home and took a bus to the Prater. She felt like a good long walk. Jeremy and she had often gone to the Prater for walks on Sunday afternoons. It was a warm sunny day and Maggie walked down the tree-lined avenues among dedicated cyclists and young lovers walking hand in hand. She tried to remember how it had felt to be so young, and experienced for the first time in her life a twinge of envy. They were too young to harbour remorse or regrets and life for them, it seemed to Maggie, was like opening a door into a lighted room. She arrived at the huge Ferris wheel dominating the skyline of Vienna. Once, she had insisted that they go up in a cabin and dangle above the city, although Jeremy had at first objected that it was such a tourist thing to do.

"But it's a landmark," said Maggie. "It's one of those things you have to do, if only once." She reminded him of Orson Welles and his damning epitaph of the Swiss on the Ferris wheel.

"I always thought that was so unfair on the Swiss," said Jeremy. "We owe them so much more than cuckoo clocks."

"Such as cheese," Maggie teased him.

"Especially cheese." Jeremy smiled.

Afterwards, they had gone to a *Heurige* for an early dinner and had drunk the sour greenish young wine and eaten sauerkraut and sausages. She remembered she had thought then how lucky she was to be able to travel abroad like this and discover the simple things that made life in one place uniquely different from anywhere else, with her tall handsome husband at her side. With Jeremy she sometimes felt as though she had shed her Englishness and was a citizen of the world. She had been sorry then for her sister, whose life had always had a sameness that Maggie thought she herself would have found very dull.

★ ★ ★

Maggie arrived back at the residence to find Esmeralda unloading a large number of bulging suitcases and parcels from a taxi whose driver was visibly impatient. He had clearly not been given a tip.

"Dona Margarida!" she said melodramatically, both hands on her breast. She was predictably dressed in black.

Maggie knew what was required of her and the two women fell into each other's arms in a fulsome embrace. Maggie found her eyes moistening as Esmeralda sobbed on her shoulder. After a decent interlude, the formalities concluded, Esmeralda wiped her eyes on a large clean handkerchief and started gathering her bags together. Maggie helped her pile them into the lift.

"I can't believe that I wasn't here for the funeral." Esmeralda was launched on a seemingly endless monologue of recriminations. "What must the ambassador have thought?"

There followed a recapitulation of all Esmeralda's emotions from the moment she had heard the news, too late to leave in time for the funeral, to the various reactions of her large extended family, her sleepless nights as she thought of poor Dona Margarida all alone in Vienna, surely not eating proper meals, to the last-minute dramas prior to departure. "But," she exclaimed triumphantly, "I have brought you some of your favourite *bacalhau*!"

That Maggie's favourite food was Portuguese cod was a myth cherished by Esmeralda, who found every excuse to include it on the menu. Jeremy would tease her about it and it had been one of their private jokes. Maggie obediently made enthusiastic noises as Esmeralda unpacked her suitcases, lining up little packages and boxes of Tupperware on the kitchen table.

Jeremy had often had cause to complain that Maggie did not know how to handle staff. Ever since, as his young fiancée, she had gone with him to a rather grand house where a butler in white gloves smoothly switched the plates in front of her and she had said a flustered thank you every time. Waiters, he explained to her sternly afterwards, were invisible. It had been the same with the help engaged for them at their residence at every posting. While the servants had always respected Jeremy, they had all actually liked Maggie because they recognized in her an innate sweetness and a desire to give as little trouble as possible. Within a very short time, however, they had completely dominated the mistress of the house and Maggie made only a pretence of choosing the menus or giving orders as to the running of the household.

Esmeralda, in particular, treated her like a wayward child, sharply criticizing outfits that she considered unsuitable for an official occasion and sending her back upstairs to change. The kitchen was Esmeralda's domain. Sometimes, after an evening out, Maggie would tiptoe in to peep into the fridge in search of a drink or a little snack and within minutes Esmeralda would appear at the door of her apartment in her floral dressing gown, her hair in curlers, demanding to know what Dona Margarida required. For this reason Maggie had persuaded Jeremy to ask the Foreign Office's permission to have the little kitchenette built into their private apartment upstairs.

In Esmeralda's kitchen everything seemed to be observing her: the rows of ladles aligned above the stove, the copper bottoms of the saucepans, the cut-crystal glasses they used for entertaining, the oven gloves with their singed fingers . . . spying on Maggie as though they too knew that she was an intruder in this perfectly ordered realm. She could almost hear them reproaching her, as a kitchen, however empty, is never entirely silent, only holding its breath.

Esmeralda was meticulously planning the packing up of Maggie's and Jeremy's things. They would start, she said, with the reception rooms and she had already spoken with Shirley about the diplomatic movers. Then together they would embark on the *coitadinha da* Dona Margarida's personal belongings upstairs. From now on, Maggie was to be apostrophized as poor. They had told Esmeralda to stay on, she said, to greet the new ambassador and his wife, although nobody knew who he would be as yet. Not that anybody, of course, could replace the ambassador, she crossed herself devoutly, or Dona Margarida. Never would she work for such wonderful people again. This elicited another flood of tears which she deftly mopped with a flourish of the big white handkerchief.

That evening, she insisted on serving Maggie a formal meal of cabbage soup followed by *bacalhau* in the official residence dining room. Maggie sat in candlelight listening to the silence, which was deafening in its intensity. The Old Masters, which belonged to the

Foreign Office, the antique china in the glass cabinets, all seemed to be staring at her in disbelief. What was this impostor doing in the ambassador's place at the head of the table?

When they had entertained, Jeremy had always attended to the seating. He knew which ambassadors had been in Vienna longest and therefore entitled to the highest places above the salt. He knew which ministers' wives spoke English and could be safely seated next to visiting dignitaries from England. The names in italic script on the cards above each plate were handwritten by someone in the embassy. One had to be so careful to get all the titles right. "Would you like me to use this tablecloth?" Esmeralda would ask in a voice that brooked no opposition. It was Esmeralda who had given orders to Heinz, the waiter who came in on these occasions, as to whom to serve first. Maggie's one contribution had been the flowers, but she had always had to stifle her flights of fantasy because of Jeremy's allergies. All sorts of pollen brought on wheezing attacks, especially in spring.

Maggie would wear her green dress and smile as she chatted in her stilted French or makeshift German, and she would unknowingly charm the guests as she was such a good listener, even remembering afterwards what they had said. "How did your meniscus operation go?" she would ask an under secretary for foreign affairs the next time they met. Or: "Did you settle for cerise for the bedroom curtains in the end?" addressed to his wife. Maggie would have been astounded had she known that in diplomatic circles, while Jeremy was considered something of a highly competent bore, everybody agreed that he had a charming little wife.

"I think the evening went very well, my dear," Jeremy would say as he climbed into bed, absent-mindedly patting her bottom. "We were lucky she didn't serve your favourite *bacalhau!*"

Next morning Maggie woke to find the precipice still yawning at her feet. Her escapade of the previous day had been only a temporary relief from the relentlessly suppressed panic that gripped her whenever she awoke. Had she been very silly, she wondered. She thought with something like dread of Jeremy's reaction to the whole episode. When people died, she questioned, could they still see one down below and watch one's reactions, listen to one's conversations? Worse still, now that they were part and parcel of the spiritual world, could they perhaps read one's thoughts?

She had little time to brood as she lay in bed with her tea, however. Esmeralda was already up and down stairs like a tornado. Maggie's role was to hover with a felt-tip pen, writing "Books", "China" or "Miscellaneous" — there were quite a number of those — on the boxes, wondering what on earth she was going do with them all. Esmeralda was intent on dispatching Zoltan downstairs to the cellar with the boxes, to await the arrival of the movers. As housekeeper to the ambassador, Esmeralda considered herself to be a cut above the rest of the embassy staff and never missed an opportunity to make them fully aware of the fact.

Maggie started taking the pictures down and stacking them against the wall. She stood for a long time holding a pen-and-ink portrait she had done of Jeremy soon after they met. Maggie had met Jeremy in London at a vernissage in an art gallery where she was working part-time. Her wages went to pay the rent while she studied art at St Martin's. He had come with her flatmate, Amanda, who knew Jeremy from county get-togethers in Norfolk. Maggie had been standing uncertainly with the catalogue in her hand, trying to look professional, when a tall figure approached her, a little cube of cheese between his slim fingers.

"Do you know much about art?" he had asked in an undeniably posh accent.

"Well, I'm studying art at the moment," she'd said, looking up at an aquiline nose and lofty brow.

"You don't look like an artist." Maggie had been wearing a little black dress that she had borrowed from Amanda and her mother's pearls. This was in the days when dress was more formal than now, after all: handbags matched shoes and women were not allowed into the Dorchester in trousers.

"Well, not all artists are bohemian!" She had laughed.

Later, he had admired her watercolours of the Herefordshire countryside with the black hills of Wales in the misty background, but said that he found the bold splashes of colour on her oil canvases "OTT".

"OTT?" she'd asked, puzzled.

"Over the top, my dear." Jeremy had been working at the Foreign Office at the time. He had been at the outset of his career then, and waiting to hear where his first posting would be. He had, Maggie realized now, been on the lookout for a wife to assist him scale rung by rung the ladder of what was to prove a brilliant career in diplomacy.

Maggie turned to see Zoltan looking over her shoulder and put the drawing down against the wall. He looked sweaty and hassled. "I'll make you a coffee," she said. "I've prepared an envelope for you. You've been very helpful and I'm most grateful."

"Are you going back to England?" asked Zoltan.

"We still have a little flat in London," said Maggie. "I was thinking of going back there. It's just that I don't really have anyone to go back to. There's my sister in Herefordshire, but she's so busy with the children. Living all these years abroad, I've sort of lost touch."

Zoltan slowly lit his cigarette. "There is something else you could do," he said.

Maggie looked at him in surprise.

"I mean, of course, it's for Modome to decide, but after what we did in Mrs Morgenstern's apartment, I was thinking . . ." Zoltan's voice trailed off and he took a long drag of his cigarette.

"Yes?" said Maggie a little impatiently.

"Well, what I was thinking," Zoltan looked hard at the ashtray, "was that we might go to Paris. On a professional basis, of course," he added hastily, seeing the alarm in her eyes.

"Why on earth would we want to go to Paris?"

Two puffs of smoke billowed out of Zoltan's nose. He stubbed the butt out deliberately with a circular motion. "Delphine," he said cryptically, his voice sounding more like a croak. Zoltan cleared his throat. "I was thinking Modome might like to go to Paris and take revenge on Delphine."

2

PARIS

Zoltan's bombshell resulted in a series of further sleepless nights.

Down in the garage Maggie sought out the remaining boxes labelled "Papers — Jeremy" and staggered with them back into the lift. There were four large boxes in all, some personal files, but mostly batches of his diaries, tied into sheaves bound together with elastic bands. Maggie extracted the ones bearing dates coinciding with their posting in Paris and put the others back in the boxes. Armed with another bottle of Jeremy's Bordeaux, she spent the night putting the diaries in chronological order and reading through them from beginning to end.

In the early hours of the morning she lay back on the sofa, resting her head on the velvet cushions and feeling unutterably weary. She would read the other diaries another day, she decided. One should only absorb so much poison into one's system at one time. Maybe she would become like the heroine of one of the detective stories she had read when Jeremy was elsewhere — he had always abhorred her taste in literature — where the wife was slowly poisoned day after day by the arsenic her husband put in the sugar lumps.

Maggie had presumed that Mausie was an isolated incident, something that could happen when marriages were getting a little stale. It had never occurred to her that Jeremy might be a serial offender. Maggie felt suddenly terribly sorry for herself. She would have liked to tell a friend about it all, someone who would pat her hand and say, "You poor, poor thing, you didn't deserve all this . . . there was nothing you could have done," and gather her up into a warm embrace of female solidarity. But who? She couldn't tell anyone in the diplomatic service; that would be against all the rules. Diplomats always lived irreprehensible lives and presented a united front to the outside world. Hilary Mackintosh would be shocked and repelled by such unseemly confidences. For Maggie too, after all these years, and despite the feelings she was beginning to harbour for Jeremy, it would go against the grain to expose his shortcomings to the Foreign Office. To be quite selfish about it, it would cast a cloud over everything not only he, but she herself, had done for Great Britain and the British Commonwealth all her adult life. And Shirley? Shirley would make no bones about the fact that, like the time Esmeralda put ground beef in the mince pies for the Christmas Carol Concert and when the bathtub overflowed in the residence during the Minister of Agriculture's visit, it had obliquely been all Maggie's fault. And Sue? How could she shatter the myth of the perfect older sister, the paragon who had left Ledbury behind to conquer the world with such a superior husband at her side? Esmeralda would swamp her in a tide of emotion and melodrama, and anyway, Maggie had been Jeremy's wife for too long to confide her personal agony to members of the embassy staff. This was a burden she was going to have to shoulder entirely on her own.

In the end, night after night, she dived into the boxes with the little Moleskine notebooks recording the betrayals of twenty-five years in Paris, Rome and Budapest until she felt a fury festering at the very core of her being that only revenge could assuage. The miscreant Jeremy was no longer there to bear the brunt of her wrath, but now that they each had a name, a face and an address, she would unleash it on his many partners in crime.

It turned out that Jeremy had met "Delphine" at a television interview he had been invited to give for a French channel halfway through the second year of his posting. As hard as she tried, Maggie could remember nothing about the interview, although she had never watched much television anyway. Theirs had been, apparently, a *coup de foudre*, a fulminating thunderbolt of love at first sight. Maggie felt the familiar dryness in her mouth and she had to steady the diary wobbling in her grasp. Their passion had also been very French, she discovered, with asterisks strewn over the pages with a disconcerting frequency.

Delphine, it appeared, was divorced, with a little boy of twelve who came home at regular intervals from boarding school, which resulted in longish gaps in the narrative. Jeremy is, however, introduced to the child, who is called Tancrède — typically French and pretentious, thought Maggie — and comments on his charm and intelligence. At one point he is buying him a present for his birthday, a fountain pen engraved with his initials.

Maggie felt something crunching her insides and a constriction in her throat. She and Jeremy had tried for a number of years to have children, on her insistence rather than his, and indeed when it became apparent that she was not going to produce an heir, Jeremy had not exhibited many regrets. She, on the other hand, had carried this failure like a tender bruise within her heart for a long, long time. Every time she saw her sister's children or a particularly enchanting specimen in the street, she would feel a physical ache throbbing behind her ribs. Many people had made her a godmother to compensate and she religiously remembered birthdays and frequently sent postcards to her godchildren at their various boarding schools. "You and your little pen pals," Jeremy would tease her. Had he really not minded that she couldn't give him a child? It was, perhaps, typical of Maggie that it never occurred to her that the problem might have been Jeremy's, rather than hers.

After Delphine was promoted from interviewing to news broadcasts, she was on the air every evening, but free in the afternoons for what the Parisians call cinq à sept in her little apartment overlooking the Seine. It seems they would sit by the open windows sipping Kir, and watch the bateaux mouches chugging along the river, Delphine in what Jeremy describes as a "very fetching" kimono. They rarely went out for a meal as Delphine was a well-known face on French television and it might have given rise to gossip. She was, however, the wretched woman, a dab hand at cuisine and her *terrines, taponades, bisques, bouillons, brochettes* and *pissaladières* were variously described in the diary. Marielise, their cook in the residence, on the other hand, had been competent but unimaginative. Maggie had always thought that Jeremy had been quite satisfied when, at official dinners, soup was served, followed by what Marielise termed *un petit gigot*. Everything was prefixed with "*petit*" by Marielise, whether it was *pomme de terre* or *pain au chocolat* or a *petit instant* or *coup de fil*, except for Marelise herself, who was not petite at all, but an overpowering figure with a large bosom and dark red nostrils. Maggie had been secretly terrified of her and Marielise had ruled the residence roost, unchallenged even by Jeremy, for the entire four years that they were posted to Paris.

It was also Delphine, apparently, who had opened Jeremy's eyes to the nuances of French wine — Maggie eyed her dwindling bottle of Bordeaux askance — and the different vintages they savoured together were all meticulously noted down. Delphine takes Jeremy to a series of gallery openings and vernissages and together they frequent literary cafes. That would have explained his sudden interest in Jacques Prévert, about which Maggie had quizzed him at the time.

All in all, Maggie had to admit that Delphine was everything that she was not. It was a devastating thought. Maybe she could wear a kimono and read Verlaine, but even if she managed to become a gourmet cook, putting on the table a *velouté de potiron* or a

Tarte Tatin, Jeremy was no longer there to savour their merits.

Maggie crawled into bed feeling a hopelessness she had never felt before. All her certainties seemed shattered and she was forced to confront the unthinkable conclusion that she had spent her entire adult life wedded to the wrong man. Maggie held to her mother's view that the first twenty years are always a preparation for life, the next three decades are the real thing and any years that follow should ideally be filled with fond reminiscences as one struggles with the last flight of stairs. It seemed now to Maggie, in her gloom, that in her case the real thing had been her marriage to Jeremy.

Yet on the bleak horizon there was one tiny pinprick of light; and with a gathering sense of resolution she saw herself sipping a *café crème* outside the Café de Flore on the Boulevard Saint-Germain. However long and dark the night, the dawn could always bring with it the fragrance of percolating coffee and warm croissants.

"Yes, Paris," she told Shirley next morning on the telephone. "Our boxes can be sent to storage in England, but I would like to spend a few weeks in Paris on my way back. It'll take my mind off things."

"But Zoltan seems to think he's coming with you." Shirley's voice registered distinct disapproval. "He was in here yesterday asking for his severance pay."

"Yes, that's correct," Maggie said firmly. "I am going to buy a car with a big boot and drive it back to

England, and Zoltan's coming with me because I never learned to drive on the Continent."

"I see," said Shirley, who clearly did not. "Well, I thought you might like to come into the embassy before you leave and say goodbye. There have been lots of messages of sympathy you might like to answer when you feel up to it."

They had set up a memorial in the atrium of the embassy after Jeremy died and hundreds of people had come in to sign the book. There had been dozens of bouquets as well, but Maggie had had them all sent to the International Hospital. A few ambassadors' wives, women she served on committees with, had called her personally, but most of the official grief had been addressed to the embassy.

"Everyone's been very kind," said Maggie. "What time would you like me to come in?"

They had all been very kind. A little buffet had been set up in the ante-room to Jeremy's old office and Moët & Chandon had been brought up from the embassy cellars. Mr Mackintosh presented her with a bouquet of flowers. He made a little speech about how much they would all miss her and he toasted her new venture in Paris and beyond. Everybody commented on how well she looked, their voices then lowering, "in the circumstances".

Maggie saw Shirley's eyes staring fixedly at her feet. "They're really rather absurd, aren't they?" said Maggie with a little laugh. She'd bought them to cheer herself up, she told an unresponding Shirley.

Heaven forbid anyone might jump to the conclusion that Jeremy's spouse was a merry widow. How many of them knew the truth about Jeremy and Mausie, Maggie wondered. Probably everybody. It seemed as though no one was on her side; all of them had been shielding Jeremy and his misdemeanour. On the other hand, they could hardly have spilled the beans, she supposed. Would she take it upon herself to tell someone that her husband was unfaithful? She had to admit that she probably would not.

Zoltan had driven her to the farewell party in her new Volkswagen, paid for out of Jeremy's little nest egg. The bank had cashed a large cheque and seen no problem about transferring money to Paris, they said, as they had an affiliated bank there. If they felt nervous about the fact that Maggie had spent more in one week than the ambassador had been accustomed to do in a year, they made no mention of the fact. Now, with Zoltan waiting patiently outside, Maggie hugged and kissed everybody in the embassy goodbye then stepped through the august portals and out of one life into another.

It took Maggie and Zoltan almost a day and a half to reach Paris, in a car stuffed to the roof with their belongings, a large space being allotted to the remaining "Papers — Jeremy". Zoltan felt that as it was a new car it would be a mistake to overtax the engine and then there were frequent stops on the way for his coffees and cigarettes and Maggie's visits to the Ladies. In the evening they stopped for a very satisfying dinner at a Routier restaurant, which they had seen lots of trucks parked outside — always a good sign, Zoltan said. They sat in the corner of a crowded room in a cloud of evil-smelling smoke and ate at a table covered with a plastic tablecloth. Zoltan did not hold with French cuisine himself, he explained, but fortunately there was a *pot au feu* on the menu which had echoes of his favourite goulash dish, and between them they drank a carafe of local red wine.

Jeremy had not believed in fraternizing with the lower echelons, and Maggie realized that she knew very little about Zoltan's life before he joined them fifteen years ago. She knew he had a brother who worked in Budapest in one of the ministries. That had made it easier to obtain a visa for him when they were posted to Rome. He went back to Hungary once a year on leave but usually spent Christmas with them. They had invited all the staff for mulled wine and mince pies under the tree at their residence every Christmas Eve and everyone had been given a present. That had been Maggie's job and one that she enjoyed. Last year she had given Zoltan one of those silver cigarette lighters that burst into a large flame and snapped shut with a loud click. She knew that his mother had died while they were still in Budapest because he had been given compassionate leave to go back to his village on the Hungarian Puszta.

Didn't he miss his home? she asked him now.

Theirs had been a very simple peasant house, Zoltan told her, with earth floors and maize stacked under the thatched roof to dry and a well in the courtyard. She knew those wells with long poles pointing diagonally into the sky; when she first arrived in Budapest she had even purchased a naïf painting of one surrounded by geese, which Jeremy had complained was rather kitsch. Zoltan's family had made a living by force-feeding geese and selling their livers to a canning factory. Maggie grimaced. All his memories of childhood were accompanied by the cackling of those geese. Out of their feathers, the soft down on their necks, his mother had made pillows and duvets and that had brought in some money too.

Then every year they had killed the pig and not a bit of it was wasted, even the cheeks and the trotters were pickled in aspic or turned into yards of salami. The family had lived off the meat of that one pig all year round. For special occasions, his mother had roasted a goose — oh, modome could have no idea of the flavour of that goose with its crispy crackling and juicy flesh. Zoltan's eyes watered at the memory. Then his mother had made the best *galuska*, pushing the dough through holes in an earthenware dish and letting the fragments drop into the boiling water. She would beat in a goose egg and serve with sweet paprika. Oh, what a cook his mother had been! His father he hardly remembered. He had drunk far too much of the plum and apricot *pálinka* he made himself in their old-fashioned bathtub and one night he had fallen on his way to the outdoor lavatory and frozen to death in the snow. All he could remember from when his father was alive were his thundering snores boring through the wall between their parents' room and the kitchen where he and his brother slept next to the stove.

When his mother died they had sold the place and slaughtered all the geese, and he and his wife had moved to Budapest. Zoltan had become quite a jack of all trades, doing several different jobs a day, but money had always been scarce and his wife had bitterly resented their low-key lifestyle.

"I never knew you were married!" said Maggie, surprised.

Zoltan lit a cigarette and inhaled deeply. "I was married for ten years," he said, "to a lovely girl I'd known since we were children. She hated life in the village and when we came to Budapest she went a little wild. She was always buying new clothes and high-heeled shoes and men would turn their heads to look at her when she walked along the Körút. I think it must have gone to her head. I didn't realize for a long time what she was up to, but then one day I came home and found them." Zoltan savagely tipped the ash off the end of his cigarette and took a gulp of red wine. "You see, Modome, you are not the only one . . ." His voice had a leaden emphasis that Maggie was to remember well many months hence.

They spent the night in a little roadside hotel somewhere in the Massif Centrale. Next morning, they decided on an early start. Maggie was quiet as she sat next to Zoltan, watching the rows of poplar trees flash by, their trunks painted white like the fetlocks of racehorses. "Zoltan," she asked the silent figure at the wheel, "tell me, what was Delphine like?"

Zoltan noisily changed gears and moved the toothpick he had been chewing to his other cheek. "Delphine," he said, "was a bitch."

"A bitch?" asked Maggie, stunned.

"She was arrogant and full of herself, like the French can be. She never bothered to say hello when she got into the car and she always slammed the door."

Maggie was silent as this unexpected windfall sank in. This paragon of *cassoulets* and *clafoutis*, this highly cultivated eclectic mind, this statuesque form draped in a kimono, was a bitch? Maggie felt suffused with warmth like hot chocolate trickling over a vanilla ice cream. Hugging this thought to her breast, she dozed off and woke up only when she found herself in the outskirts of Paris.

Maggie had reserved two rooms in a hotel on the Left Bank where she and Jeremy had spent their honeymoon. It was not, perhaps, an advisable choice in the circumstances, but it was the only reasonably priced hotel in Paris she knew. Visiting dignitaries had always stayed in expensive hotels on the Champs Elysées and Maggie didn't want to be too extravagant with Jeremy's money. As it turned out, either the hotel had lost much of its allure in the intervening years, or maybe to the young and inexperienced Maggie it had seemed more glamorous twenty-five years ago. Was it possible that the grumpy concierge who sourly handed them the keys to their rooms was the same person then too? Maggie sat on her beige candlewick bedspread and tried to remember what it had been like when she had come here as a bride.

Her mother had seen them both off at Victoria, waving from the platform as the boat train rumbled out of the station, smiling brightly as her little girl left for her big adventure. The weeks before the wedding had brought them very close. Maggie's mother had wanted so desperately that everything should be just right and that there should be no cause for criticism of her daughter on the part of her formidable new husband with his soft handshake and carefully contained smile. They had gone up to London on the fast train from Malvern to shop for her trousseau and stayed in the Basil Street Hotel. Every day they would come back with their packages and sit in the shabby genteel sitting room and relive their shopping expedition over afternoon tea. Maggie's mother had put particular emphasis on underthings and nightgowns and had sat circumspectly on the spindly boudoir chairs of the lingerie department in Selfridges, conscious of the supercilious stares of the sales staff. She was fully aware that in her homespun tweeds and well-worn brogues she looked like a bumpkin next to her pretty little daughter flitting in and out of the changing room in lacy petticoats and negligees. She hid her hands roughened by hours of gardening behind her capacious handbag and spoke in whispers, grateful when the sales girl favoured her with a smile.

Maggie was, after all, marrying into a class above her own, destined to dazzle the salons of Continental capitals. Behind her daughter's back, her mother boasted inordinately to her fellow members of the Women's Institute: "No, they don't know yet where his next posting will be. Of course they'd prefer it to be in Europe. They say that Jeremy is earmarked for a brilliant career in the service."

Maggie couldn't remember the room they had shared on that bewildering first night, she in her frilly negligee and Jeremy in his striped pyjamas, alone in a bedroom for the first time. He had been very gentle and understanding and had never, either then or throughout their married life, required her to perform in the athletic way they seemed to do nowadays in films. After her painful initiation, Maggie had actually come to thoroughly enjoy their times between the sheets, although they had become less and less frequent as the years went by.

She cast her mind back to her honeymoon. She had been so incredibly happy then. It had seemed to her such impossible good fortune that this wonderful man had actually married her, Maggie. He had said, "I do," and looked down at her fondly under the frothy meringue of her wedding veil. In Paris, they had walked across the Pont Neuf hand in hand and, even though she knew that Jeremy disliked effusive displays in public, she had not been able to resist jumping up and throwing her arms around his neck, and he had cradled her like a child before pretending to toss her over the balustrade into the Seine. It was one of the last occasions when she saw Jeremy in casual clothes. Even in his coffin they had buried him in a jacket and tie. In Paris he had worn what he called slacks and a jumper.

He had slept late in the mornings and whiled away the hours with her at their usual table at the Café de Flore, as together they watched the world go by.

Maggie sat for a long time trying dispassionately to weigh the happy years of her married life with its bitter epilogue. It was so easy to conclude, when a marriage lost its lustre, that it had never been happy, when that was not strictly the truth. After all, didn't they say that ignorance was bliss? She had been blissfully unaware that she was sharing her husband with Mausie and Delphine and their counterparts in Rome and Budapest. What Jeremy had given all these women was something that at the time it had never occurred to her to miss.

A knock on the door abruptly broke into her thoughts. She hastily put her shoes back on.

"Who is it?"

"Modome, it's me, Zoltan."

Maggie opened the door and Zoltan marched over to the television set and switched it on. A woman's face filled the screen. She appeared to have faultless skin and magnetic jade-coloured eyes speared the viewer in an almost inhuman gaze. Her pale pink lips were wide and mobile as she read what sounded like the evening news.

"Delphine," said Zoltan.

Maggie watched fascinated until the mouthing stopped and the sheaves of paper were shuffled together as Delphine wished the audience a *bonne soirée* and faded from the screen. All benevolent thoughts of Jeremy and their marriage vanished in an instant.

73

"How can she remember all that by heart?" Maggie asked enviously.

"Oh," said Zoltan, "she's reading the news, they all do."

"But she wasn't looking at the papers on her desk."

"That's because it's being fed onto a screen in front of her by a teleprompter. I used to work at Hungarian TV."

Maggie sat looking at the blank screen. "I suppose you feel like dinner?" she asked Zoltan.

She chose a little bistro around the corner in the rue des Grands Augustins. Zoltan studied the menu dubiously.

"She's so perfect," said Maggie.

"Don't worry," Zoltan said, pouring out a glass of wine. "You'll think of something, you'll see."

"We'll just have to unperfect her," said Maggie, crunching loudly on her crudités. A germ of an idea was beginning to form . . .

Next day, Maggie made Zoltan take her to Delphine's apartment with its windows looking out over the Seine and the *bateaux mouches* plugging slowly past, gusts of music and the booming voice of the guide issuing from the decks. Maggie stared up at a white curtain fluttering through the gap in the opened window. It was here that a geisha-like figure and Jeremy had sipped their Kir while tantalizing aromas were issuing from Delphine's little kitchen. She found herself grinding her teeth. Delphine, she decided, would have a public not a private *mauvais quart d'heure*.

74

That evening, she broached the idea to Zoltan over a dish of *boeuf bourguignon*.

"I was thinking, Zoltan, if you used to work for Hungarian television, I don't see why you can't get a job at Antenne 2."

"Modome, you're forgetting I'm a Hungarian," said Zoltan, picking at his plate with a critical fork, "and this beef is very French."

In the days that followed, Zoltan was often absent. It appeared he had made a few friends during their years in Paris and he assured her he was working on an idea. He drove out every day to the fifteenth *arrondissement* to the headquarters of French television and spent long hours in the Bar des Copains opposite, hobnobbing with the workers from the vast building who dropped in after work. "I'm edging in," he told an impatient Maggie during their evening dinner at the bistro round the corner. "I'm making all the necessary contacts."

"These contacts," queried Maggie. "You're making them in French?"

"*Je parle pas mal*," Zoltan said with an appalling Hungarian accent. "Especially bad words. I know lots of those!"

Every evening, they watched Delphine on television. Every evening, Maggie stared miserably at the faultless skin and the sheen on the honey-coloured hair, and admired the impeccable chic of her saucily cut *tailleurs*. She fantasized that Delphine's long eyelashes would suddenly stick together so that she could no longer read the mellifluous sentences that issued from her glossy lips. Or that she could be persuaded to drink some dark liquid just before going on air so that her *bonne soirée* would be marred by two rows of perfect black teeth. Or, in a flight of fantasy born of desperation, that a praying mantis could perhaps be trained to crawl up her shoulder and penetrate Delphine's shell-shaped ear.

It was intensely frustrating for Maggie that she had to rely on Zoltan's laborious efforts to carry out her revenge, but she had to face up to the fact that it would be quite simply impossible to enact this particular plan of action without him. If only it wasn't taking him so long! She filled in the days until they could meet over dinner in the evening as best she could. She went to museums and markets and galleries and book shops and sometimes she went to Nouvelle Vague black and white films in the afternoons. She loved to walk in the Jardins du Luxembourg and sit on a bench and watch the joggers and the lovers and the children queuing up for pony rides.

"You want to ride on Mercure?" a mother asked her little girl, flushed and excited as she waited for her turn.

Maggie felt the familiar pang that mothers and small children always evinced in her. What could ever replace the love for a little girl holding out a sugar lump to a plump dappled pony? But as she walked down the boulevards and boarded the metro, as she riffled through the rows of chiffon and gauze in the choice boutiques, she never forgot for a moment why she was in Paris, her anger burning within her like the eternal flame on the tomb of the Unknown Soldier under the triumphal arch on the Champs Elysées.

Every morning, Maggie would go to the Café de Flore and sit watching the world go by as she sipped her *café crème*. Soon, the waiters came to recognize her and brought her order on cue. She was beginning to feel in this, the hub of French fashion, not unlike her mother in the lingerie department at Selfridges. All these sleek women with that certain *je ne sais quoi*, all looking so self-assured about their place in the world and their inalienable right to go tripping down the tree-lined boulevard with firm buttocks and slim ankles. There was a French expression for it, Maggie knew. Such women felt *bien dans leur peau*. She herself had always felt at odds in her own skin and surroundings, uncomfortably trying to conform to an ill-fitting mould which fooled no one, least of all herself. It was important, she felt now, to make up one's mind who one really was. While she was married to Jeremy she had always had a ready answer: she was a diplomat's wife. Now it was time to discover her real persona, working, she decided, from the outside in. She would start by following these paragons of Gallic chic into the little boutiques in which they seemed to feel so intimately at home, chatting with the sales girls and preening in front of the floor-length mirrors. She would reinvent a Maggie who didn't have to dress for a husband or obey the dictates of the British expatriate community with its unbending rules about how a diplomat's wife should look. The outside would permeate the inside and a new Maggie would emerge expensively from her burgeoning chrysalis.

The habits of a lifetime were hard to break, however, and Maggie thought long and hard before each purchase, weighing the pros and the cons and always thinking long term. She came out carrying absurdly large carrier bags stuffed with coloured tissue paper containing what her mother would have called "a few well-matched ensembles".

Maggie was glad her mother was no longer alive to see her now. Over the years, she had come once or twice a year to stay in the various diplomatic residences and relished the grandeur of her surroundings as she sat stiffly on the well-stuffed armchairs. "I *say*, Maggie!" she would exclaim gleefully as Heinz bowed over her, his white-gloved hand bearing a tray with a little demitasse of coffee, a far cry from the pottery mugs at home. With what scintillating anecdotes could she have regaled the ladies at the Women's Institute now? Maggie's mother belonged to a generation and social class where marital infidelity and divorce were unsavoury topics tainting the lives of people far removed from their own world.

After shopping, Maggie plucked up the courage to patronize a hair salon near the Place de la Concorde, where an effete young man pirouetted and tut-tutted around her chair, draping her in soft pink towels. "*Eh voilà, Madame*," he purred, flicking the back of her neck with the soft bristles of a brush. She emerged with a short boyish cut which even she had to admit was "very fetching" and seemed to have taken years off her age.

Zoltan, despite decades of practice as an impassive chauffeur, failed to mask the incredulity in his eyes. He arrived in her bedroom for their evening rendezvous with Delphine in a crisp pair of brand-new dark blue overalls. "They're called *salopettes*," he told Maggie proudly, "like *salope*!" He stuck his thumbs into his new dark blue pockets.

Delphine was in lime green that evening, a colour that enhanced the translucent shade of her eyes. She expertly read the news items in a melodious voice, clearly concentrating more on the slant of her eyebrows and the tilt of her perfect chin than on what she was saying.

"You know, I don't think she's listening to a word she says," said Maggie, thoughtfully.

"Why do you need salopettes?" asked Maggie as she and Zoltan sat opposite each other in the little bistro.

"*Je suis un ouvrier d'entretien*," said Zoltan in his heavily accented French.

"What is *un ouvrier d'entretien*?" asked Maggie.

"I'm a maintenance man!" Zoltan said triumphantly. "*C'est mon bouleau, quoi.* You wanted me to get inside that building — but what do I do then?"

It was with some regret that Maggie finally relinquished the gummy eyelashes and praying mantis ideas. "I've got the beginning of a plan," she said slowly. In fact it was a quite irresistible scenario that had presented itself to her. "Didn't you say she read the news on a teleprompter?"

"Yes," said Zoltan, clearly nervous about what might be coming next.

"Well, there must be a way of changing the text that she is going to read at the last minute."

Zoltan sat slurping his soup, his napkin stuck into the collar of his shirt. "I only really know bad words in French," he said glumly.

"That's exactly what we need," said Maggie purposefully, digging into her terrine. "We'll make her say some of your bad words."

Maggie fully intended to go and see everybody at the embassy in Paris, as she was sure that people who would remember her were still there, and the ambassador had known Jeremy well. Once or twice she had walked down the rue du Faubourg Saint-Honoré as she researched the boutiques in her quest for a new persona, but always at the last moment she couldn't bring herself to cross the doorstep. That was all part of the previous Maggie, the Maggie who did and said all the right things and certainly not a Maggie who consorted with a shady Hungarian chauffeur in planning to sabotage Antenne 2. Her friends during her Paris days had nearly all been other diplomats' wives and they, like her, had migrated to other embassies, other legations in other lands. Jeremy and Maggie had been invited on occasion to the private homes of French politicians, socialites and intelligentsia but Maggie knew only too well that they were invited uniquely because of Jeremy's status; few, if any, would remember the demure little wife of the *chargé d'affaires Britannique*.

French women had seemed to Maggie then so remote, so slim, so chic, so cerebral, so *engagées*, so *au courant*; they had all been to see the latest play and read that year's Prix Goncourt hot from the presses. They were well versed in every detail of the latest *cause célèbre*, but Maggie wondered if they ever got together to have a giggle and a chat. Although they had something which they called *esprit*, they seemed to her not to have a sense of humour. Maggie knew that she had a sense of humour. She had made even Jeremy laugh, coaxing a reluctant burst of laughter out of the corner of his mouth. She had no illusions, however, about being a *femme d'esprit*. A barrage of *bon mots* and *boutades* whizzed passed Maggie's ears like bullets, while Jeremy occasionally managed to reply with a pithy repartee in his grammatically perfect French, upholding the honour of what they insisted on calling the *perfide Albion*. Dinner parties had been sheer torture for Maggie until she thought up a stratagem. These alarming French men, so self-assured, such *hommes du monde*, would briefly descend to her level on her left or her right. "What did you think of Bernard Henri-Levy's latest *oeuvre*?" she would ask the supercilious gentleman on her left. This would give her time to nibble her way through her pâté. "How did you like this latest show at the Beaubourg?" she enquired of her right hand, intent on mastering a slippery quail. By the time it came to pudding they were talking over her head about finance or philosophy and she could enjoy her *mousse au chocolat* undisturbed.

Maggie realized now that their posting in Paris had, on reflection, not been among their happiest times. Jeremy had been very busy; there had been issues taking up much of his time — could it have been the European Union? She tried to remember — and the evenings they had spent alone together in their residence had been few and far between. Perhaps it was for that reason that Gilberto had seemed so appealing at the time.

Gilberto had been the Argentinian ambassador for a short term, a saturnine-looking man who had not been popular with his colleagues. "He looks like a dago," had been Jeremy's terse comment. They saw very little of him socially because, unusually for an ambassador, he was not married. Perhaps his wife had died; there were rumours that some dark tragedy lurked in his past. Maggie remembered very well how they had first met at a New Year's Eve party at the Argentinian residence.

It had been so unlike a typical diplomatic party that Maggie had actually found herself enjoying it. She was sitting quietly on a chair against the wall savouring a robust red wine and listening to the orchestra playing plaintive tangos. Jeremy was at a table near by punctiliously dissecting a gory chunk of Argentinian beef. She smelled Gilberto's presence even before she looked up and saw his dark head, with a wayward lock of hair in the middle of his forehead, bending towards her. It was a male smell of fresh sweat with a hint of lime. He had been dancing and his eyes had a wild gaiety about them.

"Would you like to dance?" His teeth looked very white against his dark skin.

"Oh, no, no, thank you," said Maggie, flustered. "I don't know how to tango!"

"Everyone can tango," said Gilberto pulling her to her feet. "You just need the right partner."

Maggie found herself swept onto the floor. The room began to go backwards and forwards and round and round very fast. She felt herself swaying and melting against Gilberto's damp shirt, his arm hard and reassuring in the small of her back. Her feet and body seemed to be doing exactly what he wanted them to do as she gave herself up in a daze to this masterful embrace under the giddy sparkle of the chandeliers.

"*Cuando pasaste a mi lado se me apretó el corazón,*" he murmured to the music, looking down into her face with that unbridled gaiety she found so infectious.

All at once it was over and Gilberto accompanied her back to her chair. She sat down, suffused with a warmth which had very little to do with the temperature of the room, trying to bottle up again all this passionate abandon and primeval yearnings. But from then on they would go on bubbling slowly and silently like the gooseberry preserves in the screw-top jars in her mother's summer larder.

"You really seemed to get into it back there, old thing," said Jeremy in the car on the way home.

"Into what?" asked Maggie, who had not been concentrating. She could still feel the pressure of Gilberto's strong arm against her back.

"Into dancing the tango."

"Oh, yes." Maggie laughed. "It's funny: they always say it takes two to tango, but actually it takes only one."

Maggie realized now as she wandered down the boulevards of Paris over a carpet of autumn leaves that, unlike in other cities where they had been posted, there were very few sentimental landmarks bringing back memories of their passage there. They had participated together in many official occasions. Maggie had stood next to Jeremy on chill winter mornings as wreaths were laid on the grave of the Unknown Soldier. She had sat in the front row through interminable speeches and smiled graciously at receptions in her uncomfortable shoes. Speeches, wherever they were posted, were invariably too long and excruciatingly dull. Only the Americans knew how to be punchy and pithy and evoke an enthusiastic response. Everywhere else tedium had taken on a new dimension. She had shaken hands with many people making history and curtsied to royalty and, occasionally, hobnobbed briefly with pop singers and prima donnas from the opera or stage. But the sum of the real impact of all these encounters could be noted on the back of an envelope. Nobody had said anything memorable, few people's eyes had locked with her own. Meeting famous and powerful people did not mean knowing anything about them. "Oh, did you really meet *them*?" she would be asked in awe by her mother's friends. "What were they like?" The real answer was that they all looked exactly as they did in photographs, only occasionally taking one by surprise because they were often much smaller.

Everybody thought that being a diplomat's wife was the height of glamour, but in fact it was hard work. She and Jeremy had been on call day and night, often working the room at three or four different receptions in an evening. Maggie sometimes felt like an actress shaking out her costume in her dressing room and applying mascara before going on stage night after night in their own version of a Gilbert and Sullivan operetta. In some of the embassies where they had been posted, wives had been considered an integral part of the team, involved too in promoting the image and agenda of their country. Paris had not been one of these. All that had been required of Maggie was to remain in the background and make sure that their household was efficiently run, and for that she had relied on the formidable Marielise. It was essential, as a senior diplomat's wife, to interact with the other spouses within the embassy, as they were called in diplomatic circles, and be active within that sphere. In Vienna, for instance, she and Hilary Mackintosh had organized charity bazaars for the local orphanage and even a ball on the occasion of the Queen's birthday. But the British ambassador in Paris had been a confirmed bachelor who rarely chose to socialize; there had been rumours that he might even be gay, but these kinds of things were not openly aired in the British Foreign Service, remote as they were from the life of our own dear Queen. Unlike the Dutch, who always sent out invitations to the ambassador "and partner", as though Jeremy were harbouring something rather more exotic than his lawfully wedded wife.

Maggie knew that sooner or later she would have to breach the threshold of the Hôtel de Charost, but in the end it was Shirley who put an end to her procrastinations.

"Well, how *are* things?" she asked briskly one morning on the telephone from Vienna. Maggie had reluctantly left a telephone number where she could be reached as Shirley had been adamant that there would be all sorts of loose ends to tie up in the forthcoming weeks.

"Well, I'm slowly coming to terms with everything," said Maggie evasively.

"Because I've just heard from Elizabeth Fairchild and she said she didn't even know you were in Paris!"

"Ah, yes, well," said Maggie, flustered. "I haven't really got round to going to the embassy yet." There was a pause laden with unvoiced disapproval. "You see, it brings back so many memories," she went on, weakly.

"They said they'd love to see you," said Shirley. "After all, they knew Jeremy very well. I think Roger Fairchild was at Oxford with him."

"Mm, yes, I know," said Maggie. "And of course it was high on my list of things to do."

"Well, they're giving a dinner party next week for the head of the OECD who did a lot of negotiating with Jeremy back then."

"Ah," said Maggie, trying to remember what OECD stood for.

"So they're expecting your call," said Shirley, bringing the conversation abruptly to an end.

The dinner party was the following Tuesday. She would miss the evening news and she told Zoltan that he would be dining alone. She looked long and hard at the contents of the plywood cupboard in her hotel bedroom and chose a black jacket and skirt which she would wear with her mother's pearls, the sort of thing, she decided, a widow would be expected to wear.

"Maggie, my dear," said Elizabeth Fairchild warmly, clutching her in an embrace that left traces of face powder on the collar of her black jacket, "How *are* you?" She held a limp Maggie at arm's length. "I wouldn't have recognized you!"

"Yes, well," said Maggie, "I thought it was time to take myself in hand."

"Yes, of course you did," said Elizabeth, patting her arm. "Now I would like to introduce you to the Russian ambassador, Sergei Plutonov. He remembers Jeremy well from disarmament talks."

The Russian ambassador was reassuringly the same height as Maggie but considerably wider. "Ah, yes, Madame, indeed, indeed." His grasp of English was clearly not proficient. "We are having very nice weather for the time of year," he ventured hopefully, his eyes, squeezed between a lowering forehead and wide cheekbones, looking at her warily.

A waiter stood at her elbow and Maggie took what appeared to be a glass of water that turned out to be laced with gin. She took a gulp before replying. "Yes, it is very mild, isn't it?"

"And then," said Elizabeth, "I'm sure you remember Mercedes, the wife of the Mexican ambassador. They were here at the same time you and Jeremy were. Her husband was also *chargé d'affaires* in those days."

"Of course, I remember them well," said Maggie taking another gulp. "The previous ambassador was called José Luis, wasn't he?" He had been a round little man with a bristly moustache that always tickled when he effusively kissed her hand.

Mercedes looked at her incredulously, her plump face unwontedly solemn. "Didn't you hear?"

"Hear what?" asked Maggie, draining her glass.

"José Luis went waterskiing on the Zambesi. He was posted to Africa after Paris. I thought you would have heard." Her voice lowered to a confidential whisper. "All they found was his hat!"

Maggie felt an irrepressible urge to giggle and helped herself to another glass of clear liquid.

"It was a terrible tragedy," said Mercedes.

"Oh, yes," said Maggie, trying to sound suitably heartfelt, instantly ashamed of her lack of gravitas. "Did he drown, then?"

"Oh, no." Mercedes' cheeks wobbled with emphasis. "It was a crocodile!"

"Most distressing," said Elizabeth Fairchild, implacably shepherding Maggie around the room. "Now I'd like you to meet the new ambassador from South Korea, Mr Song Ju."

How had she ever lived through these evenings year after year, wondered Maggie.

"And Mrs Song Ju," said her hostess, bending encouragingly over a very small person standing next to her husband.

The very small person was smiling and nodding at her. "We love your country," she said, having evidently mistaken Maggie for someone else.

"And now," said Elizabeth dramatically, "I have a surprise for you."

Maggie found herself face to face with two of Jeremy's best friends.

"Geoffrey and Camilla came up especially from the south of France when they knew that you would be here!" The ambassador's wife was triumphant.

Although quite a few years older, Geoffrey had been in the service with Jeremy. They even looked alike, tall with smoothly parted silver hair and a supercilious expression, the embodiment of generations of privilege. Camilla had always been the perfect, stalwart diplomat's wife, adept at bridge and golf tournaments, indefatigable organizer of flower-arranging courses and cookery classes for diplomatic spouses. Her gravlax marinated in Lapsang Souchong tea leaves was a regular at every embassy event. Jeremy and Maggie had sometimes spent weekends with them in the south of France where Geoffrey had retired at the end of a distinguished career. Jeremy and Geoffrey would sip their whisky in the library and reminisce, while Camilla would take Maggie into the garden to deadhead the roses. Maggie had secretly found these weekends rather claustrophobic but she had been happy to see Jeremy so relaxed and mellow as they sat by the fire in Geoffrey and Camilla's little cottage, an oasis of Kent in the heart of Provence.

"Maggie, my dear, how *are* you?"

"Such a shock . . ."

"So sudden . . ."

"Did you get our letter?"

"Oh, yes, thank you so much," said Maggie guiltily, remembering the batch of correspondence that Shirley had given her in Vienna and which was still in the boot of her car. "I haven't been able to reply to everyone yet."

"No, of course you haven't. Well, as I said in the letter, it was a loss not only to us but to the service, an incalculable loss."

"Oh, absolutely," said Maggie fervently.

"And the two of you were such a wonderful couple."

"Such a boon to the service."

"Thank you both. You are being very kind."

"You're *looking* very well."

"It must be the haircut," said Maggie running her fingers nervously through her new short crop.

"Very becoming, I must say." Geoffrey was looking at her rather intently.

"What are your plans now?" asked Camilla. "Are you going to go back to England?"

"Well, yes, eventually, I suppose. Right now I'm thinking of going to all the places where Jeremy and I were posted."

"A sentimental journey?"

"Actually, more like laying Jeremy's ghost."

Camilla gave a shrill little laugh. "Oh, Maggie, I'm so glad you can joke about it!"

"I couldn't be more serious," said Maggie earnestly, turning as she found a slight pressure on her arm.

"We're going into dinner," said Elizabeth Fairchild.

Maggie drained her glass and set it back with a loud clink on the tray.

At dinner she was seated next to a tall taciturn man who, Elizabeth said, had worked a great deal with Jeremy when they were in Paris.

"I was very sad to hear that your husband passed away," he said solemnly. "He was a great help during his time here." Then he turned to his other side and started talking to a bubbly French lady on his right.

Maggie knocked back her glass of white wine. She remembered those glasses from their own posting. They were still the same cut crystal. The damask tablecloth looked the same as well, as did the plates with the lion and the unicorn on the rim. She was becoming increasingly aware that she had had no lunch to speak of and all this alcohol was going to her head. As a general rule she never drank gin, just wine and sherry.

"I'll be interested to hear what you think about the wine, Legay," said Roger Fairchild from the head of the table. "It's made by a friend of Elizabeth's."

"He's not exactly a friend," said Elizabeth with a deprecating little laugh. "I went to school with his wife."

The waiter presented her next-door neighbour with the bottle of wine, unwrapping the napkin so that he could see the label. Maggie saw that it had Château Bosquières written in gold under a coat of arms surmounted by a crown. The waiter poured some into her glass too.

"*Intéressant,*" said her neighbour, "*un bouquet exceptionnel . . .*"

Maggie drank her consommé greedily but there appeared to be sherry in that too. She turned to her other neighbour. He had been introduced as the director of the Paris Opera and was sitting in stony silence, his prominent Adam's apple jerking up and down every time he took a sip from his glass.

"The opera season is just starting, isn't it?" asked Maggie assuming once again her role as well-primed guest at a French dinner party.

The man turned to look at her with a weary expression. "Yes, the day after tomorrow is the premiere."

"I was at the opera only once while we were posted here," she said. "It was a command performance for Prince Charles."

"*Così fan tutte,* wasn't it? Yes, that was before my time."

"Which opera are you putting on at the moment?" Maggie asked him politely.

He was holding his wine glass up to the light. "We are opening the season with *Otello,*" he said.

The waiter poured some more of the ruby-coloured wine into Maggie's glass and she took a large mouthful. "I always felt so sorry for Othello," she said.

"Ah, Madame," he said, his Adam's apple diving down into his collar, "*la jalousie*."

"But don't you think that jealousy is the most human, the most natural of human emotions?" asked Maggie, taking another gulp.

"I think a real *homme du monde* should rise above such things," said her neighbour, trying to capture the little egg floating in his consommé, "don't you?"

"No, I don't," said Maggie, unaware that she was raising her voice. "He loved his wife so much and he was devastated when he thought that she was unfaithful to him." The man's face was beginning to look blurred and Maggie felt herself shaking with dry sobs. The room had gone quiet and she felt Elizabeth's powdery cheek against hers.

"My dear," said a voice in her ear, "wouldn't you like to lie down?"

"Oh, I'm quite all right," said Maggie truculently, "it's just that I really don't agree about Othello and Desdemona."

"No, no, of course you don't," said her hostess soothingly, and she found herself being led into the drawing room. "I think you should put your feet up for a while. You've been through a lot lately."

Maggie lay down on a stiffly upholstered sofa, her chest heaving, dimly conscious that something unspeakable had happened.

The ambassador had joined his wife. "If you like, Maggie," he said kindly, "we can make up a room for you and you can sleep here tonight. I'm sure you'll feel much better in the morning."

"Oh, no," said Maggie, sitting bolt upright in panic. "Please, I'd like to go home."

Next morning, Maggie went down to breakfast at the hotel suffering from a hangover and ruefully aware that she had made a complete exhibition of herself. What on earth would Jeremy have thought? She would have to send Elizabeth Fairchild flowers.

Zoltan ceremoniously rose to his feet. She noticed that he had egg on his moustache.

"*Boldog születésnapot*, Modome," he said.

"Oh, Zoltan, you remembered it's my birthday!"

"It's easy for me to remember," he said. "It's the same day as the Hungarian Revolution."

It was decided that they would celebrate somewhere special for lunch.

"I'll take you to the Brasserie Lipp," said Maggie. "They specialize in cabbage. You like cabbage."

When they arrived at the brasserie they were seated at one of the little tables against the wall. Zoltan was looking spruce. He was wearing a tie for the occasion; it clashed cheerfully with his checked jacket. She carefully studied the wine list. Very few names of wines even began to ring a bell. Except Château Bosquières — now where had she seen that before? Of course, last night . . .

Maggie ordered the most expensive vintage on the list. After all, it was her first birthday since Jeremy's death. He had always punctiliously remembered the day, a bouquet of flowers being delivered to the residence, presumably ordered by his secretary. Jeremy thought that birthday cards were rather common and preferred to include his personal embossed visiting card with formal wishes written in his neat handwriting: "Happy Birthday to my Dear Wife", or "Happy Birthday, Maggie dear". He always gave her a present as well, but he didn't believe in surprises, perhaps because he didn't like surprises himself; he preferred gifts to be practical. They would discuss the gift in the morning while he was having his bath and Maggie was sipping her tea. The Russell Hobbs kettle had been a birthday present from Jeremy. Last year he had given her a high-powered hairdryer because Maggie had always washed and blow-dried her own hair. Sometimes, as for the Queen's birthday, she would go to the hairdresser, then stand with her hair tightly curled and her high heels sinking into the lawn as she greeted the local British community, who came out of the woodwork every year to toast her Majesty with draught beer and bangers from the barbecue.

Zoltan was critically analysing his *choucroute*. "The French," he said, "are supposed to be the best cooks in the world and they can't even make a *töltött káposta*! My mother —" he began.

"Zoltan," Maggie interrupted him, "how is our project coming along?"

"It takes time," he said lugubriously, "and very careful planning. If we are to sabotage the teleprompter, then I have to get into the building — and it's not as easy as you think . . ."

"Excuse me," said a voice from the table next to them. "I couldn't help noticing you are drinking my wine. Do tell me, how do you like it?"

95

Maggie turned to look at the man sitting next to her. She had been brought up to be diffident of strangers who started up conversations without being introduced, but he had a ruddy, smiling face and she instantly felt reassured. "It's delicious," she said.

Zoltan nodded. He was looking at the man's plate. "May I ask what that is you are eating?" he asked.

"Ah, the soufflé! They do it so well here. Let me order some for you too." He made a sign to the waiter, who instantly appeared at the table, his attentiveness very unlike the lackadaisical service he had reserved for Maggie and Zoltan.

"You know, I am from the Dordogne," said their neighbour. "That's where I make my wine. I have a little chateau."

Maggie found herself wondering what a little chateau looked like.

"But with the soufflé maybe you would like some Calvados? Jules," he called the waiter again. "I also raise pigs, prize pigs," he said deprecatingly, as though he were ashamed of boasting but could not resist. "The sow was just voted National Champion. I am looking for a suitable husband for her." Running his short fingers through his hair, which made it more tousled than ever, he raised his glass and held it up to the light. It was a deep ruby with shards of light dancing in it. "It's a lovely colour, isn't it? To your very good health!" He toasted them.

"*Egészségére!*" said Zoltan.

Maggie just smiled and raised her glass. Jeremy had schooled her that it was non-U to say, "Cheers".

"Are you and your husband here for a holiday?" the man asked.

Maggie gasped. "Oh, but we're not married!" She laughed, acutely embarrassed, horrified that anyone would think that she was married to Zoltan in his checked jacket and droopy moustache, and at the same time deeply ashamed of her reaction.

"We're here on business," said Zoltan importantly.

"Ah, I know you English don't believe in asking personal questions, but I'd love to know — what sort of business?"

"Import-export," said Zoltan portentously.

Their new friend was called Luc and he insisted on accompanying them back to their hotel. He had also insisted, despite Maggie's protests, on paying the bill because, he said, the wine had been his fault after all. "It's not every day that I sit next to someone who chooses my wine, and such a good vintage too," he said, looking at Maggie approvingly.

"Ah," he said, as they arrived at their hotel. "I know this street well. I always come here to buy my cheese." At the entrance he vigorously shook Zoltan's hand and brought Maggie's fleetingly to his lips. "*Au revoir, mon amie*," he said.

As she passed through the glass doors, Maggie looked over her shoulder and saw him still standing there in his baggy trousers, his hands buried in his pockets.

"'*Au revoir, mon amie*'!" said Zoltan with his execrable accent as he made his way to his room.

"Zoltan, you just concentrate on the project," said Maggie sternly, closing her door. She sat down on her candlewick bedspread and kicked off her shoes. Despite herself she felt elated by their encounter. No one since Gilberto had given her this guilty feeling of euphoria.

During their posting in Paris she had seen Gilberto one more time. One day in early spring, she had found her way to a book shop in a side street off the Boulevard Saint-Germain des Prés. She had been told about it by an artist whom she had met at a reception. It specialized in art books and she had gone to find a book on Vuillard, whose work she had just discovered. She was staring up at the shelves, scanning the titles. Music was playing in the background and she became aware that it was a tango that sounded vaguely familiar.

"*Cuando pasaste a mi lado se me apretó el corazón,*" said a voice in her ear.

She turned round to see Gilberto's sharp profile and dark eyes looking down at her.

"I think they're playing our tune," he said and smiled. He looked so different when he smiled, disarmingly youthful, almost mischievous.

"Oh, hello," said Maggie, blushing in confusion. She found herself babbling something about Vuillard and the spring-like weather. Gilberto liked Vuillard too, and recommended a book on the Nabis, which they purchased together.

He insisted on carrying it in its plastic shopping bag. He would walk her home, he said, taking her arm and

98

steering her along the narrow pavement, the plastic bag bobbing against his leg.

In England, Maggie had been used to taking a man's arm, slipping her fingers into the crook of Jeremy's elbow. There was something unnervingly intimate about the same gesture the other way around. A tingling sensation seemed to be radiating like a burst of sunlight from her sleeve where his hand was firmly ensconced and she wondered if Gilberto were feeling the same thing. She looked up at his face and noticed that a muscle was twitching in his cheek.

They walked along the boulevards where the horse chestnut trees were coming into flower and rummaged among the wares of the *bouquainistes* on the banks of the Seine. They stopped at a cafe, sitting at a table outside on the pavement, and relished the promise of the spring breeze ruffling the tablecloth. Gilberto told her about his childhood in Buenos Aires and Maggie told him about growing up in Ledbury, which sounded so very different. They paused to listen to an old man playing his violin at a street corner and Gilberto dropped a ten-franc note in his violin case as they walked away.

"That was generous," said Maggie.

Gilberto smiled for the second time. "He was playing so terribly badly," he said by way of explanation, "we should encourage him."

When they arrived at the Hôtel de Charost, Gilberto kissed her on both cheeks. Once again Maggie smelled a hint of lime.

"That's the way we say goodbye in Argentina," he explained, when she looked momentarily taken aback. "And we say hello the same way when we meet again."

Maggie stumbled up to the first floor, her mind in a whirl. Monique, Jeremy's secretary, was sitting at her desk looking sternly at Maggie's red face over the top of her steel-rimmed spectacles. "The ladies from the British Women's Association have been waiting for you for over half an hour," she said.

"Oh, how perfectly dreadful!" Maggie gasped. "I must have lost all sense of time."

After a long and tedious meeting, Maggie returned to their residence to find Marielise advancing into the drawing room bearing a large vase, her nostrils flaring above a mass of long-stemmed red roses.

"Flowers?" asked Maggie. "Who are they from?"

"There was no note," said Marielise, "only this." She handed Maggie a package which contained a cassette: a medley of tangos.

Maggie bent to smell the deep velvety petals. Somehow they did not look like the flowers habitually exchanged in diplomatic circles. "Marielise, I'd like you to have these," she said.

Marielise looked undecided as to whether to show pleasure or disapproval.

"You know," said Maggie, "my husband's allergies . . ."

Soon after, to Maggie's intense relief, the Argentinian ambassador was recalled. Maggie never mentioned that spring afternoon to Jeremy although it was the first time she had ever withheld any part of her life from her husband. In the end, she banished the whole episode and the lingering feeling of guilt to the back of her consciousness, from where it surfaced from time to time whenever she heard the poignant strains of a tango. How absurd to have carried that burden of guilt for so long; how innocent it all seemed compared to the iniquities detailed in Jeremy's diaries! She did not want to admit that it had been far less innocent than she liked to think now.

The telephone was ringing. "Maggie, dear," said Camilla crisply at the other end of the line. "We've just got back to Seillans. Geoffrey and I are both very worried about you."

"I know, I'm so sorry. I behaved terribly last night. I don't know what came over me."

"You are going through a very difficult time right now," Camilla went on firmly, "and Geoffrey and I were wondering if you shouldn't have some kind of counselling. Lots of women in your position go to a psychiatrist."

A psychiatrist! Maggie felt her blood go cold. In her and Jeremy's world, only people who thought they were Napoleon went to a psychiatrist.

"Oh, I don't think it's that bad," she said hurriedly, "really I don't. I'm not usually like I was last night, I promise you."

"Well, think about it, won't you? And Geoffrey also says" — he could be heard rumbling in the background — "that maybe you might like to come and stay with us in the south of France. It might do you the world of good."

"Oh, thank you," said Maggie, "you're being very kind. I can't thank you enough."

She was grateful when the conversation came to an end. Was she really going to pieces, she wondered. With her thoughts of revenge, could she be losing her mind?

Zoltan, meanwhile, seemed to have made revenge on Delphine his mission in life. He wilfully suppressed his own personal motives, preferring to think of it not only as a professional and potentially lucrative undertaking, but as a quest that appealed to the latent heroics of his Magyar soul. Modome, though she could hardly be described as a damsel, was undoubtedly in distress, and he would not rest until he had achieved his goal.

He spent a very large part of his day in the Bar des Copains in front of the French television building. He had become friendly with many of the workers, joking with them in his appalling French, playing cards with the patron when business was slow, watching a football match between Paris-St Germain and Marseilles on television and making himself useful in the neighbourhood in all sorts of little ways. *L'Hongrois* became a popular figure, called upon to repair light fixtures and burst pipes, a real *ouvrier d'entretien*. He slowly pieced together who worked where and with whom and what took place at what time on each floor. Delphine, he was not surprised to discover, was not well-liked. She worked on the third floor in a corner office together with a small army of technicians and assistants and the director of the evening news, Leroy.

It was to be three weeks to the day after Maggie had set their strategy in motion that he at last got his big chance. It was lunchtime and the coffee and soft-drinks machine gave out on the first floor of the television building. The resident *ouvrier d'entretien* was out to lunch and could not be reached and meantime the entire staff on the first floor was clamouring for liquid refreshments. Zoltan was sitting in the cafe in front of an *omelette au fromage* and a *ballon de vin rouge* when Léon, one of the doormen, came bursting in.

"*Alors, viens, mon vieux, on a besoin de toi!*"

Léon propelled Zoltan across the road and pinned a staff badge on his dark blue lapel. Fortunately, it was not hard to find the cause of the trouble and Zoltan had the drinks dispenser back to normal in less than half an hour. He was slapped on the back: "*C'est génial, l'Hongrois!*" Zoltan refused any form of gratuity with a regal wave of his hand. Several people promised him a drink that evening at the bar. Before he left, he carefully put the staff badge into his toolbox and walked out into the crisp autumn sunshine.

He called Maggie as soon as he got back to the Bar des Copains. "Modome," he announced dramatically, "at last, our moment has come."

It was agreed that Maggie would sit all afternoon by the telephone and wait for his next move.

Zoltan had discovered that Delphine arrived every evening at about seven and stayed until late. For the rest of the afternoon he could hardly sit still; this, he was convinced, was his big opportunity. At a quarter to seven he stood leaning on the door jamb of the Bar des Copains smoking and watching the entrance to the television building. He was rewarded halfway through his second cigarette by the vision of Delphine's long legs snaking out of her Mini Cooper and striding towards the doors. He stubbed the cigarette out under his heel and grabbed his toolbox. "*A tout à l'heure, Gaston,*" he shouted over his shoulder.

The doormen changed shifts at six. He knew that, as he often shared a drink with Léon when he got off work. He had therefore never met the man they put at the door on night duty, which was just as well. Life under a Communist regime and fifteen years as an embassy chauffeur had trained Zoltan to be effectively invisible. He walked past the desk unchallenged, his badge prominently displayed, and made for the lift. He turned left on the third floor and, at the end of the corridor, stood hesitating in front of three identical doors. One of them opened with a flourish and a young man with an unruly lock of hair and a black shirt and tie burst into the corridor, yelling at someone behind him. Zoltan could see a large man with a red face gesticulating at his desk and, beyond, Delphine was perched on a stool above a tangle of wires and cables while a woman in a white coat brushed her cheeks with rouge. He walked straight into the room before the door could close.

The large man stopped gesticulating and stared at him. "*C'est quoi, alors, là?*"

"*VIRus CONtrole*," said Zoltan flatly. Like all Hungarians he always put the emphasis on the first syllable of every word.

The red-faced man's tie was hanging loosely round his neck. He gave it a jerk. "*Maintenant?*" he fumed. "*On sera en direct dans une demi-heure!*"

"*Je fais vite*," said Zoltan.

"*Vous n'êtes pas français?*" asked the big man, fumbling in his pockets.

"*Je suis Hongrois.*"

Leroy, because Zoltan surmised that this must be he, was visibly mollified as he searched for his cigarettes. "Ah, Budapest," he said, "*j'étais là, moi, en '56.*"

"*Moi aussi*," said Zoltan gravely.

"*Alors, faites vite. Je vais fumer une cigarette . . .*" Leroy swept out and disappeared around the corner of the corridor, no doubt on his way to the third-floor coffee machine.

Zoltan sat down at the big man's desk and looked at the screen. Typed across it in big letters were the news headlines shortly to be transmitted by Delphine. He looked across at where she was sitting, with her perfect coiffure teased and sprayed, and was confident that there was no danger of her recognizing him: she had never once looked at him when he opened the car door for her. Nonetheless, he felt the adrenalin all over, tingling at the roots of his hair and pricking the tips of his fingers. He took out his mobile and called the hotel where the concierge grudgingly put him through to Maggie's room.

"I'm here," said Zoltan, suddenly in a panic. "I'm sitting in front of the teleprompter. What do I do now?"

"Read it," said Maggie tersely.

Zoltan's eyes slowly went down the news items, familiar words and names leaping out of the text at him. He pressed the downwards arrow and minor news unfurled on the screen. Just then, right at the end, he saw the word "*ambassadeur*". "*Son Excellence, l'ambassadeur des Etats Unis, Monsieur Seton Salter . . .*" he read to Maggie in his halting French. "What about Seton Salope?" he asked eagerly.

"No, I think Salaud would be better," said Maggie firmly. In Delphine's French accent this would become *C'est un salaud.*

"How do you spell that?"

"S-A-L-A-U-D."

"T or D?"

"D like . . . like Devonshire."

"Or Debrecen?"

"Debrecen."

"*Curva jó,*" said Zoltan, which is a Hungarian rude word. ". . . *a été reçu,*" he went on, "*par le Ministre des Affaires étrangères au Quai d'Orsay . . .*"

"Quai, Quai?"

"*Con?*" suggested Zoltan helpfully.

"Let's concentrate on Orsay."

"What rude word sounds like Orsay?" he asked.

"*Ordures?*" ventured Maggie. She spelled it out. "What comes next?"

Zoltan inserted "*ordures,*" typing with both his forefingers. Then, ". . . *pour fêter . . .*" Zoltan was triumphant. "That sounds like *péter* — you know, to fart?"

"I know what *péter* means! Then what?"

Zoltan ran his long fingernail along the line of text. ". . . *ensemble l'anniversaire de la consegne de la statue de la Liberté par le gouvernement français à la mairie . . .*" Zoltan pounced on that one. "*Merde de New York!*"

Maggie was in the throes of objecting that "*merde*" might be too obvious when Zoltan cut off the phone. Heavy footsteps were approaching along the corridor.

Zoltan swiftly pressed the upwards arrow and stood up as Leroy's big frame appeared in the doorway. "*Ça va,*" said Zoltan. "*Tout OK.*"

"*Merci. Alors, à la prochaine fois.*"

"*Pas de quoi,*" said Zoltan, hastily taking his leave. It was twenty past seven. He went back down in the lift and walked silently out of the glass-fronted doors and into the street. He would watch the news at the Bar des Copains.

Zoltan took his usual seat, wiped the sweat off his face with a handkerchief and dialled the number of the hotel again. "Are you watching?" he asked Maggie.

"Of course I am!" said Maggie. She rang off nervously. Her eyes were glued to the screen waiting for Delphine's nightly apparition.

As a treat, Zoltan ordered a whisky and soda. The television was already beaming the weather forecast from its perch in the corner of the bar. Delphine was shown sorting out her papers against a sky-blue background. "*Mesdames, messieurs, bonsoir.*" She flashed her dazzling smile and launched into the news that Zoltan already knew. As usual, she remained expressionless throughout, even when she was describing a fatal accident involving a bus in the Parisian *banlieue*. Zoltan felt his breath coming faster as Delphine neared the booby trap he had prepared for her.

She mentioned the American ambassador's name, effectively calling him a bastard without a flicker of an eyelid, and the fact that he was now farting rather than celebrating with the foreign minister on the Quai of Muck rolled off her tongue unchecked. She only started visibly losing her composure when she landed on the word "*Merde*", instead of "*Mairie*" of New York. Her cool gaze became distinctly troubled and the telephone on her desk rang. Grabbing the receiver she said in flustered tones: "*A vous le reportage de Mireille St Just.*"

"*Elle a dit 'merde'?*" asked Gaston, puzzled, from his position behind the bar.

"*Elle a dit 'merde',*" said Zoltan, smiling broadly. He finished his whisky in one swig and picked up his toolbox.

"*Adieu, Gaston,*" he said and left the Bar des Copains for the last time.

Maggie was waiting for him in her room. She had turned the television off. Her mind was spinning in all directions. Her first reaction had been shock. Her revenge on Mausie had been something private, which, she felt sure, would never be divulged to anybody else.

It had been her idea that their revenge on Delphine was to be a public affair, but now she had definite misgivings that this time, with millions of French viewers involved and quite possibly a national scandal, there might be repercussions. Then there was the question of Jeremy. What if he had actually witnessed from some lofty celestial eyrie this totally reprehensible lack of taste on the part of his wife? How horrified he must be! *Merde*, indeed! It went against the grain of everything he had ever stood for in his private and public life. And then there was Zoltan. Had she created a monster, a son of Frankenstein who was going to cut a swathe through Europe wreaking revenge on Jeremy's mistresses in particular and unfaithful spouses in general?

With a determined shake, she put her misgivings aside. Zoltan had brought off a brilliant coup and should be commended. By herself she would never have been able to smash the prismatic goldfish bowl in which Delphine had swum so effortlessly and with such naiad grace night after night. And after all, she reassured herself as Zoltan came triumphantly through the door, Delphine had deserved it, hadn't she?

For the first time in fifteen years, Maggie found herself giving Zoltan a kiss on the cheek as, flushed and beaming, he stood waiting for her congratulations. "Go and take off your salopettes, Zoltan," she said. "We're going somewhere special for dinner!"

"You're going to like this restaurant," Maggie said to Zoltan as the taxi drew up outside Chez l'Ami Louis.

Maggie had never been there herself but she knew that Jeremy had once taken a minister known for his gourmet tastes to this unpretentious-looking and very expensive little restaurant in the Marais during an unofficial visit. It had been mentioned effusively in Jeremy's diary, in between one rendezvous with the now disgraced Delphine and the next. Jeremy had commented on the *foie gras*, which they had consumed together with Chateau d'Yquem.

"They are famous for their goose liver," Maggie told Zoltan proudly.

Indeed, they were. Zoltan reluctantly admitted that it was better than anything he had ever eaten back home in Hungary. It was served liberally and totally without ceremony in pink fragrant slabs on toasted chunks of country bread.

Zoltan sat in his best dark suit, the one he had worn to accompany Jeremy to pick up important dignitaries at the airport, and regaled Maggie several times with the exact mechanisms that had come into play: the coffee machine, the appearance of Delphine, his conversation with Leroy. He appeared to be under the impression that the whole thing had been entirely his own idea and his own handiwork.

Maggie decided not to disabuse him. She pushed a wadded envelope over the table. "You have really deserved this," she said.

Zoltan swiftly transferred it to his inner breast pocket and continued eating with relish.

"Zoltan, do I seem my normal self to you?" Maggie asked. "Do I seem disturbed, or —" she searched for the right word — "or anything?"

"Modome," said Zoltan, his tongue loosened by the euphoria of this, his finest hour and by the Sauternes, "you have never seemed more normal to me than you are now." He voluptuously stroked his moustache with his long fingernail. "I shall miss our import-export business."

"You don't have to, you know," said Maggie. "I was hoping you and I might go to Rome. Aren't you forgetting Arabella?"

They returned to the hotel to find the concierge waiting for them, looking distinctly more animated than usual.

"A gentleman was here this evening," she said, handing them their keys. "He left this for you." She reverently put a round wooden box on the counter. "He didn't seem to know your proper name but he said it was for the beautiful English lady with the Hungarian gentleman."

Maggie and Zoltan stared at the box, which was filling the lobby with a very strong odour of cheese. Maggie took off the lid and there it was, on a bed of straw, its delicate rind the colour of lightly toasted bread, with a creamy substance oozing from little cracks around the edge.

"*C'est un don des dieux un fromage pareil,*" breathed the concierge, clearly viewing Maggie in a new light as the recipient of such a magnificent cheese.

"She says such a cheese is a gift of the gods," said Maggie.

Zoltan wrinkled his nose dubiously.

"He left a note with it," said the concierge, producing a large stiff cream envelope of the kind used to send wedding invitations. On one side it was addressed to Comte et Comtesse de Bosquières, followed by what Maggie presumed was the name of the little chateau in the Dordogne. She turned it over. Scrawled on the back was a message: "I am staying at the Crillon and would be *hors de joie* if I could see you again." It was signed "Luc de Bosquières".

Zoltan looked at both sides of the envelope carefully. "What's this mean?" he asked, pointing at the word "Comte". "I thought he said his name was Luc."

"That's his title," said Maggie.

"*Gróf*? But I thought he was a farmer. He makes wine and has prize pigs."

"Sometimes the two things go together," said Maggie.

"But what's this, then?" Zoltan's fingernail deliberately underlined the word "Comtesse". "There is a *Grófnö*," he said reproachfully.

"There used to be a *Gróf* in our village," said Zoltan as they made their way upstairs. "My mother told me. He owned our village and about ten other villages and hectares and hectares of land. He was a very good-looking man with a moustache like mine" — Maggie tried to look impressed — "and he would ride past our farm every morning on a white horse. He always wore this wide-brimmed hat and he would take it off when he saw us and say, 'Good morning, peasants.' And my parents would say, 'Good morning, *Gróf*.'"

Maggie had noticed that the only time Zoltan became loquacious was when he was talking about his mother and his childhood home.

It really was a wonderful cheese, she thought as she turned the key to her room; how Jeremy would have liked it. And how he would not have failed to be impressed, she couldn't help thinking, that she had an admirer who was a count! She realized that she too would have liked to see Luc again. In his impulsive, irrepressible way, he brought with him a burst of *joie* that she had never encountered before. But a woman of her upbringing could no more have walked into the Crillon and asked for the Comte de Bosquières than she could have mastered the mysteries of tantalum or explained the quantum theory. Quite apart from anything else, there was the unresolved question of the *Grófnö*.

A thank-you letter was, of course, another matter. It was a habit so ingrained in Maggie's way of life it would have been quite simply unforgivable not to acknowledge Luc de Bosquières' gift of a cheese. Maggie's mother had drilled the obligation of bread-and-butter letter-writing into her as a girl and later it had been an indispensable part of diplomatic protocol. Realizing she had no suitable writing paper, Maggie went out to buy some in a little shop she had seen on the Boulevard Montparnasse. She chose ivory-coloured vellum with envelopes lined in tissue paper the colour of Luc's red wine. "Dear Mr de Bosquières," she wrote. No, that wouldn't do. The man was a count, but "Dear Count" sounded wrong. Jeremy

113

would have known what to do, she thought. She would write in French! *"Cher Monsieur le Comte,"* she began, *"Merci pour le fromage."* No, that was far too pedestrian. She chewed on the end of her pen. What was it the concierge had said? *"C'est un don des dieux un fromage pareil!"* she wrote. Somehow her usual *"sentiments les plus distingués"* sounded the wrong note so she just wrote *"Merci"* and formally signed her name. That, she thought, as she addressed it to the Hôtel Crillon, is the letter of a *femme d'esprit*.

3
ROME

They had ample time before they left Paris to savour their triumph. The morning after their celebratory dinner at Chez l'Ami Louis, Zoltan knocked on Maggie's bedroom door while she was still sipping her tea in bed. Her Russell Hobbs kettle had accompanied her on her travels, together with Jeremy's urn.

"Look," said Zoltan, dropping a pile of newspapers on her bed. Delphine's faux pas had been reported widely, as well as the consequences. There had been a formal complaint from the American secretary of state. Poor Leroy had been bombarded from all sides and it looked as though his job at Antenne 2 was hanging by a thread. He was quoted as hinting obscurely at an attempt at sabotage on the part of an East European secret service, but nobody took this seriously. While publicly beating their chests in abject apology, the French secretly found the whole episode very funny. *Les Americains* took themselves so seriously, they deserved a little poke in the ribs now and then, *n'est-ce pas?* It appeared that Delphine's lovely face was to be absent from the screen for quite a while. She, after all, should have read the news prior to going on air instead of primping in the studio. A rival television channel aired the episode several times in slow motion while *Le Canard Enchaîné* really went to town on the whole affair. Maggie began to feel a little proud that she had been the moving force behind what was turning into a national *cause célèbre*. She was, however, anxious to leave France as soon as possible, before there was a chance of the two of them being found out.

Early the following morning, Maggie paid their outstanding bill at the hotel as Zoltan carried down her suitcases, stuffed with all her Parisian purchases, to their waiting car. They were going south and Zoltan was sporting mirror sunglasses and a flashier outfit than usual in honour of the occasion. Maggie stood on the steps of the hotel, offering ineffectual suggestions on the packing, when she saw a familiar figure on the opposite side of the street.

"*Ce n'est pas vrai, ça!*" the Comte de Bosquières called out as he ran over to greet her. "Please tell me you are not leaving already?"

"Modome and I are going to Rome," said Zoltan pompously.

"To Rome! But what a coincidence! I shall be in Rome in a few weeks myself. I have to pick up my son. He is doing a language course there. He is going to study modern languages at university."

"Thank you so much for the cheese," said Maggie. "I have never seen such a wonderful cheese."

"Ah, yes, and you know that is only one of so many wonderful cheeses they have. It is a pity you are leaving — I could have shown you the shop. It was de Gaulle who said that it was quite simply impossible to govern a country that made so many different cheeses."

Zoltan had finished loading the car and was standing expectantly, keys in hand.

"It is a pity, yes," said Maggie, "but we have things to do."

"Ah, yes," said Luc, "the import-export. Where are you both staying in Rome?"

"Modome will be staying at the Hotel d'Angleterre and I shall be lodging with friends," said Zoltan getting into the front seat.

"The Hotel d'Angleterre, how appropriate! I must give you my card." Luc tried all his pockets before fishing out a card that was none too clean. "*Je regrette,* this is all I have. This," he stabbed at a number at the bottom of the card, "is my number in the Dordogne. Of course, first you will have to dial 0033 for France."

"Dial 0033," repeated Maggie automatically.

"And then you take a zero off the prefix for the Dordogne if you are calling from *l'étranger.*"

"Take off a nought."

"On the other hand, perhaps it would be easier if you called my mobile telephone. Somewhere I have a mobile telephone." He patted his pockets. "Here, you see."

Maggie looked at the tiny row of figures.

"You will have to dial 0033 for the mobile phone as well."

"I see, 0033." Maggie was in a daze. "Goodbye, then," she said. She joined Zoltan in the front seat.

"*Au revoir, bon voyage!*"

They looked back to see Luc waving expansively with both arms as the Volkswagen turned the corner.

★ ★ ★

Zoltan was silent as they drove away, his expression inscrutable behind the mirror glasses. Maybe for Christmas she would give him a pair of Italian shoes, Maggie thought as she watched the square pale grey toes of his woven moccasins negotiating the accelerator and the clutch. After all, he had done a masterly job on Delphine; she would have been lost without him.

As it turned out, Zoltan had not only made no objection to their descent on the Eternal City, but it transpired that he had his own very good reasons for wanting to return to the scene of Jeremy's crime. He had had a girlfriend during the Rome years with whom he had since kept in touch and with whom he could stay while Maggie's next ploy was put into effect. He was, he said, his customary gloom momentarily lifting at the prospect, looking forward to their reunion.

For Maggie, after perusing box three of "Papers — Jeremy", the worst aspect about Jeremy's paramour in Rome had been that it was somebody she knew, somebody with whom she had sat on committees, had helped at her stall at the annual British Women's Bazaar, had hobnobbed with at embassy receptions, had even, on occasion, invited to tea. This seemed to her a double betrayal. Arabella Stuart Watson had been, she had thought at the time, a friend. She had been and no doubt still was the headmistress of the Holy Mary Asquith School for Girls, an exclusive academy for the daughters of the elite and those who aspired to become one of its members. Sometimes, subject to meticulous vetting by Arabella Stuart Watson in person, the aspiring even succeeded in their goal and their fees were gratefully accepted into the school coffers. She had always seemed to Maggie a paragon of upper-class breeding and moral rectitude, the kind of woman one imagined astride a saddle rather than astride — Maggie felt quite faint at the very idea — a man.

Arabella was younger than Maggie by a few years, but nobody could have described her as pretty. This was something that Maggie found particularly insulting; she had been passed over for a large-boned woman with a prominent nose and a loud voice. Mausie and Delphine had both been beautiful, Delphine particularly so, and definitely feminine and desirable. But Arabella had, Maggie had to admit, a certain style, and therein lay the sting: could Jeremy have been attracted to someone because he felt she belonged to his own social class? Maggie had been acutely conscious when they married that, although all her vowels were above suspicion and she had an innate gentility enabling her by instinct to behave appropriately in any situation, she lacked the self-assured aplomb that came with generations of debutante seasons and country-house life. Even after twenty-five years as a diplomat's wife, Maggie tended to slip rather than stride into a room; hers was a vessel that sped silently across the calm surface of the sea. Arabella, on the other hand, was more like a streamlined skiff with a westerly wind in its spinnaker, ploughing the waves at a regatta.

It had been decided that they would spend the night in the south of France and take Camilla and Geoffrey

Henderson up on their kind invitation "Why, how lovely," Camilla had said when Maggie called. "We'd both love to see you."

"Your chauffeur? How grand," Camilla went on. "Yes, of course he can stay with us too. It's a big house, as you know."

Camilla and Geoffrey lived in a renovated farmhouse near Seillans in the Var. Maggie and Jeremy had last visited them the previous Easter when Jeremy had managed to get a few days off. Maggie loved the south of France and had sometimes fantasized about retiring there with Jeremy when his career came to an end. She could have painted a sea of lavender while Jeremy played golf on the eighteen-hole course near by. Lately, however, Jeremy had been talking increasingly of retiring to a wine-growing village on the Danube, a short drive from Vienna. Could it have been, thought Maggie in a moment of spleen as they drove up to the front door, because he wanted to be near to Mausie?

Camilla and Geoffrey were waiting for her on the steps of the old stone farmhouse. Despite their encounter with her new hairstyle at the Fairchilds', they were clearly expecting a crestfallen Maggie in widow's weeds and were taken aback when she sprang from the car looking radiant in what the shop assistant had called eau de Nil. It did not help that a genially beaming Zoltan in mirror sunglasses and loud check followed in her wake. He still insisted on calling her Modome, but as a result of their joint escapades and long hours spent driving across Europe a certain familiarity had crept into their relationship, which was

122

unusual between a late ambassador's widow and her chauffeur. Although he ate with the cook in the kitchen and in no way insinuated himself into their circle, along the way he had lost some of his impassive anonymity and Maggie felt a distinct chill of disapproval in the air.

Maggie came down to dinner to find her hosts sitting silently on the chintz sofa. A small man in a bow tie, with a cloud of white hair, stood up as she came in.

"Oh, Maggie, dear," said Camilla jovially, "I'd like you to meet our next-door neighbour, Dr Franklin Stern. He recently retired and moved here from New York."

"That must have been a big change," said Maggie.

He took her hand in both of his and looked fervently into her eyes. "Sometimes, big changes happen in one's life. It all depends how one confronts them," said Dr Franklin Stern.

"Yes, quite," said Maggie.

"Would you like a glass of orange juice?" asked Camilla.

Maggie's eyes wandered to the drinks tray. "Well, a little sherry would be nice."

Geoffrey brought over a small crystal glass and carefully put it on the coaster in front of her. Maggie felt everybody's eyes on her as she took a first tentative sip.

"Dr Stern has bought a lovely farmhouse on the other side of the hill," said Camilla.

"I thought Jeremy and I might also retire here one day," said Maggie.

There was an awkward silence broken at last by Dr Stern. "I understand that you have recently been bereaved?"

"Yes," said Maggie brightly. "I was married to one of Geoffrey's oldest friends."

"Friends are always such a boon in moments like these," said Dr Stern.

"Oh, yes," said Maggie taking another sip, conscious that everybody was still looking at her.

"Shall we go in to dinner?" asked Camilla brightly.

Camilla served a vichyssoise and the inevitable roast lamb, which could have benefited from a shorter sojourn in the oven. The mint in the mint sauce came, she told everyone smugly, from her own garden.

"I hear you have been travelling a good deal lately?" Dr Stern asked Maggie as he manfully chewed on a sinewy slice of lamb.

What else had he heard, Maggie wondered. "Yes, it's taking my mind off things," she said, surreptitiously taking a sip of red wine.

"Often," said Dr Stern, "travel can dull the pain but put off the inevitable reckoning."

"Yes, I've realized that," said Maggie.

"I hope you like the wine," said Geoffrey, hovering at the doctor's elbow. "We tasted it in Paris at the embassy. It's made by friends of the ambassador."

"I'm afraid I am not much of an expert," said Dr Franklin Stern. "I drink very little as a rule."

"I picked up a few bottles at a little shop in Seillans," Geoffrey went on regardless. "It's rather pricey, but Camilla and I rather like it, don't we, Camilla?"

Maggie had noticed before that couples who had been married a long time constantly asked each other for corroboration of what they were saying. She wondered if she and Jeremy had been like that.

"Shouldn't you have decanted it?" asked Camilla.

Maggie remembered that Jeremy had always gently poked fun at Geoffrey behind his back. He understood nothing about wine, Jeremy said, but thought that being a connoisseur was like belonging to the right club.

"Oh, no," said the connoisseur, "this is a fairly young wine."

It was strange, thought Maggie, how Luc's wine seemed to be constantly coursing through her life right now. "I know the man who makes this wine," she said. "He's called Luc de Bosquières." Everybody turned to stare at her. "I met him in Paris."

Geoffrey was standing at the head of the table, still holding the bottle and looking a little bereft. Maggie felt like an ingénue who had stolen the matinee idol's best line.

"Well, he's a friend of the Fairchilds, of course," said Camilla.

"Actually, I met him in a restaurant."

"In a *restaurant*?"

"Yes, we were drinking his wine and he leaned over to ask how we liked it."

Camilla was clearly pondering on the word "we". "Well, that seems rather forward," she said.

"Oh, but you don't know Luc," said Maggie, suddenly very animated. "He is somebody who never bothers with convention. He is like," she fumbled for a metaphor, "a force of nature." What on earth was she doing, wondered Maggie in surprise, talking like this about a person she hardly knew? She realized she was showing off.

"I see," said Camilla. "Well, time for pudding."

Maggie took another sip of Luc's wine and turned to Dr Stern. "Were you a medical doctor in New York?" she asked.

"Oh, no," said Dr Stern. "I am a medical doctor as well, but I had a psychiatric practice in Manhattan."

"I hope you won't find life a little slow here after being at the hub of the world?" Maggie was beginning to feel thoroughly irritated.

"Oh, I assure you, there is plenty of material for someone in my profession here too." Dr Stern fixed her with a hypnotic gaze.

Maggie felt panic rising. "I don't know, of course, but I can't help feeling that people in this part of the world have many other ways of coping with their problems."

"Ah," said Dr Stern deliberately, "and what would those be?"

"Well, good food," she eyed her apple crumble askance, "and good wine," she rebelliously drained her glass, "and love . . ." She saw Camilla and Geoffrey exchange a rapid glance.

"All palliatives, my dear lady, mere palliatives."

"Well, all the same, now you are here you might like to try a palliative or two yourself . . ." said Maggie defiantly.

Camilla leapt to her feet. "Let's go into the drawing room for coffee," she said.

Camilla had evidently been mentally prepared for sisterly condolences as she led Maggie to her bedroom when they all retired for the night. "I have given you a different room this time," she said to her guest with a wan smile. She clearly wanted to be credited with exquisite tact. "Are you feeling a little better?" she asked, patting the Provençal cotton bedspread.

Maggie tried hard to slip back into her role of inconsolable widow but could not help feeling that it was an unconvincing performance. "You know," she said, "I think the full impact of what has happened will only hit me when I go back to London. Maybe that's why I'm still travelling around Europe . . ."

"Yes, probably that's the case," said Camilla primly.

"You've been very kind to worry about me like this," said Maggie a little testily despite herself, "but I shall be quite all right, I really will."

Camilla pursed her lips. "We were very fond of Jeremy, you know. He and Geoffrey go back a long way."

"Yes, of course, I know that. It's all been very sad." And it had been sad. In this, at least, she managed to sound sincere.

That night, Maggie dreamed she was back at the restaurant Chez l'Ami Louis, eating slabs of pink *foie gras* with Zoltan. The door opened and Camilla and Geoffrey came in and sat down at another table. Dr

127

Franklin Stern appeared dressed as a chef in a long white apron, bearing a tray of crumpets.

"I think I shall have some Marmite with those," said Camilla, looking disapprovingly over at their table.

Dr Stern came back with a large jar of Marmite and then, all except Zoltan, they stood up as the strains of "God Save the Queen" issued from the kitchen. Maggie was trying to hoist Zoltan to his feet when she woke up to see Camilla bending over her with her early morning tea tray.

Later that morning, as she and Zoltan drove away, Maggie turned to wave to her hosts standing stiffly outside their creeper-covered farmhouse, and felt intensely relieved that the visit was over. The new Maggie, who had somehow become an outlaw in the weeks since Jeremy's death, found herself reviewing the whole episode in a humorous light. How was it that she had never realized how stuffy Camilla and Geoffrey were, she thought, as they disappeared around the bend.

She found herself looking sideways at Zoltan at the wheel and thinking about him as a man for the first time. She had rarely been aware of anybody as a man during her marriage, so unquestioningly embedded was she in her role as Jeremy's wife. When, despite the impenetrable hedge of thorns she had allowed to grow up around herself, she became nonetheless dimly conscious of an animal attraction to another man, she had rejected the thought as unworthy of her and chivvied it out of her mind. Only Gilberto had managed to unsettle this well-ordered state of affairs and breach the screw top of the gooseberry preserves. Zoltan, she decided now, was not unattractive if only he would shave off that ridiculous moustache. He had the greyish pallor that she always associated with people in Eastern Europe, but then Maggie had been brought up by her mother to think that there was something a little vulgar about a healthy tan. Jeremy had most decidedly been a white man and her mother had always commented to her cronies on how "distinguay" her son-in-law was. Maggie had to admit that Zoltan's lean form had a sinewy masculinity that was not unappealing. On the other hand, how silly of Camilla and Geoffrey to think that she might be having an affair with him! Jeremy would have been horrified at the very thought; in the very worst way it would have been letting the side down. Maggie was grateful to Zoltan for standing between her and the precipice which had opened at her feet after Jeremy died and she somehow felt safer when he was by her side. And, in the meantime, this new adventure in Rome was, as the ghastly Dr Stern had insinuated, a palliative and would put off for a while the inevitable return to her previous self and her as yet unformulated future.

"Rome?" Shirley's voice had lost the deferential tone she had used to the freshly widowed Maggie.

"Yes, well, I thought I'd come and see a few old friends," said Maggie. "I just wanted you to know so that you could forward any mail or anything to the Hotel d'Angleterre."

"Isn't that rather expensive?" asked a distinctly disapproving Shirley.

"Well, they've given me a special rate as it's out of season, and Zoltan's staying with friends."

"Oh, Zoltan's still with you, is he?"

"Yes, he drove the car. Remember? I told you . . ." Maggie felt herself getting into ever deeper water.

"Well, please ask him to contact me," said Shirley as she rang off. "We've been approached about his Italian visa."

Maggie did have a few friends left in Rome. Guinevere was married to an Italian civil servant and helped in the running of a homeless centre that Maggie had patronized while they were posted there. Unlike some of Maggie's other previous acquaintances, Guinevere still answered her old telephone number. They met for tea at Babington's and Maggie was filled in on the missing years after she had left in Jeremy's wake for Paris and Vienna. The expatriate community in Rome was even more transient than most and many of their acquaintances had moved on. There had been one death and a couple of divorces. And the new ambassador was not popular, it seemed. He spent much of his time travelling and was not available as often as the local Brits would have wished for the events punctuating the ex-pat calendar year. But Guinevere was reassuring on one point.

"Arabella Stuart Watson? Oh, yes, she's still around, very much so. She has the daughters of a sheik attending the school now and never lets you forget it."

★　★　★

Maggie had loved Rome. For the first twenty-four hours after she and Jeremy had arrived, she had felt disorientated by the noisy traffic, the rubbish spilling out of bins and the skinny cats roaming the squares of the city, but as the days went by she found herself falling increasingly under its spell. She sat at a table outside a trattoria in Campo dei Fiori on one of their first evenings and basked in the peach caress of a Roman sunset as the old-fashioned street lights flickered on, little pools of light glowing against the ochre-yellow plaster. The old walls with their crumbling cornices and the flagstoned streets seemed to take their antiquity in their stride, as unimpressed as the Romans themselves by the passage of centuries. This was not real, Maggie said to herself. It was a stage set and sooner or later those faded green shutters would be flung open and a woman would rest her large bosom on the sill above the washing line and burst into song. A little boy came by their table with a bunch of roses and offered Maggie one which, with an uncharacteristic gesture, Jeremy bought for her. "They steal them from the cemeteries," he said. He looked so handsome sitting opposite her, playing with the *grissini* in his elegant fingers. There was a balmy breeze ruffling the corner of the tablecloth as they sipped their white wine from glasses jewelled with condensation. She leaned across the table and took Jeremy's hand. "Thank you for bringing me here," she said.

Rome had been her favourite posting. She had felt enveloped in the unconditional warmth of its embrace.

She had loved the Italians, the shopkeepers and the passers-by who looked appreciatively at her legs. "*Che bona!*" they would whistle as she went past, something that had never happened in Ledbury or in Budapest, not even in Paris. Italians knew how to make one feel feminine; even the ministers and the under secretaries who came to the embassy were gallant in their formal way. At receptions they would squeeze her hand or even bend over to kiss it when they took their leave. She had known it was nonsense, of course, but she had often felt that they really found her attractive, that to them she was a woman and not just a diplomat's wife.

Italian politicians had reminded her of pigeons, strutting and pecking around her tall husband, who stood head and shoulders above them all, bending to greet them with his mildly disdainful smile. And the women who thronged the charity teas in their elegant two-piece outfits with far too much jewellery were like the nursery rhyme, with rings on their fingers and bells on their toes; they too would have music wherever they went. They had tiers of gold chains around their necks like the Madonnas behind glass in the churches of Rome; Maggie had been brought up to know that one should wear only one good piece. They had reclined on the damask sofas of the drawing room under the inevitable chandelier and chattered and fluttered their hands with a jangle of bracelets, and laughed and called her "Maggie, *cara*". They were womanly in a way Maggie felt she could never aspire to be, their breasts soft under cashmere twinsets, their dark eyes mischievous and shining with a knowledge she felt she could never share. It was something to do with the air, she decided, so suave and balmy as the sun set in an apricot haze and people strolled in the streets as though Rome were one big *salotto*.

Women brought chairs downstairs and put them outside their front doors to watch the procession eddy past, the *vasche*, or laps as it was called, as though Romans felt constricted within their four walls and needed to interact with the rest of the city as the day drew to a close. During the hot summer nights, whole families would sit around the brims of fountains, the men in undershirts, the women fanning themselves, the children running around the square. There seemed to be so many children in Rome. Maggie loved the unhurried rhythm of Roman days, the long lunch hours, and the total lack of urgency in their day-to-day lives.

Even Jeremy had seemed infected with the lackadaisical charm of life in Rome and had been more mellow and relaxed than she ever remembered him. Sometimes in the lunch hour they would drive out to Ostia along highways fringed with dusty oleanders and rent deckchairs and umbrellas on the beach at the Bagno Marinella. Jeremy never sat in the sun as his was a skin too delicate for tropical temperatures, but he would dive into the sea and swim far out with bold strokes, returning to his deckchair dripping wet and running his fine fingers through his hair. Maggie, on the other hand, had for the first time in her life turned biscuit-brown. It was all so different from her holidays by the sea as a child, when she and Sue had sheltered behind a windbreaker in their Fair Isle woollen hats, waiting with their buckets and spades for the sea to come back from wherever it had gone beyond the horizon. The Mediterranean had no tides worth mentioning and the children went splashing in and out of the water all day long. How wonderful to grow up in a land where the sun always shone. These were children who had never felt the cold, never waited at the corner of the lane before the first light of day — the winter dawns in Herefordshire were grudgingly late — to board the double-decker bus, its windows laced with frost, which would take them on their way to school. In the same way Maggie felt bemused when she and Jeremy would sit eating ice cream in the cool of the evening beside the Bernini fountain in Piazza Navona. How was it possible that people lived like this not just when they were on holiday but all year round?

After lunch, their backs still itching with salt, Jeremy and she would drive back from the beach into the centre of Rome in the heat of the afternoon so that he could return to the office. The spell was soon broken as Jeremy sat fuming behind the wheel in a sea of honking cars. It pained Maggie that Jeremy didn't really like the Italians. He thought them chaotic and corrupt and their propensity for procrastination infuriated him. He considered them inferior partners at the negotiating table and had been far happier later on to have dealings with the Viennese. She remembered once he had even lost his temper with a blue-jowled man lounging at a table outside a bar.

"Can you tell me the way to the Pantheon?" he asked in his perfect Berlitz Italian.

The man rolled his hooded eyes and almost imperceptibly jerked his head to the left. "*Appresso,*" he said languidly.

"*Appresso?*" Jeremy had shouted, his face an unbecoming shade of red. "Do you realize all he can say is 'near by'?"

Maggie was very conscious that she was being extravagant by staying in such an exclusive hotel and she was very careful not to incur any extras. She washed her underthings in the basin and hung them on the radiators at night. She spent the first few days walking all over Rome, up the Spanish Steps and through the Borghese gardens, pausing at familiar landmarks. She would not succumb, she decided, to the tempting boutiques lining the shopping streets in the Via Condotti, but she was determined to visit Ferragamo. Had not Jeremy splurged, after all, on Mausie's slim feet while the two of them were in Rome? After much deliberation she bought a pair of slinky winter boots which hugged her calves, quite unlike any of the practical footwear she had worn to the country weekends that Jeremy had occasionally taken her to. She persuaded Zoltan to accept a pair of lace-up shoes of the kind that Jeremy used to wear — this had been a powerful argument — for special occasions. Meanwhile, a plan was slowly hatching in her mind.

Maggie no longer awoke to the feelings of panic and desolation which had characterized the first weeks of her widowhood, but her anger at Jeremy's infidelity still simmered. Each new revelation was yet another arrow in her heart, until she felt not unlike the figure of San Sebastiano, eyes rolling up to the heavens, in the painting that she and Jeremy had once seen in a church in Florence. Her Vienna and Paris adventures had alleviated these feelings only up to a point. She began to understand why relatives of the victim often insisted on watching capital executions in the United States, their brother's murderer squirming in the electric chair. The trouble was, however, that this revenge was being wreaked on Jeremy's partners in adultery and not on the errant Jeremy himself.

"How simply wonderful to see you again," gushed Arabella, seated behind her desk in the Holy Mary Asquith School for Girls. "We were all so frightfully sorry to hear about Jeremy. And so sudden! It must have been terrible for you." Arabella was looking at Maggie with a quizzical eye. The new Maggie that had emerged from the familiar chrysalis was evidently something of a surprise. "How are you coping?"

"Oh, quite well in the circumstances," said Maggie, slipping back into her previous self for a moment. "As you say, it was so very sudden."

Arabella made sympathetic noises. "So, how can I help you? My secretary mentioned that you have nieces who might be interested in joining the school?"

"Yes," said Maggie, back on more comfortable ground, "Daisy and Janet. They are fourteen and sixteen now and my sister thought they might benefit from a little Continental polish."

"Yes, indeed," said Arabella, instantly reverting to her role as professional headmistress. "Of course, as you know, we have very few vacancies, but I'm sure there would be no problem for Jeremy's nieces. It is, of course, a board decision."

Maggie thought how horrified her nieces would be if they could have witnessed their aunt's perfidy at that moment, Daisy with her pierced lobes and Janet with a tattoo peeping out of one of the jagged holes in her jeans.

"Are the girls interested in sports?"

"Ah, yes," lied Maggie. "Janet plays good tennis and Daisy . . ." she paused, searching for inspiration, "likes croquet." Had she gone too far?

"Well, I am afraid we can't rise to a croquet lawn," said Arabella with a little laugh, "but we do take the girls to the golf course once a week and some of our girls like to ride."

"My sister particularly wanted them to absorb a little culture at first hand," said Maggie piously.

"Of course, we put a great deal of emphasis on art history and the girls are taken frequently to museums and to visit the sites of antiquity. Our main object in the formation of our girls, however," Arabella was in full spate, "is to concentrate on strengthening their character and instilling in them a sterling moral code. This is increasingly important today with the total collapse of family values, the spread of teenage sex and pregnancy."

"Yeah, whatever," Maggie could hear Janet saying.

"It is terrible, isn't it?" she concurred. "So unlike the way we were brought up." She smiled sweetly at Arabella.

"Would you like to see the school?"

Arabella led the way down the marble-flagged corridors and they peeped through the glass panels in the doors into the classrooms. "It's end-of-term exam time," she whispered. Young faces chewing their pens squinted at the blackboard. All the girls wore blue skirts and white shirts with blue and red striped ties. "The Holy Mary Asquith colours," said Arabella.

Maggie walked obediently behind Arabella, who had not changed much in the intervening years. Perhaps even more equine than before, she thought cattily; the phrase "long in the tooth" crossed her mind. She fantasized about how it would be to aim a kick with her new Ferragamo boot at Arabella's widely undulating bottom. She had reread Jeremy's papers in her room at the Hotel d'Angleterre and knew much more now about Arabella than she had before. What had particularly wounded Maggie was that Jeremy had frequently discussed politics with Arabella, and current events, occasionally even philosophical topics. They had listened together to Beethoven quartets. They had watched political talk shows on television and exchanged views on weighty subjects. He had admired the lucidity of Arabella's thoughts and had often sought her advice. Maggie herself had never discussed that sort of thing with her husband — issues, which he pronounced in an irritating fashion with a sharp "s".

She had considered them part of his job and no doubt confidential. Jeremy had, it is true, often consulted Maggie on matters of embassy staff and reciprocal relations with fellow diplomats as he had respected her gentle instinct in these things, but he had never asked her opinion on global matters or the meaning of the universe. Had they, she wondered, also discussed Maggie, and her and Jeremy's life together? It was too much to bear.

Arabella led the way into the gym where the rings and bars lay idle. There was a dancing class being conducted in a corner of the room. "Don't stop, girls," said Arabella in her parade-ground voice. "Just go on with whatever you are doing." Two plump little girls, their faces framed in dark curls, were pointing their toes at the bar. "The daughters of His Excellency Ibn Daoud from Dubai," said Arabella fulsomely, smiling at her charges. "We encourage the girls to engage in physical activity," she went on. "*Mens sana in corpore sano.*"

"*Plié*," called a stentorian voice from the end of the room and the two little girls wobbled uncertainly on bent knees.

"We also have ballroom-dancing lessons," Arabella went on. "It is important for our pupils when they go out into the big world to be able to distinguish themselves with grace on the dance floor at social occasions. We even have an end-of-term dance with the boys from the Jesuit school. Heavily chaperoned, you understand. Girls should grow up to feel at ease with the opposite sex but we vigorously discourage any form of promiscuity."

"I am very glad to hear that," said Maggie.

Back in Arabella's office, Maggie prepared to take her leave. "I'll tell my sister everything," she said. "Maybe if you have a brochure with the fees and things . . ."

Arabella strode over to the bookshelf where a pile of leaflets was neatly stacked next to piles of brand-new morocco-bound books. "We have Speech Day coming up," she said, "and we always give the girls prizes in the form of uplifting literature for their performance during the year." She showed Maggie one of the books. It was an attractively bound copy of *Little Women*.

Maggie opened the book at the flyleaf where, in expensive gold lettering, it stated that the prize was to be awarded to Theodora Schellenberg for Deportment.

"Ah, yes," said Arabella, looking over her shoulder, "that's the daughter of the Austrian ambassador."

Maggie looked at the piles of books on the shelves. "Does everybody get one?" she asked.

"Indeed! We don't believe in encouraging competition for material rewards," said Arabella self-righteously. "Everybody should be commended for something in which they have excelled. All eighty-three of our students will receive one of these."

The telephone rang and as Arabella went over to answer it, Maggie surreptitiously slipped Theodora's copy of *Little Women* into her handbag, casting a valedictory glance at Arabella Stuart Watson's broad rear.

The headmistress was talking fluent Italian with a Cheltenham accent into the telephone. She waved and put her hand over the mouthpiece. "See you at Speech Day!"

"This is going to be very expensive, Modome," said Zoltan. It was the day after her visit to the Holy Mary Asquith School for Girls and Maggie had arranged to meet in a neutral little bar halfway down Via Cavour. Zoltan was accompanied by his former girlfriend, Simona, whom Maggie was meeting for the first time. Indeed, much of Zoltan's time had been spent with Simona, who smiled encouragingly at Maggie from under a peroxided fringe. "I'm afraid it'll take more than just the two of us to pull off something like this," he said. "Simona will come along, of course. She can be our lookout person. But I had to take her brother into our confidence as well, as none of us is an expert in alarm systems. He works in property surveillance."

"And I used to work with an investigations agency here in Rome called Tom Ponzi," said Simona eagerly.

"I thought you only worked in the accounts department?" Zoltan seemed shocked.

"That doesn't mean I didn't know how things were done there. *Ainsi!*" retorted Simona, sticking her tongue out at him.

"So, it will take four of us to carry it off." Zoltan waggled four fingers.

"I hate involving you all in such a risky undertaking," said Maggie doubtfully.

141

"Oh, I've done riskier things in my time," said Zoltan loftily.

"Actually, so have I." Simona laughed.

"This time we would be really and truly breaking the law," said Maggie. "What happens if we are caught?" she asked.

"Modome," Zoltan pulled at the ends of his moustache, "if I didn't crack under Communism I am hardly likely to blab to the carabinieri."

Maggie did not find this as reassuring as it was intended to be. She was also not at all sure how she herself would react if she was caught red-handed committing a felony. If she were ever interrogated by a blue-uniformed official under a naked light bulb she suspected she would cave in at once. "Just how complicated is the alarm system?" she asked.

"That's why we need Simona's brother. He will know how to neutralize the alarm."

"But aren't there regular patrols?"

"He can find out about those too," said Zoltan confidently. "He knows the security company."

"And what about the bookbinder?"

"I have a friend."

"All right," said Maggie at last. "But we must all be very careful. And don't forget that we have less than a month until Speech Day."

Walking back to the hotel under her umbrella, as it had started to rain, Maggie wondered what on earth was she getting herself into now. Then she thought about Arabella and her sanctimonious lecture on morals, and

142

any lingering scruples splashed onto the pavement together with the raindrops. Arabella too would have her "bad quarter of an hour".

On her way back, Maggie stopped at the international book shop. She scanned the shelves one by one, concentrating on the more lurid titles. Every now and then she took her copy of *Little Women* out of her handbag. It took her forty-five minutes to come up with the perfect match. Not only was it a recently published book corresponding in every way in size, thickness and quality of paper to her prototype, but the title fulfilled her wildest expectations. She bought the book, trying to look casual as she handed it over the cash desk. No doubt they were used to middle-aged ladies purchasing dubious literature. She hummed as she waited with an innocent air for the shop assistant to slip it into a bag.

Maggie had never been good at technical things and had never learned to work a computer so it was with some trepidation that she ventured for the first time in her life into an internet cafe.

"I wonder if you could help me?" she asked shyly. "I want to place an order with Amazon dot com."

A pleasant young man with a little pigtail at the nape of his neck patiently explained to her what she had to do and she managed, not without a few false starts, to order eighty-three books to be delivered to the Hotel d'Angleterre.

★ ★ ★

"There is a lady waiting for you in the lounge," she was told as she folded up her umbrella in the hotel foyer.

"A lady?" Maggie walked past the desk into the lounge, her curiosity aroused.

A figure in black was sitting hunched on a sofa, a large handbag on her knees and a very large suitcase propped against the arm. She looked up as Maggie came in. "Dona Margarida!"

Completely taken aback, Maggie allowed herself to be enveloped in one of Esmeralda's capacious embraces. "How wonderful to see you," she said, trying to decide in her own mind whether or not she was sincere. She ordered coffee. Esmeralda embarked on a torrent of explanations.

The new ambassador had not been, Esmeralda raised her eyes to the frescoed ceiling of the Hotel d'Angleterre, a gentleman. He had not known how to behave and had not appreciated her cooking, least of all, imagine, her *bacalhau*. He had even, her voice lowered to a whisper, slept in his socks and not elegant blue knee socks like the ambassador wore but short ones with patterns on them. Esmeralda had had a vision of her late husband, Luis, in a dream, bending over her and whispering in her ear: "Dona Margarida needs you." And here she was.

Maggie had her little bedroom upgraded to a double and watched nervously as Esmeralda filled the cupboard with her belongings, many of which appeared to be of an edible nature. A number of bottles of wine from the Alentejo were wrapped up in her voluminous nightgowns and there were several boxes of ominously familiar Tupperware. Maggie realized, however, that in her heart of hearts she was pleased to see Esmeralda. Esmeralda, with her large shapeless bosom beneath her white apron, was a motherly figure; a mother, moreover, whom she would never be expected to compensate or impress.

In all her years of marriage to Jeremy, with their frequent uprooting and migrations to new places, among new people, Maggie had not found the time or inclination to form close relationships. She was separated by her role from many people and some of the women to whom she felt drawn were diplomats like her, also destined to fly off to another continent and another life. For a while they sent Christmas cards. There was nobody to whom Maggie could bare her soul and confide her secrets. All in all, she realized now, members of the "Diplomatic Corpse", as Janet had unwittingly called it once, were more often than not very boring. Accustomed as they were to be sent abroad to lie for their country — was it Talleyrand who had said that? — they were rarely sincere or spontaneous in their private lives either, keeping up a front, never unbuttoning or unburdening themselves. They would pretend against all evidence to the contrary that they lived in a perfect world, representing as they did an irreprehensible government from an idyllic country. Diplomatic wives never complained. Even in darkest Africa or during the darker days of Eastern Europe, they would stand smiling staunchly by their husbands' sides, united in a sisterly conspiracy that everything was

145

as it should be, much as women of Maggie's mother's generation would never admit that childbirth actually hurt. Was she boring too, Maggie wondered. It was certainly true that she had spent the last twenty-five years pretending to be someone she was not.

In Esmeralda, she realized, she finally had a friend and confidante. The social barriers between employer and employee slowly broke down and, when Maggie was not actively engaged in strategy sessions with her fellow plotters, they would sit together on benches in the Borghese gardens or in the coffee houses of Rome and talk of this and that and especially that.

"Men," Esmeralda explained to Maggie, patting her hand, "are not like you and me. They have different appetites. Now the ambassador adored you. I know that for a fact. You had fun together. Remember that. I heard you laughing as you went upstairs after our dinner parties."

"Yes, but if he adored me and I made him laugh, why did he have to spend so much time with all these other women?"

"Men," said Esmeralda, "they never grow up. Now take my Luis. He could never resist a pretty face, but when he was dying it was me he wanted. He held my hand and squeezed it in his, right up until the last minute."

"But I wasn't with Jeremy when he died . . ."

"You can be sure that he wished you were. That Mrs Morgenstern, Fatima told me, she was a boring woman, *chata, muito chata*." Esmeralda started to laugh. "She guessed it was you, you know, with that crazy idea of the fish. Fatima told me that she wanted to sue you and then realized that she would only look foolish. You've no idea," she went on, "the scandal you caused! The neighbours started complaining about the smell and they had to call in the city sanitary service to find out what the problem was. It took Fatima weeks to wash the smell of rotting fish out of Mrs Morgenstern's clothes and cupboards and they had to throw all the shoes away! Then they had to change the carpet in the dining room. It was such a delicate colour and the octopuses had bled ink all over it. The veneer on the dining-room table was completely ruined. Oh, she was so furious! The insurance wouldn't pay for anything as there was no evidence of a break-in. And that carp! It had completely decomposed!" Esmeralda scraped her little plastic spoon around the bottom of the paper cup which had contained her pistachio ice cream. "Oh, you wicked girl, Dona Margarida!"

Occasionally, Zoltan called to give a progress report, which he couched in cryptic language as though their mobiles might be bugged. "Modome, I have arranged the interview you requested with Matthew Raven for tomorrow at twenty forty *post meridiem*."

Matthew Raven was Zoltan's code name for his bookbinder friend, a reference, Maggie guessed, to Matthias Corvinus's historic library in Budapest. Matthew Raven's workshop was in a part of Rome rather less salubrious than the Hotel d'Angleterre. He received them in his basement after working hours and they sat around a deal table under glaucous neon lights.

He was a ratty little man with a nervous twitch, but he had an ingratiating manner, talking nineteen to the dozen in impenetrable Romanaccio. He used his hands with manic frequency to make gestures even Maggie understood. He often drew a line with his thumbnail down his cheek, tapping the side of his nose for emphasis, and more than once he rubbed his fingers and thumb together in a gesture that Maggie knew meant money. Once he mimed sewing up his lips with needle and thread, but even more alarming was a rapid slash of his forefinger across his neck as though slitting his throat, although fortunately this was followed by a lewd wink. Maggie came away feeling far from reassured.

All Maggie had to do now was wait. To kill time, she and Esmeralda wandered through the streets of Rome and spent many hours in department stores which Esmeralda preferred to boutiques. Maggie took her friend to the Colosseum, and they threw a coin into the Fontana di Trevi. "*Que lindo*," puffed Esmeralda following stolidly in her wake. They lunched at the little trattorias in Trastevere where she and Jeremy had sometimes gone on summer evenings and where everyone had joined in when groups of roving musicians had sung *stornelli*. In Rome, Jeremy had had more evenings off to spend with his wife; as head of chancery, his days were full, but they did not have to socialize as much in the evenings. Jeremy had put his hand over hers when she joined in the refrain. "I'm not sure if this is quite suitable for your ears, old thing."

Unlike Maggie, Jeremy had been an outstanding linguist, which had proved a huge advantage in his career. He could quote Dante to the Italians and Montesquieu to the French and Rilke to the Germans with a more than passable accent.

Maggie took Esmeralda to her and Jeremy's favourite restaurant in a lovely square; it had a fountain with little stone tortoises climbing all over it. The waiters Maggie remembered had all gone and the decor seemed different. She asked after Giuseppe but nobody knew what had happened to him. They went to the market in Campo dei Fiori and Esmeralda waddled delightedly from stall to stall, exclaiming in eloquent Portuguese at the mounds of mushrooms, the tender little salads, the *puntarelle*, the Roman lamb, the *abbacchio*, which she would have loved to have been able to cook in her kitchen in Vienna. They went together to visit Guinevere's homeless centre where there were several old-timers who still remembered Maggie and insisted on kissing her hand with their bristly chins.

"You need some more *peperoncino* in this soup," Esmeralda admonished the young immigrant chef in the kitchen as she dipped spoons into the large cauldrons. "Now off you go and wash your hands before you eat," she ordered Gino, who spent his days under a bridge; and, to everyone's surprise, he meekly wandered off to the washroom.

At the beginning of December, the Christmas market was set up in Piazza Navona and Esmeralda squealed and clapped her hands like a child at the Neapolitan cribs with their figurines of shepherdesses and little mills churning trickling brooks and suns setting rosily in the background.

On one crisp wintery day when they had been in Rome for nearly three weeks, they were wandering around the Forum when Esmeralda sat down suddenly on top of a severed column. It seemed that pillars where senators had once leaned and debated in their togas in the days of Ancient Rome were now to bear the weight of Esmeralda's bottom. She fished for a peppermint in her large handbag and offered one to Maggie. "You know, I've been thinking," she said, "maybe it's time to bury Caesar."

A puzzled Maggie sucked on her peppermint.

"It's time to put the past behind you," said Esmeralda, "and move on. You are an attractive woman and now with all these new things," she looked at Maggie from top to toe, "you will soon find someone who will love you as you deserve."

Maggie shook her head.

"Oh, yes, you will. It's time to forget the ambassador's little failings," Esmeralda crossed herself and kissed her fingers, "and forgive. Enough of this vendetta!" She stood up and brushed the dust off her behind.

"You don't understand," said Maggie. "If I had found out while he was alive, we could have talked about it together. I would have screamed and yelled and hit him, and he would have explained, or tried to explain. It's because I can't do that any more that I can't find peace. It all seems so terribly unfair!"

Maggie's mind kept going back to all those times she had seen Arabella and Jeremy together and never suspected for a moment. She had thought they were talking earnestly at embassy receptions about the Holy Mary Asquith School for Girls, their heads almost touching, Arabella being a much taller woman than Maggie. She remembered Jeremy reading articles from *The Economist* with whole passages underlined and she had always thought it must be his secretary vetting the press for him, but now she was not so sure. Sometimes Arabella had called their residence. There was no reason why she shouldn't. After all, they were friends.

"I just wondered if I could talk to Jeremy," she would say. "Something has come up at the school and I need his advice."

And Maggie had passed on the message, buoyed by the infinite trust she had in Jeremy. One felt such a fool. Maybe Jeremy had confessed to Arabella that he and his wife never talked about all these sibilant "issues" and she had despised Maggie as an intellectual inferior. Oh, no, it was too much!

In the Roman Forum the two women started walking towards the exit. "But just think," said Esmeralda, "you never knew, you never guessed. You had happy years together. You have to weigh the pros and the cons."

Pros and cons were old acquaintances of Maggie's. "You don't understand," she said. "These women have stolen my life!"

It was the first Sunday of Advent, almost a month since they'd arrived in Rome and Esmeralda insisted on going to Mass. She chivvied Maggie into a pew in St Peter's Basilica, brushing past people who had to flatten themselves against the back of their seats at her bulky passage. Maggie craned her neck to look upwards at the soaring immensity of it all, the swathes of different-coloured marble, the opulence of the stucco and gilded flourishes, the flamboyant frescoes. It all reminded her of a monumental dessert of the kind her mother would have described as "rich". The columns holding up ornate canopies looked like Brighton rock, the stucco like icing on a cake, while some of the niches veined in green marble reminded her of the gobstoppers they had bought at the sweet shop on the way back from school.

Maggie had been brought up in the Church of England, although her mother had tended to consider religion a badge of respectability rather than a faith. Papists were, of course, different. Nothing the matter with them as people, but they were, of course, different from us. It had always been very important to Maggie's mother to be "one of us", to belong to an unspecified group of people who thought the same way and knew what was right. Maggie had attended Sunday School at the village church and helped her mother and her friends decorate the altar for the Harvest Festival every year. As a little girl she had knelt by her bed and said her prayers. "And if I die before I wake," she intoned every evening, "I beg the Lord my soul to take." And every evening she had hidden under the bedclothes and added a postscript: "But please don't let me die yet, oh Lord."

Later, she and Jeremy had attended the Church of England services in the various cities where they were posted, although in Budapest these had been rare as the chaplain had to come especially from Vienna, which he did only two or three times a year. They always sat in the front pew as befitted their station and Jeremy joined in the hymns in a robust baritone. She herself had always taken part in the carol concert. "Ding-dong merrily on high," she would warble along with the others, thrilling to the music rather than the significance of it all. Christmas was a time for children, she had always thought, while for Jeremy and Maggie it was just another of their commitments, involving a spreading of goodwill on the part of Great Britain and the British Commonwealth.

St Peter's was a very different proposition. Maggie looked over at Esmeralda who sat rapt, her mouth slightly open, staring at the glittering flock of prelates flapping around the main altar, which was lit by a blaze of candles. The music was solemn and awe-inspiring, very different from the jolly singalongs of the C of E, gaining momentum as it sped upwards, together with the fragrant clouds of incense, towards the cavernous dome towering above their heads. It was, of course, ridiculously pompous, Maggie thought, but despite everything she found herself feeling uplifted and transported. For the first time since Jeremy died, she felt the dull pressure on her heart lighten. For a brief moment, she forgot why she was in Rome and contemplated, albeit fleetingly, the enigma of eternity.

As they walked out of the church into the winter sunshine, Esmeralda squeezed her arm. "I said a prayer for the ambassador," she said.

"I think I did too," said Maggie. "It's very different from what we are used to in England, you know."

"Dona Margarida," Esmeralda explained as they made their way through the crowd, "it's like a reception at the embassy. Some embassies put on more of a show, others less," she said. "But in the end it's all about the same thing: welcoming an honoured guest."

Speech Day at the Holy Mary Asquith School for Girls loomed nearer and nearer. Maggie had become increasingly nervous as she waited for the arrival of the books, but, just as she was about to panic, Amazon dot com duly delivered the goods, which she found stacked by the reception desk when she and Esmeralda returned from one of their Roman forays.

Esmeralda went up to their room to rest and Maggie was just studying one of the cardboard packages when she heard a rumpus behind her, the rustling of newspaper, the clink of china as though a coffee cup had overturned and the thud of a number of heavy objects hitting the floor. She turned round to hear a familiar voice.

"You are here at last!" Luc extricated himself from the mess around him and came bounding over. "I thought you'd never come! You see, I have only a few hours before I have to pick up my son at his language course."

Maggie found herself inordinately pleased to see him.

"Ah," said Luc, pouncing on the pile of books. "Import-export!"

"Yes, well . . ." She guided him back to his table in the lobby and started righting his coffee cup and picking up the scattered pages of *Le Monde*.

"I do hope you don't mind," said Luc, suddenly sober as though uncertain of her reaction. "You are the only person I felt like seeing in Rome at the moment and I was hoping we could have lunch?" He looked disarmingly boyish as he ran his fingers through his unruly hair with a supplicant expression on his face. "I mean, of course, if you don't already have another engagement."

As it happened, Maggie did not have another engagement. If she had paused to think for a moment that accepting a strange man's invitation to lunch was rather "infradig", as her mother would have called it, she would have pushed the thought out of her mind. After all, Luc was hardly a stranger: indeed, he was one of those people one felt one had always known. And hadn't she told Geoffrey and Camilla he was someone who never bothered with convention? Neither, surely, did the new Maggie, she thought to herself, as she stepped out of the Hotel d' Angleterre at Luc's side into a city that seemed to be sparkling with promise in the crisp winter sunshine.

Luc took Maggie to the ghetto, where she had never been, because he wanted to eat *carciofi alla giudea*, a Jewish way of making artichokes so that they were flattened into little stars and fried. "You see," he told her as he marched her along the narrow streets, her heels catching in the cobblestones, "my grandmother was *juive*. I always remember when we went to see her at her house in Neuilly she would give us Jewish food. I shall never forget her *cholent*. And on Fridays, she lit a candle and everybody said prayers. But, of course, we were raised *catholiques*."

Growing up in Ledbury, Maggie had had very little to do with Jews. There was Mr Ross, the tailor at the end of the High Street, but she had only known that he was in any way different from everyone else when, as they walked past his shop, her mother had said, lowering her voice, "They're Jewish, you know." As for Jeremy, his opinion had been that, like all foreigners, they were people for whom, in one's line of business, allowances had to be made.

Luc and Maggie sat opposite each other in the little trattoria and it was as if Maggie had always known this bulky rumpled figure, gesticulating and laughing and appreciatively gulping his wine. She felt totally at ease with him, as if there were no longer any need to pretend or impress; and indeed, Luc seemed to like her just the way she was, unconditionally accepting her imperfections as part of her charm.

The artichokes, it appeared, were not yet in season, but he suggested she eat grilled mushrooms with *nepitella* instead. "I am very good at finding mushrooms," he said, looking as embarrassed as he had when he boasted about his prize pig. "Even as a child, I had an eye for a little *chanterelle* hiding among the roots of the tree trunk — they are very shy, the *chanterelles* — and HAH!" — the American couple at the next table looked over in alarm — "I pounce!"

By the time they had finished, he was late for his rendezvous with his son and had to put her in a taxi, telling the driver three times where he had to go. He thrust a large square hand through the window and squeezed her arm. "*A bientôt,*" he said.

Later that afternoon, Maggie hailed another taxi and, piling the cardboard packages into the back of the car, headed for their usual meeting place at the bar in the Via Cavour.

Zoltan looked even more solemn than usual. "Everything, Modome, is going according to plan," he said with the air of one who should be saying, "It is a far, far better thing that I do now than I have ever done."

Simona tossed her yellow mop of hair with a reassuring nonchalance. She was someone who took life lightly and laughed at everything irrespective of whether it was funny or not. She didn't just laugh with her uneven teeth or lively brown eyes; Simona's laugh involved her whole person, her shoulders, her short mobile fingers, her legs in their pointed cowboy boots. She called Maggie their avenging angel and nudged her in the ribs. "That's our code name for you!" She laughed. "Look over there," she said in the rich cadence of the streets of Rome, "you've made a conquest. He really seems to have taken to you." She indicated a burly man at a corner table who looked as though he spent most of his time behind the wheel of a truck.

Zoltan glared at her reprovingly to no avail.

"See, he's smiling!" said Simona. And indeed the man put down his coffee cup and looked over in Maggie's direction with a most unattractive leer.

It appeared that Simona was genuinely fond of Zoltan. They had managed to meet infrequently over the last few years but theirs was a very solid attachment. She had been married, she told Maggie, to a *figlio di puttana* who had abandoned her for another woman when her son was eight years old and she had raised the boy on her own. However, her son was nearly twenty now; he was apprenticed to a mechanic and lived with his girlfriend in a suburb of Rome. So if she wished — Simona squeezed Zoltan's arm — she was now free to follow Zoltan wherever he led.

"Thank you all," said Maggie, after they had stacked all the packages in the back of Simona's Fiat. "And see you on Monday for the dress rehearsal!"

Maggie realized that nothing in her Parisian wardrobe was suitable for breaking and entering the Holy Mary Asquith School for Girls. She went to buy herself a pair of jeans and some trainers, two items of clothing she had last worn in her teens. She studied the effect in the mirror of the hotel wardrobe and was suddenly struck by the complete absurdity of what she was planning to do. Maybe Camilla and Geoffrey were right and she was slowly losing her mind.

That Monday, according to plan, Zoltan came round to the hotel with Simona to accompany her to what he called "the target" to carry out what he also called a "reconnaissance mission". He was accompanied by Simona's brother who, at Zoltan's insistence, was operating under the code name "The Terminator".

"Now you, Modome," Zoltan said to Maggie in tones that brooked no opposition, "will be stationed here, at the corner of these two streets. If you see a police car or anything suspicious you must whistle three times."

"But I don't know how to whistle," objected Maggie.

"I will obtain a whistle for you," said Zoltan.

The weather forecast for the night before Speech Day, he informed Maggie, was good. It would be cloudy and that would mean no moon, but it would not rain. He pointed out that it would be better if she arrived at the target on public transport so that no one would remember her getting into a car in front of the hotel or arriving by taxi. They would rendezvous at twenty-one hours.

Maggie made a mental calculation. "Isn't nine o'clock too early?"

"No," said Zoltan, "it will be already dark and everyone will be watching the European cup on television." He seemed to have thought of everything.

At twenty-one hours, Maggie was stationed at her street corner with her whistle in her hand. Her fellow conspirators were lurking in the school gardens and Simona was round the corner in what Zoltan insisted was the getaway car. It was dark but the windows in the houses were all alight and in some she could see the flickering of a television screen — of course, it was the football match! Football was a collective hysteria in which she had never shared, as Jeremy had considered it a proletarian sport.

Maggie would have liked to blow her whistle just once to make sure it worked, but it was too late for that. Wasn't it Humphrey Bogart who had given Lauren Bacall a whistle and told her to blow it every time she wanted him to come? It would be wonderful if she blew and Luc came bounding round the corner in one of those manic bursts of energy and enthusiasm he had lately been bringing to her life. She wondered what he would have thought of her present escapade. She knew exactly what Jeremy would have thought.

Maggie was feeling so nervous and jangled on her street corner; she could feel her breath coming in little gasps. Oh, if only it was all over. She heard a number of thuds behind her and tried to peer through the darkness at the school facade. She could see the light from the lamp post reflected in the sash window and dark shadows passing back and forth. More thuds.

"Are you waiting for someone?" asked a voice at her elbow. It was all she could do not to scream. A small skinny little man was looking her up and down at a few feet from her face.

"Er, yes, I'm waiting for my husband."

"He shouldn't leave you alone all by yourself on a night like this," leered the stranger. "You're not Italian, are you?"

"No," said Maggie in a panic. However was she going to get rid of him? "He's gone to get the car to take me to hospital," she said at last. "I have a fever."

The skinny man's interest began to wane.

"Maybe I'm getting" — she didn't know the word for mumps so she cupped her hands to her chin and blew out her cheeks. "I could have caught it from my son." Men, she knew, were terrified of mumps.

"*Orecchioni, mamma mia. Buonanotte.*" The skinny man shuffled off.

She heard more thuds.

"Modome!" An agonized whisper came from behind the fence. "Come and help!" Zoltan held a bulging sack over the fence and then ran back for another one.

As Maggie grabbed the sack, she could see Simona's brother, leaning out of the ground floor window of Arabella's office.

"Here," hissed Zoltan, "the *vigilantes* will be around again in seven minutes!"

From behind, Maggie heard a car revving up the engine. As she reached for another sack, she heard a rasping sound and then a rattle and then the car was silent again.

Zoltan met her eyes over the fence. "It's Simona," he said. "She never could drive a car."

The little Fiat was hiccuping and sputtering at the curb. Maggie ran over to it. "Let me try," she said. Bundling Simona out, she dived into the front seat and played with the clutch which was alarmingly located on her right-hand side. Eventually the car gave three little hops and grudgingly rumbled into motion.

In an instant, Zoltan had the boot open and was piling sacks into the car. "They'll be here any minute," he said hoarsely. As he was tipping the last sack into the car, it split open down the side and books started spilling into the gutter. Simona and her brother scrambled to collect them, just as they saw lights at the end of the street. "The *vigilantes!*" squealed Zoltan, leaping into the car.

Slowly, Maggie moved away from the kerb, leaving Simona and her brother standing there. Even in her petrified state she realized it would be a mistake to drive too fast. She slid round the corner just as a car came driving slowly past the school. Inside she could just make out two uniformed figures in the front seat looking up at the darkened building. Through her rear window she could see them coming to a halt. They stopped to speak to Simona and her brother who were trying to look like innocent bystanders on a quiet street of Rome after dark. Just at that moment a roar issued from every lighted window in the neighbourhood until the night seemed full of noise.

"Italy has scored a goal," said Zoltan. "They won't be interested in Simona now. Let's go!" He slapped the dashboard and Maggie had no choice but to drive off with their cargo of purloined books in the boot of the car leaving Simona and the Terminator to their fate.

Simona had, of course, risen to the occasion as she told them at length, punctuated with peals of gaiety, when they met once again at their usual bar. She had pretended to be a hooker taking a client back to her apartment. She had wiggled her bum as she put it and been so utterly convincing, she said proudly, that the *vigilantes* had driven off without further ado!

Maggie was still in shock. It was the first time in her life she had done something so flagrantly against the law: she who had never even cheated at exams or tried to get away without paying her bus fare and she couldn't quite believe it. And they had nearly got caught in the act! She had visions of everyone she knew, of Hilary Mackintosh and Shirley and Geoffrey and Camilla and Elizabeth Fairchild, all reacting to the news that Jeremy's wife had been arrested for breaking into the Holy Mary Asquith School for Girls.

"You need a drink," said Zoltan. He came back with something dark and alarmingly potent. "A Hussar cocktail!" he said triumphantly. "You'll feel better after that."

Maggie felt the warmth seeping back into her frozen limbs. She took out her whistle and blew it. Of course, nobody came, but everyone in the bar turned to look at her and some of them smiled. Nobody seemed to think it abnormal; after all, Italy had won the match.

Zoltan, Simona and her brother had been detailed to manage the next phase of the operation. It was decided that they would go to the bookbinder's workshop at dawn, and would then return to the school without Maggie, after the *vigilantes'* last round at five-thirty.

After going over the plans one last time, they drove Maggie back to her hotel. She went to bed, falling immediately into a troubled sleep, her dreams peopled by Hussars on horseback tucking their tall red hats under their arms and saying, "Good morning, peasants." She awoke bleary-eyed at dawn with a cry of alarm. The Hussars had turned into carabinieri blowing whistles.

"Dona Margarida!" murmured Esmeralda, roused from deep slumber in the bed next to her. "Everything is going to be all right."

Maggie lay imagining the scene, the opened sash window and the sacks being passed over the fence and back into Arabella's office. What if Simona couldn't start the car again?

In the end, Maggie overslept and she had to rush to be on time at Speech Day, for which she was careful to dress up in her Parisian best. She knew some of the parents of girls at the school, daughters of the British diaspora. She bowed her head with grace when they all said how upset they had been to hear about Jeremy. She received several compliments on how she looked, and many of them seemed genuinely pleased to see her again, but Maggie couldn't concentrate, her mind in turmoil. Zoltan had turned his mobile off, no doubt so that he and Simona could catch up on their sleep, and she had been unable to check with him how the night had come to an end.

Nervously, she slipped into a chair in the back row and sat staring in front of her in frozen anticipation. On either side of her, smartly dressed families were taking their seats, often accompanied by grandmothers and younger siblings.

The lady next to her took out a fan and smiled at Maggie. "Do you have a daughter in the school?" she asked.

Maggie felt the familiar fist punching at her stomach as she said no, she was there because her nieces might like to join the school next year.

"Oh, they'll love it, you'll see," said the lady, fanning vigorously. "Our Mathilde can never wait for the holidays to end."

What, thought Maggie in panic, if something had gone wrong? What if, in the meantime, somebody had found out?

As it turned out, everything went off swimmingly at first. A prominent female member of the Italian establishment gave a rousing speech. There were so many openings for women now and the world needed women to govern, to manage businesses and, she turned ingratiatingly to Arabella sitting next to her on the podium, to teach.

The school orchestra clambered onto the stage and settled themselves in a large semicircle with a lot of scraping of chairs and stage whispers and raucous tuning of instruments. The music teacher was a pale young man who clearly modelled himself on Daniel Harding at La Scala, his tails flying, a lock of hair bobbing on his forehead. The orchestra performed an awkward rendering of a piece by Monteverdi and then with feigned reluctance, in answer to tumultuous applause, an overture by Schubert. The daughters of Ibn Daoud danced a *pas de deux* together and were enthusiastically applauded by what appeared to be a large delegation from Dubai in the front row.

At last, Arabella Stuart Watson stood up to deliver her customary uplifting address, in which maidenly virtue and family values played their usual part. She was dressed in a navy-blue suit and white blouse and her hair had been swept up into a bun, every inch the headmistress. This had been, she said, a particularly successful year with twelve students going on to university and a series of victories for the school hockey team. They could now boast thirteen different nationalities in the school — here a dazzling smile was directed at the front row — and Arabella liked to think they were a little United Nations in microcosm.

She would like, she said, to call the girls, one by one, to the dais to receive their prizes. She picked up the first of the large pile of books on the table and called out: "Isabelle Devereux."

A little girl with ringlets and red cheeks came shyly up to the platform. "For exceptional merit in elementary mathematics," Arabella continued. The little girl curtsied to the headmistress and returned to her seat with the book tucked under her arm.

"Magdalene Goodson . . . Petronella von Heinrich . . ."

For a while, this part of the ceremony went smoothly as few pupils or their parents bothered to open the book beyond the flyleaf with their names on it. In the end, it was somebody's little brother in the row in front of Maggie who, bored with the proceedings and with little else to do, actually started leafing through his sister's prize.

"Hey, Mum, look at this," he said in a hoarse whisper. He was staring at a pen-and-ink drawing which left little to the imagination.

Maggie saw his mother grab the book from his hands and hiss something in her husband's ear.

Meanwhile, a murmur began buzzing from row to row. The murmur became loud. The parents sitting on Maggie's other side started whispering angrily in a language that she didn't recognize. After a while, they rose to their feet, gathered up their belongings and walked out.

"*Alors là!*" the lady with the fan said loudly. She sprang to her feet, stepping on Maggie's toes as she made her way to the end of the row, followed by Mathilde and a man in a turban who was presumably her husband. Others followed suit.

Arabella was still in full spate: ". . . and above all I am proud to say," she went on, "that our girls are ready, girt in armour, to face the many insidious perils confronting our youth today. They know their worth and they will leave this school like little foot soldiers of virtue marching into a battle against the forces of decadence and dissipation . . ." More and more people seemed to be making for the exit and her voice began to falter. For once uncertain how to proceed, she evidently decided to round up her speech. "And on that note, I would like to thank you all for coming today and we look forward to seeing you again next term."

"We'll see about that," said a red-faced man making for the door.

Arabella made her way rapidly towards the doors of the school hall which had been flung open to accommodate what was becoming a mass exodus. A copy of *Little Women* was thrust into her hands by an irate man in a dog collar. Bewildered, she turned the pages until she came to the title page: "Kama Sutra," she read. "An illustrated introduction to the amatory arts of the Orient."

A vociferous Italian lady was berating her in broken English, stamping on her daughter's morocco-bound prize. "*Eine Schande!*" said a distinguished gentleman who could well have been Theodora's father. The last to file out was the delegation from Dubai in a compact group, averting their gaze from Arabella, who was left standing all by herself, hugging the book to her breast, breathing heavily and perspiring in an evident state of shock.

Maggie was the last to leave. She went over to Arabella and patted her arm. "You never told me that sexual education was part of the curriculum," she said, then, mindful of Matthew Raven, she drew her thumbnail down her cheek. "I am sure Jeremy's nieces will be most appreciative." And as a parting shot she attempted one of the bookbinder's lewd winks.

It had been decided to celebrate with lunch at a restaurant that Zoltan knew of outside Rome in the Castelli Romani. Simona came with her brother and the bookbinder, who talked incessantly, telling rude jokes in Romanaccio that Maggie only vaguely understood. Esmeralda was in her element, laughing and crying and embracing everybody in turn. Vast quantities of food were consumed and a mound of *abbacchio scottadito* was brought to the table and rapidly disappeared. Simona noisily licked the grease off her fingers as she chewed on the fragile ribs of lamb and even Zoltan seemed to approve of the menu. The yellow wine came in thick glass litre jars and the meal seemed to go on for ever. An itinerant musician came to their table with an accordion and the bookbinder led them in a series of *stornelli* which involved a lot of ribald laughter. Toasts were drunk.

"To our avenging angel, Maggee!" said Simona.

"*Hasta la vista*, baby!" said the Terminator who had taken off his jacket to reveal blue tattoos on either arm. "Viva Maggee!"

"Viva Maggee, viva Maggee!"

Their hilarity attracted the attention of the neighbouring tables. "Viva Maggee," said total strangers, raising their glasses of dark yellow wine, their flushed faces smiling in Maggie's direction.

Each member of the team took it in turns to relive the various stages of the coup. How they had neutralized the alarm, how Simona's brother had torn his trousers on the gate, then the broken sack and the *vigilantes* and Simona pretending she'd picked up her brother, who was desperately trying to hide the tear in his pants. They filled Maggie in on what had happened when they went back the following day just as dawn was breaking. There had been an electrifying moment when they had thought the patrol was on its way and they had not yet finished the job, but it had turned out to be only some inebriated teenagers returning from a disco. Then Zoltan had tripped over a bench and landed with a crash and a light had gone on in the house across the street. They all laughed uproariously to think of it now and of how when they'd finally got to the getaway car as they called it, Zoltan couldn't find the key. It seemed hysterically funny in retrospect.

Then it was the bookbinder's turn. He had been up all night substituting the *Kama Sutra* for *Little Women*. He made a sweeping horizontal gesture across his forehead and then wrung his hands vigourously as though he had wiped off copious amounts of sweat. Towards the end, he said, he had fallen asleep at his desk and had woken up only when Zoltan called to say they were on their way. His indeed had been the fattest envelope of all. As Zoltan had promised, the whole venture had been very expensive. Meanwhile, it seemed that nobody had slept a wink that night as they waited to load the books into the car and stack them back on the shelves before morning. They had finished as the first light of dawn shone lemon-yellow behind the cupolas of Rome.

Was this really her, Maggie from Ledbury, she thought, as she found herself laughing as uproariously as the rest. What would Jeremy's reaction have been? Then her mind went to the odious Arabella, her husband's Roman muse. Her resolve hardened and she ordered another sambuca.

They stayed there until the day began to darken beyond the wide windows looking out over the Roman countryside and Maggie was not a little drunk as they drove amid the evening traffic back into the city with Simona still laughing, the bookbinder cracking jokes and Esmeralda softly singing *fado* on the back seat beside her.

★ ★ ★

The *Kama Sutra* scandal, meanwhile, was the talk of expatriate Rome and had even been written up in the English-speaking newspaper. Guinevere was full of the story when she met Maggie at Babington's for tea a few days later. His Excellency Ibn Daoud of Dubai had gone so far as to remove his daughters from the Holy Mary Asquith School for Girls and quite a number of parents were likely to follow suit. Arabella's official explanation had been that the whole affair was the work of a vengeful parent whose child had not been accepted by the school. However, there were rumours, Guinevere said.

"What sort of rumours?" asked Maggie innocently.

"Well," said Guinevere, "apparently, despite all her talk about the virtues of maidenhood and all that jazz, Arabella was having it away with a married man."

"No!"

"Yes, can you imagine? Behind that po-face and pious talk there was quite a firebrand."

"Well, who would have thought it?" Maggie shook her head.

"So they say it wasn't a vengeful parent, but a wife with *le corna*." In Italy a husband or wife whose spouse is unfaithful is always described as wearing horns.

"My goodness," said Maggie.

Maggie had decided that Zoltan and Simona would drive the car back to England with all Maggie's belongings and Esmeralda's bags and "Papers — Jeremy". She and Esmeralda would travel by aeroplane.

171

They would all meet up in Jeremy's bachelor flat in Ebury Street. The least she could do, Maggie felt, after everything they had done, was to offer them a little holiday in London.

If the truth be told, Maggie dreaded the return to England all by herself after so many years abroad. Though in no way mollified or resigned to the situation, she had reluctantly postponed any idea of avenging herself on Jeremy's paramour in Budapest, as she had perused the diaries thoroughly and there was nothing in them to suggest where she might be found, even if she had been still at the same address. The time had come, therefore, for her to face up to the fact that she was now a woman on her own with a future that was only hers to forge. The respite was over, the hiatus between what had been and what was to be.

Before they left Rome, she and Esmeralda went to a little trattoria in Trastevere for the last time. At the end of the meal, Maggie joined in the *stornelli* humming the refrain and even translating one of them for Esmeralda, who burst into raucous laughter.

"Oh, Dona Margarida," she said. "You will see, you have a wonderful future in front of you. If you don't find another boring Englishman, we can find you a Portuguese!" She went on laughing, unaware of the enormity of what she had said.

As they walked back down along Via della Lungara, past the Roman prison of Regina Coeli, Maggie remembered how one evening she had walked with her mother on the Gianicolo above the prison and they had heard the voices of the prisoners' relatives shouting down from the top of the hill to the inmates in their cells. "*Ahoh, Mario, semmo quà!* Light a match if you hear us, we're all here!"

"I don't like it," Maggie's mother had said, quickening her step. "I don't like it, Maggie."

How little she would have liked Maggie's antics over the last months or two, Maggie thought ruefully. Now, as they hailed a taxi, Maggie stood bathed in the amber light of the old-fashioned street lamps, realizing that it would be harder than she'd thought to tear herself away from Rome.

That night, Maggie had a nightmare. It was Speech Day at the Holy Mary Asquith School for Girls. Arabella Stuart Watson was giving out the prizes. She was dressed differently this time, like a clergyman with a white collar and, quite incongruously, a tricorne hat and she had brought her golf clubs with her onto the dais. The sheik from Dubai and his entourage were in the front row; under his headdress the Sheik looked remarkably like Jeremy, but with a pointed beard and moustache. He was sitting, like Jeremy used to do, with his long fingers joined at the fingertips, a signet ring on his little finger. Everyone was being called to the dais to receive a prize.

"Every pupil should be commended for their merits in some field," Arabella had told her and Maggie too was waiting for her prize. Everybody she knew seemed to be receiving an award for their performance. Hilary Mackintosh was summoned to the dais, followed by

Shirley, and she was surprised to see even the hairdresser from the Place de la Concorde receive a morocco-bound volume. The ceremony came to an end and everybody had received a prize except Maggie. She was crestfallen as she followed the others out to the atrium where Arabella was standing swinging a seven iron.

"Why didn't I get a prize?" asked Maggie in a small voice.

Arabella looked around at the assembled company, a scornful expression on her face. The sheik of Dubai was just leaving with his family and laughed shortly out of the corner of his mouth. Shirley snorted as she walked out through the door. Hilary Mackintosh averted her gaze.

"You should have loved your husband more," said Arabella sternly, taking a swing at a golf ball poised on a tee in the middle of floor. The golf ball popped like a balloon with a plaintive phut. "What did you expect?"

Maggie woke up with her heart pounding. Esmeralda was lying in the next bed snoring softly. Their suitcases, ready packed, were queuing up near the door. She could hear the first cars starting up, their wheels hissing on the wet tarmac in the streets of Rome. Every now and then solitary footsteps sounded on the pavement as someone walked past the hotel on their way to work. Maggie lay looking at the reflection of the headlights washing across the ceiling.

Of course she had loved Jeremy, she thought indignantly. How did you quantify love anyway, she wondered. There was madly in love and just in love and then loving someone, which might or might not be the same thing. Then there was loving someone with all one's heart, which Yeats had considered eminently inadvisable when she had studied the Irish poet at school. Then there was being fond, very fond, *extremely* fond. Surely love mutated as the years went by from the mad to the staider variety? She would discuss it with Esmeralda in the morning. She couldn't help thinking, however, as she tried to go back to sleep, that in the Portuguese language there was unlikely to be an equivalent for being staidly fond.

4

LONDON

Maggie turned the key in the lock of Jeremy's flat with a sinking heart. It was just as she remembered it — although imagining it might have changed in any way was, of course, irrational. There was the drawing room with Jeremy's hunting prints all hung too high up on the wall, his desk between the windows, the dining room with its Chippendale chairs and menacing sideboard. Occasionally Jeremy had rented it to colleagues at the Foreign Office, but they left few if any traces of their presence in the apartment when they were gone. Maggie and Jeremy themselves had lived there together only at the outset of their marriage and for brief intervals in between postings. Above all, Maggie dreaded the bedroom with the quilted chintz bedspread and rigid headboard and the dressing room full of Jeremy's flotsam and jetsam and the lingering smell of Floris soap.

Esmeralda was in her element. "We'll have everything nice and clean and sorted out in no time," she said, hugging Maggie's limp form. She started bustling around with the suitcases, pulling the dustsheets off the chairs, flicking on the lights and running her finger along the dusty mahogany surfaces. Hers was a little room behind the kitchen in which she felt instantly at home. She aired Maggie's sheets and put her to bed with a hot-water bottle and supper on a tray.

Maggie woke up to the sound of the hoover and it took her quite some time to understand why the window was in a different place from the Hotel d'Angleterre.

"Where is Zoltan going to sleep?" asked Esmeralda with a loud sniff. It was decided that the only sensible thing would be to empty the dining room. "After all," said Esmeralda, "we won't be giving dinner parties for a while."

Maggie secretly wondered if they ever would. She watched as Esmeralda deftly dismantled Jeremy's prized dining-room table and together they carried it, leaf by leaf, down to the cellar. The whole flat was being shaken into life again, the washing machine rumbling, the hoover droning on and on, a smell of beeswax competing with Esmeralda's cherished bleach. Maggie sat in her dressing gown with her legs tucked under her sipping her tea, immensely thankful not to be alone.

In the days that followed, Maggie's little band of followers was reunited under what slowly became a very merry roof. Zoltan and Simona spent the days sightseeing in London and came home with dubious souvenirs. Esmeralda cooked dinner and they ate on their laps leaving rings on Jeremy's coffee table that made Maggie wince. Simona laughed, Zoltan stroked his moustache with his long fingernail and relived the salient moments of their various triumphs. Maggie found herself watching football matches with them on Jeremy's little television set and drinking beer out of a can, wondering, not for the first time, what her husband would have made of it all.

After a week or so, Maggie began to feel restless. "You know," she said to Zoltan one morning at breakfast, "next year would be high time to have a go at Budapest and take our revenge on Ilonka. Things seem incomplete, somehow."

"Yes," said Zoltan looking pensive. "I wonder whatever happened to Ilonka." He did not seem inclined to find out.

"Well, maybe when you go back to Budapest you could start making a few discreet inquiries," said Maggie tartly.

Christmas was approaching and Maggie realized that soon she would be alone. Zoltan was leaving for Budapest, Simona for Rome and Esmeralda for Portugal. She phoned her sister in Ledbury.

"But of course you must come! We were expecting you," said Sue, the noise of barking dogs and some kind of farm machinery drowning her words.

Maggie drove down to Herefordshire at the wheel of her new car. Much to Zoltan's chagrin she had exchanged their capacious Volkswagen for a little right-hand drive English car. She had filled the back with some of Jeremy's clothes which she hoped would fit Sue's husband, Jim. She and Esmeralda had picked these up from storage, along with some choice items from her kitchen in the embassy in Vienna. Jeremy's bachelor kitchen had left, in Esmeralda's view, much to be desired.

It was quite a while since Maggie had driven down the country roads of her childhood and it was a comforting feeling that she was going back where she belonged. The windows beneath the thatched roof of her sister's cottage sent beams of light into the dark night as she drove into the yard. A couple of boisterous dogs leapt up at the car window and her nieces burst out of the front door.

"Hey, what a brilliant new haircut!" said Janet, who had gone alarmingly orange herself. Everyone hugged and kissed her and Maggie felt an incredible sense of warmth against Jim's broad chest as he ceremoniously enveloped her in a strong embrace.

Her sister looked tired but happy, thinner than she remembered her, dressed in an old sweater and jeans. Maggie instantly felt a little silly in her well-matched Parisian ensemble. In the family it was she whom everybody considered the success story, the daughter who had married the diplomat and gone off to foreign climes to dazzle the salons of Continental Europe, or at least she had been portrayed thus by her proud mother. Sue, on the other hand, had settled for second best, it was felt: a solid, honest, homespun branch manager at the local bank. Sue managed the house and garden and raised chickens, cooking homely meals on the Aga and rarely going out anywhere but the local pub, occasionally invited by friends for dinner or accompanying Jim to a bankers' convention.

The cottage was warm and cosy and the girls had decorated the tree. Somewhere a radio was playing "Away in a Manager". As Jim brought her a drink, a cat climbed onto Maggie's lap and started to purr. The girls sat on either side and plied her with questions. Was it true that Sting had come to the embassy when she was in Vienna? Had she really had a butler and was he like the one in *Upstairs, Downstairs?*

Sue carried the turkey to the table and Jim bluntly said grace. Maggie had forgotten how good gravy could be. She sat watching as the steam rose from the turkey and Jim sliced the breast and Sue spooned brussels sprouts onto her plate. One of the dogs nudged her with a wet nose. She patted his head. She and Jeremy had never had a dog because he was allergic to animals. They had never even been able to stay in a house where dogs were kept. Maggie looked at her family around the table. To her horror, she found herself crying.

"Oh, please don't, Auntie M.," said Daisy, putting an arm round her shoulders.

Maggie couldn't tell them why she was crying, but it wasn't for Jeremy.

After dinner, Jim opened a bottle of brandy and the girls cooked chestnuts on the open fire. Maggie chose her favourite chocolate from a box of Black Magic.

She had brought her sister a Hermès scarf from Paris which Sue reverently folded and unfolded. "What beautiful silk," she said.

Jim cradled Jeremy's clothes awkwardly in his big hands. "Try them on, please go ahead," said Maggie.

183

He stood, blushing and handsome in Jeremy's pinstriped suits from some London tailor. "I'll be the best-dressed bloke at the bank," he said and they all laughed.

"This must all seem rather tame to you," said Sue as they peeled the chestnuts and the girls opened their presents.

"Oh, no," said Maggie. "Oh, no, you don't understand. I have been dreaming of a Christmas like this. I am so happy to be here."

The telephone rang in the next room. "Who can that be?" said Jim. Maggie could hear his puzzled voice questioning the caller at the other end. "It's for you, Maggie," Jim said. "It's from overseas."

"*Boldog karácsonyt*, Modome!" said Zoltan's voice, which seemed to be coming from a long way away. "Happy Christmas! I just wanted you to know that I bumped into Ilonka."

Back in London, Maggie went to the box room and pulled out the earliest box of "Papers — Jeremy". She would start at the very beginning all over again. Budapest had been a long time ago and she wanted to refresh her memory. She opened the bottle of sweet champagne that had been Zoltan's parting gift and went through the little books one by one until once again she fell asleep on the sofa.

Their first posting together had been Washington and it was in Washington that Jeremy first started writing his diaries. There was no record of the year they had spent in London immediately after their wedding. A junior diplomat in those days, in Washington Jeremy had commuted every day from Alexandria, leaving his young wife alone in the bungalow they had been issued by the ministry, its drab interior barely alleviated by the few personal possessions they had brought with them. It was still only the outset of Jeremy's career and they had as yet gathered little moss. Maggie had spent her days pottering in their small garden and making all the machines in the house spin at once: it was the first time she had had a dryer, let alone an ice-making machine or a waste-disposal unit. She would drive in the little Mazda they had bought which said D for drive and S for stop and go to the vast malls where she walked dispiritedly for hours along interminable rows of T-shirts with unfamiliar slogans emblazoned on their fronts. "That will be nahnteen-nahnty-nahn," the large somnolent black girl would say at the cash desk, removing the item from the hanger with languid gestures and long curved silver nails.

Maggie had never been more miserable in her life. Of course she wrote glowing reports to her mother who embellished them still further before passing them on to her cohorts at the Women's Institute. Jeremy had actually met the President, they had stood side by side in the receiving line at the reception for the Queen's birthday, Maggie had started flower-arranging lessons with other diplomatic spouses and won first prize.

Occasionally they were invited to a big gathering and Maggie was introduced to a host of bit players, all of whom were identified by the initials of the organization they worked for, making Maggie even less the wiser. "Mr Hogarth from the SPQR and Anthony Bigelow, former president of the RIP." On one occasion, right at the beginning, she was invited to tea by the ambassador's wife, Lady Smythe, at the magnificent embassy built by Lutyens, and had accompanied her hostess on a tour of the herbaceous border, an event to which Maggie referred more than once in her weekly letters home to Ledbury.

At weekends, Jeremy came home and mowed the lawn and Maggie produced a Sunday roast. The rest of the week she used her new microwave to heat up the delicious ready-made meals she had discovered in the local Safeway. This was before the days when Jeremy discovered cuisine. He would spend his Sunday afternoons catching up on the editorials in the *New York Times*.

Meanwhile, Maggie started making cupcakes with all the different mixes you could buy at the supermarket and learned to say "Have a nice day!" After a few months she was saying: "Have a nice day, *now!*" She watched hours of television series from the seventies and learned all the advertising jingles by heart. In the end, Jeremy started complaining, especially when she told him at dinner one evening that the chicken was "finger lickin' good". "Shouldn't you be doing something more worthwhile with your time?" he asked.

Maggie bought herself a sky-blue tracksuit and joined an aerobics class. She asked her mother to send her all the volumes of *A Dance to the Music of Time*. American women, Jeremy told her reprovingly, were all

186

involved in voluntary work. So Maggie adopted a tree. She went to watch it being planted in Rock Creek Park and occasionally went back to visit it after that. She joined other women at the embassy in organizing Cake-Bakes for charity, putting her new talents and the products of the local supermarket to the test.

Her next-door neighbour was a harassed housewife called Delia whose husband worked in the Pentagon and with whom she made friends. Delia was a jolly person, the mother of two little boys, and Maggie enjoyed her company. She must have been a pretty girl once but was now bordering on obese, something she made no effort to hide in her shorts and tight-fitting tops. She had never lost the weight she put on with the boys, she told Maggie, and diets were often mentioned with the same enthusiasm that Maggie reserved for the opus of Anthony Powell. Meanwhile, she and Maggie ate fudge brownies for tea.

Maggie would occasionally babysit for Delia while she went to what she called the store. She would sit between the boys on the sofa drinking soda pop and watching cartoons. She felt a physical thrill as their close-cropped heads drooped sleepily against her shoulder or one of their hands rested distractedly on her knee. Once, the boys were sleeping over with their grandmother and she and Delia sat on the deck drinking Bloody Marys and listening to the mocking bird trilling in the tree. They slowly became garrulous and not a little drunk and a stern Jeremy came to fetch Maggie home.

At Christmas time, which seemed to start as soon as the last bonfire of autumn leaves had fizzled out, red-nosed reindeer would prance across what Delia called their front yard, with little lights flickering along their harnesses all night long. Maggie would lie in bed and watch their reflection dappling her ceiling and wonder if this life on another planet was ever going to come to an end.

There was little of interest in the Washington diaries. As a junior member of the embassy staff, Jeremy did not have much standing in the pecking order of the capital and pretty young secretaries or lobbyists were unlikely to smile in his direction. Important as his job may have been behind the scenes, in the social arena he and Maggie counted for very little. It was the ambassador and his wife who met the movers and shakers on the world scene and were photographed in colour with people who were making history every moment of the day. Jeremy recorded in his diaries a number of social functions with colleagues that involved barbecues on the porch, their hosts in jokey aprons and their fellow guests in Hawaiian shirts and shorts. Americans in suburbia were obsessed with the idea of comfort, Maggie thought; they invariably dressed in clothes that Maggie associated with the gym or the sports arena, carrying their bottles of water and juice with plastic teats wherever they went. A friendly, childlike folk, "Where are you *from?*" they always asked Maggie in wonder. They had a disarmingly credulous approach to life; Maggie sometimes felt that if she had said she was related to Santa Claus and his reindeer they might even have believed her. Meanwhile, everybody smiled at her in the street and in the store. "Take care," she said cheerily as she smiled back, and she put a "Keep Smiling" sticker on the bumper of the Mazda which took her to and from the mall.

One afternoon Maggie had gone next door to find Delia still in her dressing gown, her hair plastered to her forehead, her eyes swollen from crying. The two little boys sat with hunched shoulders in front of the television, watching Woody Woodpecker. "What's the matter?" asked Maggie, following Delia into the kitchen where she collapsed onto a chair.

"It's Dan," she said. "I found out he's having an affair."

She had been hanging up his trousers when a piece of paper fell out of the pocket. She was going to throw it away but she thought she'd check whether it was important. She fished into her dressing-gown pocket. Maggie unfolded the crumpled page of a notebook. "Come today at four. I'm alone, Helen." Maggie turned it over in her hands, her heart beating fast.

"But that's not conclusive proof," she said doubtfully.

"But I confronted him when he came home," said Delia. "I started off joking, saying this couldn't be what it looked like, and he went all solemn and said he'd been wanting to tell me but that he couldn't find the right moment."

"Tell you what?"

"That he was in love with someone at work and that he wanted a divorce." Maggie sat down heavily on the other kitchen chair.

"Oh, Delia," she said. While she felt overwhelming compassion for her friend, at the back of her mind she also found herself thinking with relief that such a thing could never happen to her. She banished the thought and made Delia a coffee, reciting platitudes as she did so. Maybe he would change his mind. Maybe this was just a passing phase. He would come back to Delia, of course he would. What about the two boys? He couldn't let that go. Knowing all the time that he could and he would. Delia rolled her Kleenex into a ball and then shredded it, wiping her nose with the back of her hand. They drank their coffee and Delia cried until it was time for Dan to come home, then Maggie slipped out through the door.

Next day, Delia left to go back to her mother, taking the boys with her. Maggie stroked their soft bristly heads for the last time. She waved goodbye from what she had learned to call the sidewalk in front of Delia and Dan's front yard. In the weeks that followed the grass grew long in front of their bungalow and a "For Sale" sign was put up on the edge of the lawn. The chimes left hanging on the porch tinkled mournfully in the breeze. That Christmas there were no reindeer, with their harnesses sending flickering lights across her ceiling. Cosy in bed on her husband's right side, Maggie nestled into the crook of Jeremy's arm, secure in the knowledge that behaviour and calamities of this kind were far removed from their world.

Of this particular drama, in which Jeremy showed little interest, there was no mention in his diaries. The jottings were mainly dry and down to earth. A number of lunches and one dinner were mentioned with a certain Jessica, but little seems to have come of the liaison. Jeremy had always been ambitious and Washington had been a major stepping-stone in his career; the diaries were almost exclusively full of the minutiae of his daily work.

The box devoted to their time in Budapest was, on the other hand, a very different kettle of fish — as Maggie's mother might have put it.

5

BUDAPEST

After Washington, Jeremy had been posted to Budapest. In those days, Hungary was still Communist with little prospect of change and Maggie's mother assuaged her disappointment by telling her cronies that this was, after all, a very "sensitive" appointment. Jeremy had been appointed second secretary, dealing with the political side of embassy life, and this was indeed, in the Eastern Europe of those days, a sensitive assignment.

At first everything had been very dreary and dire as she walked the unlit streets, between soot-encrusted facades still pock-marked by the bullet holes of the war and the '56 Revolution. Maggie had relied heavily on the diplomatic shops, but the quest for daily provisions took her to the dismal markets where knobbly dirt-encrusted carrots spilled out next to piles of cabbages, and broken old people stood stoically in queues with sagging plastic bags hanging from their wrists. For the first time in her life Maggie felt rich and privileged and did not find it an enjoyable sensation. People turned their heads and stared as she stepped out of the embassy car as though she were Grace Kelly. In those days the embassy car was the only Daimler in Budapest. Little Trabants farting brown exhaust politely eased out of their way as Zoltan drove them down the darkened boulevards. They had joined the haves in a country of have-nots and Maggie was appalled at the dignified poverty of the people. She bought up bunches of flowers from the old ladies in headscarves standing in the cold outside the metro station. "*Aranyos*," they whispered as she pressed the coins into their hands. "Don't worry, it wears off," said her fellow diplomats who had been there longer and become immune to such things. "You stop noticing after a while. If you want to see poverty, go to Romania."

When Maggie accompanied Jeremy on a reconnoitering tour of Romania, she had to admit that they were right. She had never imagined that a European nation could languish under a regime more consonant with her idea of Haiti and Papa Doc. Within twenty-four hours she too found herself talking in whispers as the fear furled like fog around corners and under doors. There was something unnervingly sinister about the face of Romanian officialdom, a honeyed smile on their lips and eyes like the opaque glass of ambulance windows. "Let's go home," she had said to Jeremy, as she stood in the bathroom of their concrete bunker of an hotel where the brackish water had trickled to a halt. Ceausescu was still solidly in power and huge signs loomed over the skyline extolling his achievements, while the giant gas pipeline snaked over the grey cityscape like a malevolent polyp. Back in Budapest Maggie felt as though she really was back in a civilized country.

Few diplomats learned Hungarian, an impenetrable language in which Jeremy rapidly became fluent, and in any case, as Western diplomats they were not allowed to fraternize with the local community. Social life was confined to other Western diplomats and their wives, all of whom were manifestly making the best of a very bad job. Maggie and Jeremy would be invited to formal little evenings where, in brilliantly lit apartments, they made polite conversation, always careful of what they said as anywhere they went could be bugged. "Beware of the moaners," the wife of the ambassador told her when she arrived. These were women who were letting the side down. "Of course there were women in the hospital who screamed during childbirth," Maggie's mother had told Sue before Janet was born, "but they were members of the lower classes."

Maggie looked forward eagerly to weekends when she could go riding with fellow members of Janet's Diplomatic Corpse down acacia avenues and across flat fields on the edge of the Puszta. They would stop in a clearing and the grooms would hold the horses as goulash soup bubbled in iron cauldrons above an open fire and they sat on hay bales and were served straw-coloured white wine out of plastic beakers. It must have been like this, Maggie thought, in India under the British Raj. Maggie was not an expert rider, but she was always given a safe mare which stood patiently while she struggled up into the saddle and never went faster than a gentle canter. Sometimes Jeremy came with her. In his younger days he had ridden to hounds and the sculpted haunches of his powerful mount would kick up the dust and leave her far behind. In winter they would be driven through the

197

snowbound landscape in a horse-drawn sleigh, rugs over their knees, warming themselves with shots of burning *pálinka*.

They had lived in an uncompromising cube of a house on a residential street in Buda with a large garden back and front where children could have romped with golden retrievers if only Maggie had been able to have either. During those years Maggie had devoted herself wholeheartedly to the business of making children, every time feeling an elated sense of certainty until the monthly recurrence regularly dashed her hopes.

Winters were long and snowbound and the whole city turned brown. Brown not grey was the real colour of Communism, Maggie decided: the brown snow beneath the trunks of the bare brown branches of the deciduous trees, the pervading smell of brown coal and brown smog, the brown curtains and dark brown wooden furniture in the few international hotels.

Then came the first stirrings of democracy. Maggie and Jeremy were there when the Berlin Wall came down and people poured into the streets and held candlelit vigils, when the red stars were wrenched from the facades and the heroes of the '56 Revolution reburied in state. It had been an exhilarating time and Maggie's letters home had been genuinely enthusiastic as she had felt that for the first time in her life she was living history. She and Jeremy had shared this moment intensely and she remembered it as one of the happiest times they had spent together. Never then would she have imagined that Ilonka was trespassing on their idyll.

Maggie remembered Ilonka well. In those days the staff at the embassies was rigorously vetted by both the British secret service and the Hungarian secret police. Gizineni, who had cooked and cleaned for them, was a motherly soul; however, she regularly went through their wastepaper basket and spied on their every move. It was recommended by the British Foreign Service that diplomats should never leave any documents of a financial nature on their desk or travel within the country without their spouse. Their telephones made ticking noises every time they lifted the receiver.

Ilonka, however, must have made the grade because she was allowed to come to their private residences and massage the taut muscles of the embassy staff and attend to the toes and surplus hair of their wives. She would arrive every Wednesday after lunch, standing on the doormat apologetically, a plastic bag hanging from her wrist with the tools of her trade. She would then hang up her coat, remove her woollen hat and place her shoes neatly underneath. She always brought with her a pair of slippers for indoor wear and a white housecoat. Jeremy would retire to the bedroom for a massage to ease his aching back and occasionally Ilonka would manicure his pink oval nails. Maggie herself had sometimes indulged in a pedicure, her feet often sore from the hours spent standing at official receptions. Ilonka was one of the people whom Maggie regularly invited to their Christmas mulled wine and mince pies evenings and for whom she reserved a little package under the tree. Hungarians never opened their presents in front of one, she remembered. They slid them into their plastic sacks with a polite thank you and the subject was never mentioned again. Maggie was always left with the uncomfortable feeling: had it been too little, had it been too much?

Ilonka, it turned out, had not been nearly as apologetic as she had seemed. Jeremy's massages had culminated in virtuoso sexual exploits, it transpired from the diaries, despite Jeremy's terse prose. They also met in her tiny apartment while her husband was out at work and her nimble fingers had elicited a response in Jeremy which had surprised even himself.

Maggie had happy memories of her love-making with her husband. When it was over she had lain with her cheek on his chest, her fingers playing with the sparse hairs and listening to the subsiding beat of his heart. "My sweet little Maggie," he would say, as he fondly kissed the top of her head. In those moments she had often fantasized about the child they would have. He would be a boy, of course, tall like his father and he would be called Edward like the father who had died when she was a little girl. Maggie already saw him in school uniform with his school cap and his satchel on his way to school. One of the few heated discussions she had ever had with Jeremy was about whether or not this hypothetical son would be sent to boarding school. Jeremy had been for putting his name down for Eton at birth, while Maggie had maintained that children needed to grow up in the heart of a family.

"But what will happen when I'm posted to the Orient or the Sublime Porte?" Jeremy had asked.

"We'll see when the time comes," Maggie had said. "But I couldn't bear to think of him having a little nervous breakdown in the locker room."

"My dear," Jeremy had teased her, "he's not even born yet and we are already worrying about him having a nervous breakdown in the locker room?"

"And what about all that hanky-panky that goes on in boys' schools, then?" Maggie had demanded irately.

"Oh, that?" Jeremy had said. "Surely that's only part of growing up." And he'd turned over in bed and closed his eyes. "Go to sleep, old thing, it's late," he'd said, bringing the subject to a close.

What more, Maggie wondered, her heart in smithereens as she perused Jeremy's Budapest diaries, could this Ilonka have given her staid English husband in her dreary apartment where a brown curtain separated the kitchen from the bedroom and a smell of cabbage lingered over it all?

"Hello, Zoltan," said Maggie. "I'm coming to Budapest tomorrow on the 12.15 Malev flight."

"I'll be there, Modome," said Zoltan. "We have missed you, Simona and I."

Before she left London, however, Maggie made a visit to the lingerie department in Selfridges. This time she invested in rather less castigated underwear than the trousseau her mother had insisted on all those years ago. The mirrors in these places were always merciless, but she had to admit as she stood sideways, tucking in her tummy with a deep intake of breath, that her flesh still looked firm on her round buttocks and now that she had been liberated from diplomatic entertaining she even seemed to have lost weight. If she was going to be massaged by Ilonka she could at least start out on an equal footing. She reflected that the outer transformation of Maggie was now at last complete. She was less convinced by the revolution going on inside.

Both Zoltan and Simona were at the airport to greet her, Zoltan in his new car, a Fiat Punto of which he was very proud. Simona was shivering in a fake leopard-skin coat, complaining bitterly of the cold but still laughing beneath her yellow fringe where dark roots were beginning to show. She rolled down the car window and lit one of her slim cigarettes. "So, Maggie, how are you? Our angel is back to avenge again!"

Zoltan was obviously eager to show her the changes that had taken place over the last ten years in his city. "We are lucky with the weather," he said.

Budapest today had brightly lit streets and shop fronts and there seemed to be restaurants and bars at every corner, while the traffic had become horrendous, Western cars choking all the thoroughfares. Maggie saw no sign of bullet holes in the freshly plastered facades and it also seemed to her that everyone looked better dressed and no one was carrying a plastic sack any more. The smog had lifted and the cold sky reflected in the river made the Danube seem almost blue. Zoltan had booked her into a small hotel overlooking the river where the bedrooms were furnished in pastel colours without a trace of brown.

"How lovely Budapest has become," Maggie told a beaming Zoltan, who flushed red with pleasure.

Zoltan lived in one of the grey concrete high-rise buildings on the edge of the city and Simona was going to cook them *spaghetti alla carbonara* there that evening, he told Maggie.

Simona laughed and said she hoped so; it wasn't the same bacon she found at home but she had brought the *Parmigiano* with her. She'd seen it for sale in a shop in one of the markets in Budapest but it had been far too expensive, she said.

Maggie was soon to discover how much more expensive everything had become.

That evening, the conspirators duly met in Zoltan's tiny kitchen over plates of *carbonara* and a bottle of Hungarian wine that Zoltan reverently uncorked. Zoltan began to tell Maggie in detail exactly what street he had been walking down and what tram he had just descended from and what his exact impressions had been when he had bumped into Ilonka. She had changed a lot over the years, it was true, but he had known at once that it was her. He had invited her for a coffee at a bar on the corner and she had asked after Jeremy and been suitably distressed to hear that he had passed away. Maggie gritted her teeth.

Ilonka now had her own salon on the Margit Körút, Zoltan said. Simona had gone for a facial and manicure and said that although Ilonka was, of course, a cow and a despicable cow at that, the salon had been quite luxurious with frosted-pink towels and soothing music and pretty little changing booths. Ilonka herself had not massaged Simona's face but sat in the corner behind her desk, wearing horn-rimmed spectacles. The girls occasionally asked her advice about particularly rebellious facial hair or a virulent pimple, but Ilonka otherwise mainly confined herself to presiding over her little pink kingdom and effusively greeting the customers in several languages. She could even speak a little Italian, Simona said, and had complimented her on the handbag which Simona had bought in Rome before she came. They had fixed an appointment for Maggie the next day. "Under an assumed name," added Zoltan conspiratorially.

Zoltan drove Maggie back to the hotel in his Fiat Punto. She was tired and they were silent as he drove through the streets that were so much more brightly lit than they had been in her day.

"But," Maggie said in a puzzled voice as she opened the door of the car, "how did you know it was Ilonka? I didn't think you ever knew her."

There was a silence. Zoltan and Simona exchanged glances. "Oh, that was easy enough," said Zoltan darkly. "You see, I didn't tell you before, because the ambassador made me promise not to, but Ilonka used to be my wife!"

Maggie found it hard to fall asleep after this startling revelation. She remembered what Zoltan had told her about his marriage when they were driving through

France on their way to wreak revenge on Delphine. How he had come home and found his wife with another man. Had that other man been *Jeremy?* She cast her mind back to the time when Zoltan had come to work for them and began to view it in a different light. She remembered the first time she had met Zoltan. Jeremy had come home from work with this slight, skinny man in tow. Zoltan had stood glumly on the doormat looking at his feet, his hands clenched. "This is Zoltan," Jeremy had said, introducing him. "I've decided to hire him as our chauffeur now that my eyes have started acting up."

Maggie had known about Jeremy's erratic eyesight for some time. They had sat in the drab corridor of the Budapest eye hospital together, with sad people in dressing gowns talking in whispers, waiting for the specialist who had delivered the verdict. It was a congenital condition, the specialist had told them, that might well remain essentially unchanged for years but which could deteriorate later on. Jeremy was to expect a certain amount of double vision when he was tired and should on no account drive at night. Later in London, a highly respected ophthalmologist in Harley Street had confirmed the diagnosis, but Maggie remembered thinking at the time that it had not seemed serious enough to warrant the hiring of a chauffeur.

Men were so funny about their ailments, she thought. It had been unlike Jeremy, however, to embark on such an extravagance, even though in those days a Hungarian chauffeur's salary had made few inroads into their monthly budget. Had Zoltan blackmailed

Jeremy into giving him a job? Maggie realized that he might have been capable of doing just that. A job as a diplomat's chauffeur would have been considered a godsend in those days, with vistas of foreign travel and foreign currency opening up before him. But how unlike Jeremy, to stoop to compromise with someone like Zoltan! On the other hand, if Jeremy's liaison with Ilonka had become known, it would have been a terrible scandal that would have adversely affected his budding career. If diplomats were not allowed to fraternize socially with people who were members of the Warsaw Pact, they were most certainly not supposed to go to bed with them. There had been cases in the past that had sometimes erupted into spy scandals and been featured luridly in the British gutter press. Jeremy had always been very ambitious and he wouldn't have wanted anything to get in the way of his career. Maggie thought now how she had often noticed that Jeremy's and Zoltan's relationship had been rather cool. She had presumed that it was just Jeremy's habitual bearing towards people he considered socially inferior. And another thing began to make sense: this would explain why, apart from the financial rewards, Zoltan was so zealous in sharing her quest for revenge.

Maggie woke early as the sun was piercing the morning mist behind the Parliament. How many times she had stood for hours under its brightly gilded and painted dome listening to speeches that went on for ever and ever and singing the Hungarian national anthem which had to be the saddest song she knew. In those days a huge red star had surmounted the whole magnificent Gothic structure, modelled after the Houses of Parliament, but which, her Hungarian hosts never failed to tell her, was actually twenty centimetres larger.

She got out of bed and went over to the wardrobe. She must choose her ensemble carefully, especially the underthings. This was going to be an important day.

The hotel called a taxi to take Maggie to the Margit Körút. As she sat in the traffic she noticed that the street name had changed since she and Jeremy were there. Then it had been Mártirok utca, but presumably they had been martyrs for the wrong cause. Later she was to realize that many streets had, like Maggie, assumed a new identity after the fall of the regime.

The salon was a low-ceilinged room, fragrant with a pot-pourri of different essences with strong overtones of molten wax. Vases of exotic artificial flowers punctuated the spaces. Ilonka sat behind a spindly little desk wearing horn-rimmed glasses, just as Simona had said.

Maggie wondered if she would have recognized in this stout middle-aged woman the slim girl standing apologetically on her doormat all those years ago. Hungarian women were very beautiful when they were young and took great care of their skin; even under Communism there had been a *Kozmetika* on every corner. Even in the dark days they had always been what Maggie's mother called "soignay". But they lost their bloom early on, perhaps because of hard work or an unhealthy diet. Ilonka, however, still had smooth skin and her hair had obviously benefited from a recent visit to the *Fodrász*, as hairdressers were called here. Maggie remembered how frustrated she had been, searching in Hungarian for a word that resembled any language other than its own.

Ilonka's smile of greeting was formal rather than warm. She escorted Maggie to her changing booth and gave her a pair of slippers and a frosted-pink gown, which she saw she was supposed to wear under her arms and above her breasts like a bath towel. A willowy young blonde girl came to fetch her for her facial.

Maggie lay down on the massage bed and her hair was secured behind a pink headband. This was the first time in her life that Maggie had had a facial. It was something of which neither her mother nor Jeremy would have approved, and deep down Maggie also thought it was a frivolous and fundamentally unnecessary pursuit. She stretched out stiffly on the bed in her pink gown much as she might have lain on a slab at the morgue. "Relax," said the girl, who looked as if she might be Ilonka's daughter, her young breath smelling of peppermint.

Slowly her fingers caressed Maggie's throat and neck, rippling over her cheeks, fluttering around her chin, describing soft circles around her eyes and smoothing away the wrinkles in her forehead. The sensation was so delicious that Maggie drifted gently into a meditative state where she seemed to be floating, her hands heavy at her sides. Another pair of hands took over from the first, stronger warmer hands that massaged her shoulders and the back of her neck.

Maggie lost all track of time and ceased to follow in her mind the activity of the fingers kneading her skin until they came to a stop pressing firmly and warmly against her chest.

"Haven't we met before?" asked a new voice very close to her ear. Maggie opened her eyes, suddenly wide awake. Ilonka's face was suspended upside down above her own staring fixedly at her over the horn-rimmed glasses. Maggie could see the pores of her skin.

"I don't think so," said Maggie, deliberately vague.

Ilonka deftly wiped the excess cream off Maggie's cheeks. "Would you like to try a mask?" she asked.

Maggie found herself coated with something that looked like spinach which slowly hardened over her face, with holes only for her nostrils, mouth and eyes.

"It may burn a little at first," said Ilonka.

As time went on it also started to itch underneath and Maggie began to wish she hadn't agreed to this part of the procedure, especially as it was removed with a brusque gesture which made her gasp as some of the down on her cheeks went with it. She realized that the masks were all being hung on the wall at the far end of the room.

"Would you like to sign it?" asked Ilonka holding out a felt-tip pen.

Maggie's mind went blank as she tried to remember the alias she, Simona and Zoltan had agreed on. Pen poised in her hand she stared hopelessly at Ilonka. In the end she signed the first name that came illogically into her mind.

"Pandora?" questioned a puzzled Ilonka.

"That's my nickname," lied Maggie, descending from her slab and searching for the little slippers. "It's the name my husband used to call me."

The three of them met for lunch at a little basement restaurant Zoltan had chosen. It smelt very strongly of onion and paprika. He was obviously in his element and ordered chicken paprikás for everyone.

"Ahoh, Maggee, you look wonderful!" said Simona. "Ten years younger." Zoltan glared at her. "Not that you needed to lose ten years, what am I saying?" Simona said hastily, spooning her soup.

"It must have been that mask," said Maggie.

Simona laughed. "The green one? I lay there wondering if they would ever come and take it off! *Terribile!*"

It was over their pancakes smothered in chocolate that the conspirators started talking strategy. "Ilonka's made a fortune with that salon," said Zoltan. "She has a villa with a swimming pool on the Rószadomb."

"A swimming pool?" asked Maggie incredulously, remembering the dignified poverty of the Hungarians she had known in the old days.

"We have lots of rich people here nowadays," said Zoltan, although it was not clear if this were a boast or an apology. "Ilonka's clients are all rich women with too much money. She charges higher prices than anywhere else in Budapest."

Maggie had indeed been shocked by the sum Ilonka had murmured in her ear when the time came to take her leave. At the same time, now that she had been given the first one, she decided that life would never be complete again without a facial. Even the mask, though uncomfortable, had left her cheeks taut and youthful and she really did look as though she had lost ten years. Maybe next time she might even let them pluck her eyebrows and dye her eyelashes black, like the lady lying on the slab next to her. The large person on the other side had been so relaxed, meanwhile, that she had lapsed into a deep sleep, a loud snore escaping her at intervals.

"What would happen," Maggie wondered out loud, "if we put itching powder into one of those creams?"

The others looked at her in awe.

"We'll need a chemist for this," said Zoltan in a masterful tone, taking the debate in hand. "Substituting the creams will be no problem at all."

Of course not, thought Maggie dismally. They had become adept at breaking the law in every country in Europe. "Where do we find a chemist?" she asked.

"I have a friend," said Zoltan.

"I think," said Simona, "we should concentrate on that mask."

The trio drove down to Lake Balaton the following Saturday afternoon. Zoltan's friend had worked for many years in a pharmaceutical company and was now retired. He lived with his wife in a little thatched cottage in a village above the lake. In winter the lake was a romantic place, Maggie thought, as they drove along the north shore, very different from the way

Maggie remembered it in summer, when the East German tourists had crowded its banks like a *Mitteleuropean* Blackpool. Now tall rushes were reflected in its grey-green surface and moorhens perched along the shore fluffing up their feathers against the cold.

It took them some time to find Dénes' cottage as it seemed that several villages had the same name. In the end, a next-door neighbour standing in her vegetable garden in a red headscarf and smiling an angelic smile, like a picture in a children's book, showed them where to go.

They sat round the fire in the kitchen drinking rough *pálinka* while delicious smells emanated from the stove. Dénes' wife had cooked a goose in their honour. A smaller sauccpan cooling to one side contained a greenish paste which looked familiar; evidently, Zoltan had been very specific in his instructions. Before they left, it was spooned into a little Tupperware box which reminded Maggie of Esmeralda.

They piled back into the Fiat Punto. This time it was Simona who drove because Zoltan was visibly suffering the after-effects of plum brandy. How strict the laws against drinking and driving had been while they were there, Maggie remembered, although, as diplomats, they could not be prosecuted. The police never flagged down their cars with light blue licence plates and the letters DT. There was a joke in the embassy that it stood for Delirium Tremens. They waved goodbye to Dénes and his wife and to the little old woman out of a fairy tale who pressed warm fresh eggs into their hands when they stopped to thank her. It was dark when they got back to Budapest and Simona delivered Maggie to her hotel.

Next day, the telephone rang before Maggie was fully awake. "At last!" said Shirley, no longer trying to veil the accusatory tone in her voice. "I have been trying to get in touch with you. Esmeralda told me you are now in *Budapest?*"

"Yes," said Maggie sleepily. "I told you I was planning to travel for a while."

"I have just received a tax rebate for Jeremy and I didn't know for the life of me where I was supposed to send it."

"I'll be back in London soon," said Maggie. "You can send it there, if that would be all right."

"And another thing," said Shirley. "The Argentinian foreign minister was here the other day and he was asking after you."

"Well, I suppose he must remember Jeremy from the aftermath of the Falklands. He had a lot to do with the Argentinians then."

"He didn't say anything about the Falkands," Shirley went on. "He said he'd taught you how to tango. Apparently he was ambassador in Paris when you were there."

"Oh — *that* ambassador . . ." said Maggie.

"Yes, I imagine it must have been *that* ambassador," said Shirley, rounding off the conversation and hanging up.

Oh, dear, thought Maggie. What with one thing and another I'm acquiring quite a reputation as a flighty wife. No wonder Jeremy had affairs.

Zoltan also called early. "Simona wants you to come over and try out the mask."

This time Maggie was very much awake. "All right," she said. "Just give me time for a cup of tea and I'll be there as soon as I can."

Sometimes Maggie felt as though her revenge had been taken out of her hands. It had become an entity of its own as though evolving by itself, a genie let out of a bottle with no intention of being stoppered up inside again. Obviously, it was something that was meant to happen, she thought, as she got into the taxi to take her to the outskirts of Budapest. Jeremy's possible views on the question had long ago ceased to trouble her.

Simona met her at the door with a plate of green paste in her hand, a spoon sticking into the middle. "I was hoping you could spread it on for me," she said.

"But Simona, why should you be the guinea pig?" Maggie was genuinely concerned. "We can put it on my face."

"It wasn't my face I was thinking about," said Simona with a cackle. "I was thinking more like spreading it on my bum!"

Simona lay on her stomach on Zoltan's double bed as Maggie tentatively spooned a small quantity of the green paste on to Simona's rosy buttocks. "You'll have to put more on than that," said Simona looking over her shoulder. "Otherwise we won't really get an idea."

"You're sure you'll be all right?" asked Maggie over her shoulder as she closed the bedroom door.

She went back into the tiny kitchen where Zoltan was making coffee. He carried it out on a little tray into the sitting room where an overstuffed sofa and armchair were vying for the limited space in front of a large television set, which was evidently switched on on a permanent basis. They sat down to watch what appeared to be an episode of an on-going reality show. This, too, was part of the new Hungary, thought Maggie as she put her coffee cup down on the little occasional table in front of the sofa. There was an embroidered doily in the middle under a little arrangement of artificial flowers. Zoltan stubbed out his cigarette making it revolve three times around the bottom of the ashtray.

"What are your plans when this is over?" Maggie asked him. Zoltan scratched his nose thoughtfully with his long nail.

"I was thinking of going into business," he said portentously. "I have a friend who sells used tyres."

Maggie tried to look enthusiastic. "Used tyres?"

"Yes," said Zoltan, "there's definitely a future in Hungary for used tyres."

Maggie sipped her coffee. There was a picture, too high up on the wall, of the Puszta; it showed a long diagonal beam poised above a well surrounded by geese cackling in the courtyard. "You don't feel tempted to go back into *foie gras* production?" she asked.

"Oh, no, God help me, it brings back too many memories . . ." He was staring out of the window. "I think it's going to snow," he said gloomily.

Suddenly, there was a shriek from the next room. "*Li mortacci tua!*" yelled a furious Simona appearing in the doorway totally naked. "Get this stuff off my butt!"

She lay down on the sofa and Maggie and Zoltan gently tried to prise the green mask from her behind, Zoltan putting his long nail to a new use. It remained resolutely stuck.

"Let's try a little water," suggested Maggie. Zoltan returned from the kitchen with a saucepan of warm water and a brush. He and Maggie renewed their efforts to no avail. "Maybe a cream?" Maggie queried, going into the cupboard-sized bathroom and searching among Simona's toiletries. They smoothed Oil of Olay into the offending part and waited a few minutes to see if the hard crust would soften.

Simona, meanwhile, was becoming testy. "*Ma, insomma*, what are you waiting for?" she yelled at Zoltan.

"I'm so sorry," said Maggie, "I knew you should have let me try first . . ." It was becoming apparent that nothing was going to shift the green carapace from Simona's backside.

"I'm afraid we are going to have to go to hospital," said Zoltan. "I have a friend at the János Kórház."

Maggie sat on a chair by Simona's bedside crushed by guilt and shame. Simona, her buttocks raw and bandaged, had fallen asleep under mild sedation. How could she have let this happen? Maggie asked herself. She had obviously lost all sense of reality. Imagine letting Simona be hospitalized like this, just to revenge herself on someone who had wronged her over fifteen years ago . . .

The worst part had been trying to explain to the doctors what had happened. "It's an Italian treatment for cellulite," said Zoltan.

"I don't have cellulite!" said Simona, outraged.

"Darling, you have a bad case of cellulite, OK?" Zoltan stroked her hand. "That's why you put this Italian cream on your bottom." Simona glared at him and at the doctor, who was staring at them all at a loss. It had taken two hours to remove every trace of the green mask from Simona's behind.

Maggie had been in the hospital all day. Sometimes she went into the unripe-banana-coloured corridors and walked up and down, but the people in dressing gowns on the benches along the wall were staring at her and she felt uncomfortable. One old lady in particular kept lurching in her direction inside a little metal cage on wheels. She felt even guiltier for being healthy and wealthy and distracting these overworked underpaid nurses with something as futile as Simona's green bottom.

Simona opened one eye. "Maggee," she said sleepily.

"Simona," said Maggie, "I am really most frightfully sorry. This is all my fault and we are going to stop this whole project right now. I can't imagine what I was thinking of."

Simona opened both eyes. "You joking?" she asked. "Just as we were starting to have fun!" She began to laugh. "Zoltan's already gone down to Balaton to get Dénes to modify the formula."

"But I really can't allow this," said Maggie with determination.

"Oh yes, you can," said Simona, wide awake now and laughing so loudly there were reproachful stares from the next bed, "because next time you're the one who's trying out the cream!"

At six o'clock the nurse came around with a trolley with the evening meal. Everyone was given a large round white roll and a chunk of spam.

Simona stared at her plate in disbelief. "I don't understand this country," she said. "In Rome if you gave a patient this for dinner, his family would lynch you."

Fortunately, Zoltan arrived at that moment from the Balaton and unpacked a plastic bag with a leg of roast goose sent by Dénes' wife and some country bread and pickles. From his pocket he fished out a bottle of *pálinka*.

"That's more like it," said Simona, biting into her drumstick. Then, stricken with guilt, she looked over at the woman in the next bed: "*Volete favorire?*" she asked.

The new cream was promised by the following week. Zoltan was often out, intent on setting up his new used-tyre concern and so Maggie and Simona found themselves thrown very much in each other's company.

"What shall we do today?" asked Simona, looking out of Zoltan's window at a sky that promised more snow. "There doesn't seem much to do in this country except eat and drink." She paused. "Not that I mind that," she said with a laugh.

"We could go to the thermal baths," suggested Maggie.

As Maggie pushed open the heavy door into the atrium of the Gellért baths, she felt Simona squeeze her arm. "Oh, Maggee, what fun!" she said. "We're going to the thermal baths — you and me." Simona was always stroking Maggie's cheek or encircling her waist with her arm or squeezing her shoulder, something that to Maggie was totally alien and yet she found she enjoyed this physical nearness. Hers had not been a very demonstrative family. Brisk kisses on the cheek when they met and took their leave. As Simona, out of sheer ebullience threw her arms around her neck and hugged her, Maggie had a feeling of belonging for the first time in her life to a vast hugging, clasping, squeezing family of humankind.

In the baths, both women were issued with a little apron which partially covered their fronts but left their backs completely bare and Simona went into a storm of giggles. She herself was what the Germans would call appetizing: little rolls of fat in all the right places. She looked at Maggie standing mortified in her apron. "Great boobs, Maggee," she said in undisguised admiration. It was true, thought Maggie, perhaps because she had never had to breastfeed children, but her breasts were still those of a young girl. Even Jeremy, she remembered, had seemed to love her breasts, often burying his long aristocratic face in her cleavage.

They sat opposite each other in the sauna and Simona started making faces at her from the opposite bench. "*Ammazzate*, it's hot!" she said in a loud voice, fanning herself vigorously with her apron which had become a limp rag in the moist heat. A large burly woman with a moustache had been glaring at her for some time: "Shush," she said fiercely. Simona turned to look at her. "Ahoh!" she answered defiantly. The woman rose to her feet, various layers of wet fat slithering into place, and stalked out, her buttocks wobbling in indignation. Simona winked at Maggie and aimed an imaginary kick at the woman's receding rump.

Maggie realized that not long ago she would have been a bit ashamed of a friend like Simona, so different from the people she normally met, so very much not "one of us". It was like stepping out of pointed-toe shoes that pinched, and slipping with relief into a well-worn pair of slippers that had taken on the contours and hollows of her own feet. Simona accepted Maggie in a spirit of undemanding and uncritical fellowship; her presence was a comfort in every sense of the word. This was a new dimension of freedom, Maggie decided. Now she was not only mistress of her time, but free to choose friends that nobody need approve of, neither her husband nor the diaspora of Great Britain and the British Commonwealth. As the sweat started forming all over her body, Maggie also realized that she was now feeling at ease with herself, comfortable, as the French said, inside her own skin.

Maggie's evenings, however, were always spent alone. She would order a sandwich from room service and lie in bed watching CNN. The evening after her visit to the thermal baths with Simona in particular she felt lonely and depressed. The taxi driver who had brought her back had been rude and unfriendly when she questioned the inflated price. He had evidently taken advantage of the fact that she was a woman and a foreigner. These things never happened when she was with Jeremy and it had left a bad taste in her mouth. She found herself wondering what was she doing here, all by herself, so far from everything that felt familiar, in a hotel room. She had always abhorred hotels and was unused to single rooms, the cramped space and the narrow bed; with Jeremy they had always been given suites.

She listlessly opened the mini-bar. She was reaching for a bottle of mineral water when her eye was caught by the row of little bottles on the top shelf. A brandy, she thought, she deserved a brandy. She sat in the only chair and kicked off her shoes, sipping the strong liquor directly from the bottle. She suddenly felt terribly lonely: Zoltan and Simona had gone to have dinner with his brother, and Budapest seemed very far away from the world she knew. If only she had someone to talk to.

Maggie reached for her address book. The telephone in Ledbury rang with the reassuring English "dring-dring". It rang for a long time. In the end, it was Janet who answered. There was a noise of loud music in the background and laughter close at hand.

"Oh, Auntie M.," she said. "How are you? Mum's out, I'm afraid. They've gone over to the Hicksons for supper."

Who were the Hicksons, Maggie wondered, as her eye alighted on Luc's card which she had slipped into her address book that day in Paris. How wonderful it would be right now, she thought, to hear his vibrant voice. She drained the little bottle of brandy and dialled 0033 followed by the number of his mobile phone.

"You're in Budapest?" he sounded delighted. "*Mais j'arrive!*"

"Oh, no, no, no," said Maggie, exceedingly alarmed.

"I was coming next week anyway," said Luc. He was obviously in a restaurant. There were sounds of plates being stacked and the glug-glug of wine being poured. "I'm coming to fetch my new pig. I'll be staying at the Gellért Hotel."

Later that week, Zoltan, Simona and Maggie foregathered in the lobby of Maggie's hotel.

"This," said Zoltan, producing it with a flourish, "is the cream. You must rub it into your face and leave it to seep in for about an hour. Then wipe it off with this." He produced a lotion in a plastic bottle. "This, Dénes says, will stop the itch." Maggie was drinking tea, or what so often passed for tea in Continental Europe. Zoltan was sipping the dark local liqueur called *Unicum*, of which he was particularly fond.

Simona, meanwhile, was walking up and down, as she was still not comfortable in a sitting position, puffing at one of her slim cigarettes. "I was at Ilonka's yesterday," she said. "I stole a couple of empty jars and I've booked an appointment for both of us tomorrow at ten."

Here we go again, thought Maggie.

Later, she sat on her bed watching the sky go pink behind the spiky silhouette of the Parliament. She smeared the cream onto her face, massaging it into her cheeks just like they had done at Ilonka's beauty salon, and then lay down to wait. She found herself drifting into a doze and so was not fully awake when, about forty minutes later, an uncontrollable itching took hold of her, her face and neck aflame. She leapt from the bed, her face in her hands, dismissing the impulse to leap into the icy waters of the Danube flowing wide and black beneath her windows. It really was unbearable. She ran into the bathroom to grab the bottle of lotion and poured some onto cotton wool before smoothing it onto her cheeks and removing all traces of the cream. She splashed cold water on her face and looked at herself in the mirror. The itching had ceased, but her skin remained mottled and blotchy and flaky patches were appearing on her forehead and chin. She reached for the telephone and called Zoltan. "It works all right," she said, "but what would have happened if I hadn't had the lotion?"

"Oh, Dénes says any astringent lotion will do the trick."

"I don't want any of these women to be seriously harmed," said Maggie in alarm.

"No problem, Modome, trust me," said Zoltan airily.

Maggie ordered her usual sandwich and turned on the television. It was a nature programme showing pigs greedily snuffling at the trough. The telephone rang. "There is a gentleman calling from the Gellért Hotel." Maggie sat bolt upright in bed. She could see her pink and puffy reflection in the mirror at the little dressing table against the opposite wall. "Please tell him I'm out," she said in panic. "Tell him I'm away on business. I'll be back tomorrow evening."

"Oh, Pandora, good morning," said Ilonka, greeting Maggie at the door of the salon and taking her coat. Maggie studiously ignored Simona who had already arrived and was winking at her from a chink in the curtains of her changing booth.

"I see you are down for a manicure? But what has happened to your face?" Indeed, there were still rough red patches on Maggie's cheeks and the skin on her nose was flaking off in strips. "Please come to the light," said Ilonka leading Maggie over to the window. "Look at this," she said to the two young girls who abandoned their clients to come and examine the damage. "When did this start?"

Out of the corner of her eye, Maggie saw Simona tiptoeing out of her booth carrying her large Italian handbag. She went over to the counter along the wall behind the reclining clients and made a play of taking things in and out of her handbag. While Ilonka and her girls studied her skin, Maggie could observe the deft substitution of two large jars of cream with two identical pots.

"The day after my facial," said Maggie, "my skin started to itch and it's been getting worse. I think I must be allergic to the creams."

"I'll see what I can do," said Ilonka, accompanying her to her cubicle. "I have some anti-allergic creams as well."

Maggie sat in a corner of the salon with her fingers soaking in a little bowl of soapy water. She thought with a pang that her last manicure had been before her wedding day. Jeremy disliked nail varnish and she had usually filed her own nails and shined them with a chamois leather buffer. Pedicures, on the other hand, had been a painful necessity.

The girls had returned to their clients. Simona was already lying on one of the slabs, her yellow fringe pinned back by a pink headband. The girl who looked like Ilonka's daughter was finishing the massage on one lady and Ilonka came to take over, helping herself to a dollop of the new cream.

The other employee, a slim dark girl, was also reaching over to dip her fingers into one of the new jars. "Relax," she said softly to a voluminous lady in a pink gown.

The music was softly playing in the background. There was a clock on the peach-coloured wall and Maggie found herself watching it compulsively. It was one of those clocks where every tick corresponded with a little jerk of the second hand. One lady was already being smothered in a spinach-coloured mask. The girl carefully washed her hands and came over to Maggie. She took one hand out of the bowl of soapy water into her own cool palm and gently dried Maggie's fingers on a frosted-pink towel. Yes, this is what Ilonka used to look like, thought Maggie, her eyes on the bent blonde head. Behind her, Maggie could see the finishing touches being given to Simona's mask. Simona made a V sign with her fingers behind the young girl's back. The clock ticked on. Another client was admitted and decked out in a pink gown. Maggie's nails were being expertly filed and buffed.

"Nail varnish?" she was asked.

"A nice bright red," said Maggie.

One client's mask was hung on the wall along with all the others and the lady was shrugged into her coat and accompanied to the door. By now, there were seven bodies laid out on slabs in different stages of treatment. Maggie was waving her red nails in the air to dry.

After a while, the lady on Simona's right started to twist and turn on her slab. She began gesticulating with her hands and picking at the spinach-green mask. Ilonka got up from her desk and went over to her. "It's itching," said a voice suffocated behind the hard crust of the mask. "Take it off!" Ilonka ripped off the mask to reveal a red face gasping and hissing underneath. "Do something!" it said.

At this point, the door of the salon burst open and, with an irate red face, the client who had just left made an appearance. "Help me, I can't stand this!" She threw

226

off her coat and rushed at Ilonka gesticulating eloquently as though she would tear her face apart.

Simona rose from her slab with a howl which Maggie could not help feeling was mainly for effect. From now on the scene was one of total anarchy. One by one the ladies leapt from their beds, shrieks emanating from behind their green masks. Ilonka and the girls ran from one to the other, ripping off masks and applying cold compresses.

"*La polizia*," yelled Simona. "I am going to call *la polizia!*" One of the girls dabbed at her face with cotton wool. "I'm burning all over," said Simona, running around the salon like a dervish while the other ladies, in several other languages, followed suit.

Maggie sat in her chair fluttering her red fingertips to dry them, unsure whether to laugh or sob in consternation. One lady, who turned out to be the wife of the Turkish ambassador, crawled into a corner of the room and started to cry. Stricken by conscience, Maggie wet a towel and took it over to her, holding it against her face. "It will be all right in a minute," she said. She fished the astringent lotion out of her handbag. The Turkish lady slowly started to look relieved. She seized the lotion and rushed over to Ilonka waving it under her face. "This is what you need," she said in a guttural accent.

Two new clients had arrived and stood in their coats uncertainly taking in the scene. The red-faced women were all rubbing their cheeks and chests and staring at each other, their hair spiking above their pink hairbands, outcrops of spinach-covered mask adhering to their faces, and expostulating in a babel of different tongues. Ilonka, who had visibly lost control of the situation and her coiffure, slammed the door and hung out the sign "*Zárva*." Simona liberally doused herself in the astringent and handed it to the voluminous lady on her left who was beginning to hyperventilate. It was quite some time before the situation returned to normality.

Maggie and Simona left together without paying the bill. It was typical of Maggie that she felt much more guilty about not having paid for a manicure than she did about the distress she had inflicted on the Turkish ambassador's wife and Ilonka's bad quarter of an hour.

To celebrate, Maggie insisted that they go to the best restaurant in Budapest and Zoltan booked a table at Gundel for that same evening. As she stepped out of the lift in the lobby of her hotel on the way to her waiting taxi, she saw with a mixture of dismay and delight a familiar figure gesticulating in front of the reception desk.

"Oh *bonsoir, bonsoir!*" Luc said effusively. "I couldn't get this man to understand who I was looking for . . ."

"*Bonsoir,*" said Maggie, suddenly tongue-tied.

"I was hoping you were free for dinner?" said Luc. "I've just got back from the country and buying my pig."

"Well, actually, I was just going out to dinner with Zoltan," said Maggie uncertainly. "You know — my business partner."

"Such a magnificent pig," Luc went on, and then, as her answer registered, he became suddenly crestfallen. "So, you aren't free? You see, I'm going back to France tomorrow . . ."

He looked so abject that Maggie found herself feeling sorry for him. All her life she had been someone who had tried to be accommodating, to arrange things so that other people would be comfortable and well looked after. Jeremy had always reproached her because she found it so hard to say no. And then, she thought, what harm could there be, after all?

"Would you like to join us? We're dining at Gundel," she found herself saying.

"I'll meet you in a little while, if I may," said Luc. "I just have to make a few calls and get some things from my hotel. Gundel — ah, excellent!"

Maggie arrived at the restaurant to find Simona perched on a stool at the bar, a flute of champagne in her fingers, looking even more dazzling and bespangled than usual. Zoltan was leaning against the bar wearing his suit from their ambassadorial days and his Italian shoes; they looked so shiny and new, Maggie surmised this must be their first outing.

"I met Luc de Bosquières in the lobby of my hotel. He is here on business," said Maggie. "I hope you don't mind but I asked him to join us."

Simona's plucked eyebrows went shooting up into her fringe. "Oh, Maggee!" She giggled. Zoltan said nothing. They filed into the dining room. Simona winked at Maggie as the waiter pulled out her chair.

Zoltan ordered a robust red wine from Eger and chose goulash soup followed by goose, which he was to pronounce almost as good as his mother's legendary dish. He was clearly enjoying himself. They toasted the absent Esmeralda, and the gypsy orchestra came to their table and played poignant melodies in Maggie's ear. With Simona, the gypsy primás struck up a more cheerful tune and the rest of the orchestra joined in the refrain.

"It's about brown eyes," said Zoltan, looking at Simona fondly. "Everybody says that blue eyes are beautiful, but my love's eyes are brown."

It was at this point that Luc made his appearance, exuberantly waving at their table from the door as he came in. As he sat down, Maggie couldn't help noticing that, although he had clearly taken some trouble over his appearance, he had a little stalk of straw poking out of his hair.

"I have just come from the country," he told them, "from" — he fished out a piece of paper from his bulging pockets — "Kiskunfélegyháza. Isn't that an impossible name?"

"It doesn't sound so impossible if you translate it," said Zoltan. "It means 'the Little Tribesman in Half a House'."

"Oh, c'est génial, ça," said Luc. "Anyway the little tribesman in half a house has sold me a most wonderful pig. Look, I'll show you." He produced a digital camera from one of his pockets. The pig was on video, progressing across a muddy paddock towards the camera, getting larger and larger until his snout filled the little screen. He was unlike any pig that Maggie had ever seen, covered in ginger hair like an Airedale terrier. "He is a Mangaleeca peeg," said Luc proudly.

"*Mangalica*," said Zoltan, with the emphasis firmly on the first syllable while the "c" sounded more like "ts".

"That's what I said," said Luc, unrepentant. "Mangaleeca."

"He is a very handsome pig," said Zoltan, looking at Luc with new respect.

"*Che schifo*," said Simona with a shudder.

Luc was delighted to find snails on the menu and a soufflé for dessert. He called back the gypsies and made them play the Monti "Csárda". "Listen to the little bird," he said to Maggie as the musician performed virtuoso acrobatics on the E string. Then he asked for "Gypsy Baron". "*Wer uns vertraut*," he sang in a gravelly tenor, looking at Maggie. "They too were wed by the birds," he said, ordering cognac for everyone and lighting a very pungent cigar. "To my new pig," he raised his glass, "and" — he consulted the little piece of paper again — "Kiskunfélegyháza!"

"*Egészségédre!*" said Zoltan.

"*Cin-cin!*" said Simona.

"Cheers," said Maggie.

"How is the import-export coming along?" Luc asked Zoltan with a wink.

"I am thinking of going into the used-tyres business," said Zoltan importantly.

"Used tyres?" Luc looked at Maggie incredulously.

She burst out laughing. "Oh, that's just Zoltan's sideline," she said.

After dinner they all said goodbye. With a regal gesture, Zoltan refused Maggie's envelope which she had prepared as the usual fee for his services. "This one is on the house," he said.

Maggie had booked a flight for very early the next day. Simona clung to her for a while.

"I shall miss you, Maggee," she said, "I really will."

"I shall miss you both," said Maggie, "but we'll meet again one day soon."

Luc offered to accompany her back to her hotel. "I'm not ready to say goodbye yet. Let's have a coffee at the Gellért," he said, "and then I'll walk you home."

"Won't it be rather cold?" asked Maggie, looking out at the fresh snow on the pavement.

"I'll lend you a jacket," said Luc, "it's not far to walk."

The lobby of the Gellért was milling with people in evening dress. Evidently, there was a convention on in town. Luc and Maggie sat side by side on the sofa, he with his coffee and she with a tisane, in a companionable silence broken by comments on the couples coming and going through the swing doors.

"They're English," said Maggie, nodding at two women standing near the fountain.

"Or German," said Luc, "but one thing is certain, those two are French." They were expostulating volubly with the concierge.

"And the one with the moustache?" asked Maggie. "Mexican, don't you think?"

"You know, I am going to have to think of a name for my pig," said Luc. "He should have a Hungarian name as he is from Kiskunfélegyháza."

"What about Attila?" suggested Maggie.

"*Mais c'est parfait!*" exclaimed Luc.

Maggie smothered a yawn.

"You're tired, *mon amie*," said Luc, "I'll go and get that jacket." He headed for the lift and Maggie stood up and wandered over towards the swing doors.

"Maggie!" said an astonished voice close at hand. Geoffrey and Camilla had just come in and were stamping the snow off their shoes. They too were in evening dress. "What a surprise!"

"What a surprise," agreed Maggie.

"We're here for the convention," said Camilla. "They invited Geoffrey to give a lecture. He's still very much in demand, you know."

"I'm sure he is," said Maggie. It was clearly her turn to say what she was doing in Budapest. At this point Luc came bounding out of the lift brandishing something that looked like an aviator's jacket. He came towards them and draped it over Maggie's shoulders.

"I don't think we've met," said Geoffrey.

"Oh, yes, sorry, of course," said Maggie. "May I introduce Luc de Bosquières? He is an old friend of Jeremy's and mine. I was sure you knew each other."

Geoffrey inclined slightly in his direction. "I don't seem to recall . . ."

Luc shook hands formally with Geoffrey and raised Camilla's reluctant hand to his lips. Geoffrey was a tall man, impeccably attired in black tie, his greying hair neatly plastered to his scalp, every inch the retired diplomat, an order of merit discreetly peeping from his lapel. Camilla, meanwhile, was raking Luc with her eyes, from the toes of his scuffed shoes to his nondescript tie which had worked its way into a rakish angle.

"We are business associates," said Luc, his eyes twinkling. "Import-export."

"Surely that is a new departure, Maggie?" said Geoffrey looking at her quizzically.

"We import pigs," explained Luc, undeterred. "Look, I'll show you . . ." He yanked his camera out of his pocket and the wristband brought a number of things with it: his cigar case and a battered box of matches, while a little wad of forint notes fluttered to the ground. Geoffrey bent elaborately from the waist and retrieved the cigar case, proffering it to Luc with two fingers, while Maggie busied herself retrieving the forint notes. Luc paid no attention; he was pressing buttons on his little video camera. "Look," he said triumphantly. He showed Geoffrey and Camilla the last sequence where Attila's revolving black snout filled the screen, its angry little eyes glittering beneath a ginger fringe.

Camilla took a step back. She was clutching her evening bag to her breast with both hands. "Geoffrey," she said pointedly, "it's been a long day."

"Yes," said Geoffrey, "I think it's time to go to bed and count sheep. Or pigs, if you prefer," he said as a parting shot over his shoulder.

Maggie thought she was going to get the giggles as she and Luc stepped out into the cold night air.

"You know, you are a very mysterioose woman," said Luc, smiling down at her as they walked along the Rakpart on the bank of the river, "with your Zoltan and your import-export and your *collet monté* English friends."

"I know," said Maggie, "it must all seem very strange. One day I'll explain it to you."

They stopped to look at the black fast-flowing waters of the Danube. The lamp posts were reflected in the river, wriggling like snakes of light.

"It's exciting, isn't it, how fast the river flows?" said Luc.

"Yes," said Maggie. "It's almost frightening, this mass of water on the move." She shivered.

He took her hands in his to warm them. "Where are your gloves?" he scolded her. It was true: she had eliminated gloves from her wardrobe. "You know, I was thinking when I was in the Little Tribesman in Half a House that it would be better if we didn't see each other again," said Luc sadly.

Maggie, who had been enjoying the warm currents running up her arms from Luc's strong grasp, literally felt her heart stop beating for as long as it took her to say: "Why did you think that?"

"Because you know, I am an old-fashioned man. I have been married for over twenty years to a lovely

235

wife. I thought when we met that we could have what we French call an *amitié amoureuse*, but now I am afraid that we might become *amoureux tout court*." He looked at Maggie soulfully. She could smell his cigar and a whiff of the garlic from the snails and a reassuring masculine odour of leather and tweed and clean sweat. She didn't know what to reply. "I shall have to leave tomorrow with nothing but my memories," said Luc. He looked so utterly miserable that Maggie characteristically tried to cheer him up, her own disappointment a secondary consideration.

"And your pig," said Maggie.

"Yes, Attila. He will always remind me of you."

"I'm not sure if I should take that as a compliment!" Maggie laughed.

They had arrived at the door of her hotel. Luc took her in his arms and hugged her fiercely before walking away without looking back. Maggie turned to go inside. She suddenly felt the winter chill of the dark night and shivered convulsively. It wasn't until she got upstairs that she realized she was still wearing Luc's aviator jacket.

6

BACK IN LONDON

It was with a heavy heart that Maggie climbed up the stairs to Jeremy's flat in Ebury Street. It must be her imagination, she thought, as she inserted her key in the lock, but it seemed to her she could hear the noise of a television and the sound of the hoover very close by. She pushed open the door to find the apartment full of light, every single lamp in the room turned on. Bent over the hoover in the middle of the room, her back to the door, her hair covered by a headscarf, was the unmistakable figure of Esmeralda.

"Dona Margarida!" She dropped the hoover and flung herself into her arms. "I wasn't expecting you back so soon. I'm not quite ready."

"I wasn't expecting you at all," said Maggie bewildered.

"Ah, Dona Margarida, I can't find work in Lisboa," Esmeralda said, her face stricken. "They think I'm too old." She sat down on the sofa and pulled the headscarf off her head. "So I went to Mass in the Estrela and Luis told me what to do. 'Your place is in London,' he said." She sat beaming at Maggie. "I'll make you a cup of tea," she said.

Maggie's last conversation with the bank in Vienna had not been very reassuring. She had, of course, been living far beyond her means. There was a sizeable sum

239

of Jeremy's money still left, but it was time for her to think seriously about the future. She realized that she was totally unqualified for an adequate job. Maybe she should sell Jeremy's flat and invest the proceeds and then go and live somewhere inexpensive like Ledbury. The one thing she knew she could not afford was a housekeeper and cook. She sipped her tea looking over the top at Esmeralda's expectant face.

"Esmeralda, I quite simply don't have the money," she said sadly.

Esmeralda leapt to her feet. "Oh, but Dona Margarida, I won't need money!" she exclaimed. "I am going to make enough money for both of us." She led the way into her bedroom and gestured dramatically at the table by the window where a portable sewing machine was enthroned under a fringed damask cover. "I have lots of work," she said triumphantly. "I'm doing the curtains for the couple downstairs and aprons for the girls at the bakery and the cleaners give me broken zips and hems to do . . ."

Maggie hugged her, suddenly moved.

"And if I can just stay in my room, I will look after you, too," said Esmeralda.

In the days to come, Maggie tried to bring herself back down to earth. She forced herself to be efficient, paying bills and doing paper work. Quite a lot of correspondence had accumulated on the doormat while she'd been away. There was even a telegram, which she opened with trepidation. "We regret to

240

inform you that your sister-in-law, Isobel Davenport, passed away, yesterday, 5 December. Our deepest sympathy." It was signed with the improbable name of Reginald Appleyard. Poor Isobel. Maggie hardly knew her, but it was always sad when someone died. Jeremy's family had now effectively extinguished itself. She put the telegram on the mantelpiece.

Maggie then forced herself to read through all the letters of condolences she had received after Jeremy's death and answered every one. "Thank you so much for your moving words of sympathy," she wrote on Jeremy's blue stationery with the address embossed in white. She and Esmeralda went through Jeremy's cupboards filling boxes full of his clothes and shoes and sending them to Portugal to Esmeralda's relations in the Alentejo. Maggie tried to imagine the genial country folk she had met there wearing Jeremy's school tie and Church shoes.

"We must make a clean break," said Esmeralda, throwing away the ambassador's shaving creams and brushes and Floris bath salts, crossing herself reverently each time.

They cleared the box room of years of bric-a-brac and Maggie tied up Jeremy's files and papers into batches with string. The Foreign Office had warned her to be careful how she disposed of them. There could be sensitive material mixed in among the old postcards and long out-of-date magazines. She would take all his papers down to Ledbury and have a bonfire, she decided, and be done with it all.

★ ★ ★

Meanwhile, Maggie was having disturbingly erotic dreams. They all revolved around scantily clad figures cavorting in spinach-green masks. One of them was Ilonka because she wore horn-rimmed glasses. The *primás* of the gypsy orchestra at Gundel was playing Argentinian tangos in the midst of it all. The worst thing was that she knew she should be somewhere else, with Jeremy at an important event on a ship on the Danube. At last she made it to the dock, only to see the ship sailing away. Jeremy was leaning on the rail at the poop, the waters of the Danube churning white below him and seagulls swooping above his head. He raised his hand, whether in admonition or in greeting she couldn't tell.

It was while she was going through Jeremy's desk that she came upon the letters. It was ten o'clock at night and Esmeralda had already gone to bed. Maggie had put on one of Jeremy's CDs and was busy putting papers into piles on the floor when her eye was caught by three little bunches of envelopes tied with a pink ribbon. She idly pulled them out and was putting them on the pile of papers to burn when she noticed the handwriting. It was round and elaborate and unmistakably feminine.

Darling, I can't believe a whole week has gone by since the wedding when I saw you walking out of my life with another woman at your side. You should know that I am, and will always be, yours whenever you need me. I love you with all my heart and always will.

    Yours for ever,
    Lavinia

Maggie felt the familiar wobbling of her knees and her mouth went dry. Who, in God's name, was Lavinia? She looked at the date on the envelope. It was, just as the note said, a week after her and Jeremy's wedding. So she must have been there in one of the pews, watching Jeremy walk out into a blaze of sunshine and a shower of confetti. Lavinia. Could she have been that tall redhead in the turquoise shantung dress and jacket who had got a little tipsy at the reception? At least, Maggie had presumed she was tipsy, as her head had rested on Jeremy's shoulder as he accompanied her to her car.

She looked at the other envelopes. The first letters seemed to refer to a period before her and Jeremy's marriage, which also corresponded with the year of their courtship. The letters were full of impassioned declarations and pleas. Maggie tried to tell herself that this was hardly Jeremy's fault. The woman had been madly in love with him and had fought for him desperately as he prepared to share his life with someone else. But why couldn't Jeremy have told Maggie? He could have involved her in the drama, asked her advice. Or maybe he hadn't wanted to hurt her. Or maybe, she thought bitterly, he had been cold-bloodedly two-timing her even then as she prepared for her wedding and sat in the Basil Street Hotel with her mother planning her trousseau.

Some of the letters were unequivocal.

It was wonderful to see you last night, just like old times. It was such a relief to know that I have not lost you for ever. That we will always find time for each other and that this immense love we share no one can ever take away from us.

Maggie looked at the date at the top of the letter and found herself going rigid in shock. It was dated a month after their wedding. She sat for a long while with the letter in her hands and the tears flowed down her cheeks. She no longer kept a handkerchief in her sleeve and made no attempt to go and look for one. Just as she had thought that she had managed to mend all the holes in the web and weave of the last twenty-five years, this new tear was ripping the whole tissue of her life apart. Where was the new Maggie, she thought in disgust, with her gamine hairdo and pretty shoes, the Maggie who had felt ready to move on to a new life, who could laugh with Simona in the sauna, and be the toast of her new friends: "Viva, Maggee"? All the lights had gone out in her life and she felt herself horribly alone and shivering with cold.

Like an automaton, Maggie started reading the letters one by one, part of her mind on a parallel track reliving that first year of her marriage, then the years when she had been so happy and head over heels in love with Jeremy.

Suddenly the door to the drawing room was flung open and Esmeralda rushed in to find Maggie sobbing uncontrollably, surrounded by pink ribbons and bits of paper which she had shredded into confetti, like the festive shower that had greeted her outside the church on her wedding day. "Oh, Dona Margarida," she said and gathered Maggie into her arms.

It was after midnight that Zoltan was roused from his sleep in his apartment in Budapest. He shook Simona awake. "That was Esmeralda. Modome needs us."

The next day, Maggie was running a temperature and stayed in bed. Esmeralda hovered over her like a mother hen bringing soup and hot-water bottles and endless cups of tea.

"We'll have our revenge on this one too, Dona Margarida, you will see . . ." She had evidently forgotten all about burying Caesar.

Zoltan and Simona called to say they had found a cheap flight and were arriving the following day.

As soon as he arrived, Zoltan reported for duty. He and Simona sat on Maggie's bed and discussed strategy. Maggie was holding Jeremy's little black telephone book in her hands.

"There is a Lavinia under L," she said. "One number has been crossed out, but there is a London number underneath."

Zoltan reached for the bedside telephone. "What is the number?" he asked in a masterful voice.

"Drrr, drrr." English telephones had a ring unlike any other country's. The telephone rang for quite some time.

"Hello, Weidenfeld and Nicolson," said a bored male voice. Zoltan handed the receiver to Maggie.

"Um," Maggie said, momentarily finding herself at a loss, "I would like to speak to Lavinia, please," she said.

"Now which Lavinia would that be, then?" the male voice replied patiently.

"Well, I'm afraid I don't know her married name. I'm looking for a Lavinia with red hair," she hazarded. "She may not be with you any more."

"Oh, goodness me, *that* Lavinia," said the voice. "She no longer works at Weidenfeld, I'm afraid. Left ages ago."

"I suppose," asked Maggie uncertainly, "I suppose you wouldn't know where she went after she left, would you? You see," she said in a moment of inspiration, "I'm planning an old school reunion . . ."

"Well, I don't know if she's still there, but I know she left here to go and work at Bagshot and Newby, the book shop in South Audley Street."

Maggie knew the book shop well. Jeremy had ordered books from them frequently while he was posted abroad. The shop had searched for copies of books he wanted that were out of print and one year he and Maggie had ordered a magnificent tome on gardening for Maggie's mother as a sixtieth-birthday present. Why he should have chosen that book shop rather than another was, of course, now abundantly clear. He and Lavinia had evidently pored over volumes together and swapped literary aphorisms behind the dusty shelves of Bagshot and Newby. Maggie decided that she would undertake this particular mission on her own.

"You must dress up well," Esmeralda admonished her.

"Yes," said Zoltan, "the weather forecast is not good at all."

Maggie left Zoltan and Simona in front of the television watching *Ben-Hur*. Esmeralda wrapped a shawl around her neck and patted her arm reassuringly. It was such a comfort, Maggie thought as she went downstairs, to close the front door behind her and know that they would all be there when she came back.

She decided to walk from Jeremy's flat to South Audley Street. She went up the steps to the front of the shop and turned the large brass knob on the door. It creaked open and a bell started chiming above her head like an old-fashioned grocer's, such as Ginger & Pickles.

It was rather dark inside after the stark light of a winter morning in London. Maggie looked around but there appeared to be nobody there. Piles of books teetered on the round mahogany tables and there were pillars of books on the floor in front of the overstuffed shelves. A gas fire was making a sizzling noise in the grate.

"Good morning," said Maggie loudly.

A figure emerged from a door at the back of the shop and looked at her over his spectacles like a vole caught in the headlights. "Good morning," he said.

"I am looking for Mr Bagshot," said Maggie.

247

"That's me. I'm Desmond Bagshot," he said. He shook her hand.

Maggie couldn't help noticing that he had a cobweb adhering to the crown of his head.

"I've been downstairs going through somebody's library we've just been offered," he said by way of explanation.

"Lavinia," said Mr Bagshot, when Maggie had explained the reason for her visit. "Ah yes, Lavinia . . . She left here a long time ago, I'm afraid. When she got married."

"Do you happen to know her married name?"

"I should, you know, but I can't remember right now. Derek might know." He went over to the door at the back of the shop and called downstairs, "Derek!" A prematurely balding young man appeared looking harassed and even dustier than Mr Bagshot. "You wouldn't remember Lavinia Thorpe's name now she's married, would you?"

"Lady Lavinia? She married a foreigner, I believe."

"Do you have her address?" asked Maggie, who was becoming impatient.

"Oh, no, we wouldn't have her address any longer, I shouldn't think. We might have the address where we forwarded some of her mail after she left. I'll have to consult our files." Derek dived under one of the mahogany tables and pulled out a large box. "I'll have a look and let you know," he said, "Do we have your number?"

Reluctant for many reasons to give her name, Maggie told them she would call them next morning and took her leave. She might feel up to telling them she was Jeremy's wife and reminisce with them about his taste in literature another time.

On her way home she stopped on impulse at Fortnum & Mason to buy crumpets. She would introduce her new family to something very English. The old Maggie would have queued at Sainsbury's, but the born-again Maggie delighted in making her purchases standing on a pile carpet and carrying them away in stiff little green carrier bags. As she walked past the wine department she heard a voice that sounded pleasantly familiar.

"So tell me," said Luc, who was sitting with his back to her at a little table covered with an array of bottles, "do you sense the blackberrees?" He was holding a glass up to the light, swirling it around vigorously. So vigorously, in fact, that she was afraid he would splash the anaemic cheeks and pinstriped suit of the Fortnum wine buyer sitting opposite with his ruby-red wine.

It was on the tip of her tongue to call his name, but Maggie had been a professional wife too long to interrupt a man about his business. She stood watching for a while, secretly hoping that he would turn around and catch her eye, but he was engrossed in sniffing and slurping and spitting his wine into a silver spittoon. "Luc, I still have your jacket," she wanted to say, and found herself smiling in anticipation.

"Can I help you, Madam?" asked a voice at her elbow.

"Ah, yes," said Maggie turning regretfully away. "Crumpets?"

"Crumpets would be over there, Madam, on your right."

When Maggie returned, her carrier bag dangling from her wrist, the broad back in his tweed jacket was nowhere to be seen. The wine buyer was busy collecting the bottles and putting them into a room at the back. Maggie sighed and stepped out into the street.

By the time she got back to the flat, she found that Zoltan and Simona had gone to *Holiday on Ice* and Esmeralda was sitting, hard at work, behind the sewing machine. Maggie toasted her crumpets and found an old jar of Marmite to spread on top, just as she had done as a child.

She thought of her childhood in Herefordshire and found herself swamped by a wave of nostalgia for the swing in the massive oak tree, Spud, her golden retriever, *Listen with Mother* on the radio and her mother's scones with home-made strawberry jam. She remembered how she would sit with Sue on the flaccid old sofa chewing Nuttall's Mintoes and smoothing out the papers on her knee, listening to the voice on the radio saying: "Are you sitting comfortably? Then I'll begin . . ." It was a voice that held in its measured cadences the promise of the safe permanence of a world she never wanted to end.

Maggie went to Esmeralda's room, her fingers still greasy from the crumpets, a dab of Marmite adhering to her nose.

"Dona Margarida," said Esmeralda gently, rising from behind her sewing machine, "what on earth have you been eating?"

"Lady Lavinia left an address in Kent," said Derek when she called next day. "Chilham. It's a village near Canterbury."

"Zoltan, we'll go down tomorrow," said Maggie. "Somebody there is bound to know whatever happened to Lady Lavinia."

Next day, it was Simona who seemed definitely the worse for wear. She had evidently caught Maggie's chill and they left her in Esmeralda's care. Maggie drove, as Zoltan confessed he had never driven an English car. He sat on the edge of his seat, clearly nervous at every change of gear. He had mellowed slightly by the time they reached Kent and was enchanted by the countryside, by the narrow roads winding between green hedgerows, the cottages with their gardens tinged with frost. "It must be beautiful here in spring," he said.

On the way to Chilham, Maggie took Zoltan to visit Canterbury Cathedral. Suitably awestruck, he walked around the tombs of the kings of England lying in state on their slabs of stone. "Like Arpad, the founder of the Magyar nation," he told her solemnly.

Maggie didn't like to tell him that they reminded her rather more of Simona and herself laid out on the massage beds at Ilonka's beauty salon.

251

They stopped for lunch at a pub in Chilham where Zoltan was considerably less impressed by the cuisine. He had never seen a brussels sprout before and couldn't understand why they had not let it grow up to be a cabbage. "You'll like the treacle tart," said Maggie to cheer him up.

"But why does it have this yellow veil all over it?" asked Zoltan dubiously, scooping up the custard with his fork. Like a true Hungarian, he pronounced all his "v"s like "w"s, smothering the treacle tart in a yellow whale.

Maggie asked him if he had news of Ilonka.

"Ah," he said jubilantly, "the Turkish ambassador's wife sued her. She lost all her foreign clientele. She has had to charge Hungarian prices. When Simona went the other day, Ilonka wanted to know where Pandora was. Who's Pandora?"

"I think she knows who Pandora is," said Maggie.

Zoltan lit his customary cigarette and let out the smoke in rings. "Do you think they have *pálinka*?" he asked.

"No, I don't," said Maggie, "and I don't think you should be drinking it at this time of day anyway." Zoltan shrugged and inhaled his cigarette with gusto. "Zoltan," said Maggie hesitantly, "there is something I have to ask you." He looked up in alarm. "Did you blackmail the ambassador?"

"I didn't have to," said Zoltan. "He was so afraid you might find out, not to mention the embassy. It was he who offered me the job."

"I see," said Maggie, suddenly relieved. "Let's go, shall we?"

Maggie had earmarked an older man who looked as if he had been many years behind the bar. "I'm looking for a family called Thorpe," she said.

"Oh, yes," said the publican, "Lord and Lady Thorpe. They used to live at the big house over there."

"They don't live there any more?"

"No they sold the property about fifteen years ago," he said. "They were getting on, you know. They went to live in a cottage down the road. I haven't heard of them for quite a while." He went into detailed instructions ending inevitably with "you can't miss it".

Maggie and Zoltan left the car outside the pub and walked through the village until they came to a country lane with a group of cottages at the end. "It must be this one," said Maggie. There was the pond the publican had mentioned on the front lawn. They went through the wooden gate and up the path to the front door. There were children's toys littered all over the porch.

"Hello," said a shy young woman who opened the door. A dog shot out barking shrilly and two little children tried to crawl between her legs. "Oh, no," she said, when Maggie explained who she was looking for, "Lord Thorpe went away after his wife died a year or two ago. His daughter came and sold up the cottage and I heard Lord Thorpe was put in a home. He couldn't manage on his own any more, you see." The old people's home was about ten miles away, she said, but she didn't know what it was called. It was a big white house on the hill.

"There it is," said Zoltan triumphantly, as he and Maggie drove round corners and down country roads that were beginning to look all exactly the same. They made their way up the drive lined by ancient elder trees.

"I think it might be better if you waited in the car," said Maggie, looking doubtfully at her companion. He didn't look like the kind of person to whom a British matron might be persuaded to divulge any information.

"No, I'm afraid I can't give you Lady Lavinia's address," said the matron severely from behind a large desk. "I believe she lives abroad now, but we receive our monthly cheque from a bank in London."

"Doesn't she ever come and visit her father?" asked Maggie in surprise.

"No, not since the day she brought him here. I understand they did not get on very well and after her mother's death Lady Lavinia severed all ties. He is a rather difficult man."

"I see," said Maggie, visibly disappointed.

"Actually, now you mention it, her husband was down here last week with his son. The boy wanted to see his grandfather. I am afraid the visit was not a success."

"Oh, why was that?"

"Well, Lord Thorpe mistook the young man for his batman during the war and started berating him for not cleaning his shoes properly. We had to restrain him as he started throwing all his shoes out of the window. They all landed on the agapanthus and the gardener was most upset."

"Could I see him?" asked Maggie. "He might remember me. I was at school with Lavinia, you see."

"Well . . ." the Matron hesitated. "I don't see how there could be any harm in that. It might do him good."

They went down a corridor and Maggie felt the familiar dread at the smell of institutions, a combination of disinfectant and stale cooking faintly reminiscent of mutton.

"He is not always very lucid, I'm afraid," said the matron, leading the way. "He has his good and bad days."

Lord Thorpe was sitting up in bed in blue and white striped flannel pyjamas. His face, which must once have been handsome, was flushed and blotchy, his white hair standing up like a halo around his head. He was clearly having a bad day. His eyes took on a menacing glitter as Maggie and the matron entered the room. "What do you want, you trollop?" he asked in a rasping voice.

"Good afternoon, Lord Thorpe," said the matron. "This lady has come to ask after Lavinia. She was an old schoolfriend."

"Ah!" shouted Lord Thorpe. "Ah, Lavinia, eh? You would want to know about Lavinia, wouldn't you? You always wanted to know everything about them all, about Lavinia, about Bertha, about Ines . . ."

"I think he has mistaken you for his wife," murmured the matron.

"Quiet, you harlot," yelled an irate Lord Thorpe. "You were always spying on me, weren't you?" He fixed Maggie with a malevolent stare. "Looking through keyholes, always listening to the telephone, you were always jealous of the women I loved. But I still managed to trick you, you have no idea how many times I managed to trick you!" Lord Thorpe started laughing a harsh laugh that ended in a fit of coughing.

"Maybe it is all too much for him," the matron said to Maggie, who started to rise to her feet.

Lord Thorpe immediately recovered himself. "As for you, you little whore, I know what you want!" His lordship sprang out of bed. He had evidently wriggled his way out of his pyjama bottoms, because his lower half was completely bare. A hugely lubricious erection was protruding from under the last button of his pyjama jacket.

Maggie got into the driving seat next to an expectant Zoltan. "The trail," she told him, "has gone cold."

She and Zoltan drove back to London in silence. They drew up outside Jeremy's flat, and Zoltan got out; Maggie was taking the car to the garage.

"Tell Simona that the avenging angel is folding up her wings," she said. "I don't see how we can ever find Lavinia now."

It was a subdued group that sat around Jeremy's coffee table that evening, glumly partaking of Esmeralda's *bacalhau*.

256

"I don't know what to do now," said Maggie dismally. "I have to find some way to earn a living and pay all these bills." Esmeralda had put a stack of envelopes by her plate. She perfunctorily leafed through them one by one.

"Can I have the stamp on that one for my nephew?" asked Zoltan, pointing at an envelope at the bottom of the pile.

Maggie picked it up. "It's from New Zealand," she said. She ripped open the envelope with her finger, something that had always irritated Jeremy who regularly used a paper knife. "My goodness me," she said. It was a letter from Appelyard and Crosby, Isobel's solicitors. Maggie was, the letter informed her, Isobel's sole surviving heir. Maggie passed the letter to Zoltan.

"But, Modome," he said, his eyes on the second page, "you now own a farm in New Zealand." They all looked at each other stunned.

"Does anyone want to move to New Zealand?" asked Maggie. She was met by blank stares.

"But look, read here," said Zoltan. "They are making an offer for the farm which they urge you to accept," his eyes widened in shock, "for one million pounds sterling."

"Oh, Maggee!" Simona laughed. "You're a millionaire."

Maggie sat back, letting the news sink in.

"With that money," said Zoltan, "you can start a business, like I am going to do in Budapest."

"But I'm not really interested in used tyres," said Maggie.

"Not used tyres." Zoltan assumed an air of elaborate patience. "You can open a fashion business, an art gallery, anything you like."

Simona put down her fork. "Why don't you open an agency specializing in matrimonial investigations?" she asked. "Like Tom Ponzi in Rome, where I used to work. It's not as though you didn't have enough experience." She laughed. Everybody turned to look at her. Maggie's first thought, instantly banished, was that Jeremy would have found something definitely seedy about an investigative agency.

When Esmeralda brought Maggie her tea next morning she was already wide awake. The more she thought of it, the more she liked the idea of their very own matrimonial investigations agency. "We'll call it Pandora's Matrimonial Investigations Agency," she told Esmeralda as she sipped her tea.

"Oh, Dona Margarida," sighed Esmeralda, waddling out of the room.

Zoltan and Simona always rose later in the day and Maggie spent the intervening time packing Jeremy's papers into boxes and lining them up beside the front door. She waited until Zoltan had drunk his coffee and rubbed his cigarette round three times in a circle before she said. "We are going to have a bonfire."

"They have forecast rain," said Zoltan.

The boxes full of Jeremy's papers were carried downstairs to the car one by one. It had been decided to make a weekend of it and Maggie was going to drive everyone down to Herefordshire. She wondered what Sue and Jim would think. Sometimes she felt like Dorothy in *The Wizard of Oz*, a film she had often watched with Delia's little boys in Alexandria. She too now had a motley following of loyal companions.

The weekend turned out to be a huge success. Jim helped them make a bonfire at the bottom of the garden and he and Zoltan chopped up an old fence and some fallen branches to add zest to the flames. They all stood around warming themselves at the blaze and watching Maggie's marriage go up in flames. She gazed at the smoky curlicues of wispy blue and green as they escaped upwards into the night sky. Twenty-five years of honourable service to Her Majesty's Government would soon be smouldering embers, together with twenty-five years of dishonourable infidelity.

The bonfire triggered memories for everyone. Esmeralda told about the village feasts in the Alentejo when she was growing up, Zoltan remembered burning the husks of corn in their farmyard on the Puszta, Simona recalled the fires they used to make with the fallen chestnut leaves on the hills of the Castelli Romani. Sue thought of Guy Fawkes night when she and Jim were courting. For Maggie it was her first bonfire of any significance and it was magnificent.

As the others turned back towards the house, she surreptitiously brought out Jeremy's urn. She would scatter his ashes on top of the pyre. "Goodbye, Jeremy," she whispered. The ashes in the urn mingled with the ashes of "Papers — Jeremy", looking exactly the same. Ashes to ashes, she thought. Surely the last twenty-five years could not have been a huge, unfortunate mistake, smouldering at her feet under the night sky? Couldn't she be like a phoenix and rise from the ashes? She heard a loud snuffling noise behind her. It was Esmeralda, thwarted of her moment of explosive grief at the ambassador's funeral, who was not going to let this occasion pass without the requisite tears.

Maggie rubbed her arm. "Do you remember in Rome when you said we should bury Caesar?" she asked her.

"Yee-es," sobbed Esmeralda.

"Well, I think you meant the hatchet," said Maggie.

Afterwards, when they were all indoors again, Sue made mulled wine and brought out home-made ginger biscuits. Esmeralda chivvied Sue out of the kitchen and roasted two of the family's chickens. Zoltan renewed his acquaintance with the brussels sprout. Jim opened a bottle of whisky and Janet and Daisy put some of their music on, insisting that everybody join in the dancing. Simona told jokes in Italian which Zoltan translated into English and everybody laughed as they became more and more nonsensical as the night wore on. They all sang "Auld Lang Syne". As Maggie climbed into bed, still humming, she realized that her hair smelled strongly of woodsmoke.

Perhaps no man or woman found their ideal in one single person, she thought as she drifted off into a fitful sleep. Perhaps Jeremy had found elegance and comfort with Mausie, who represented the local establishment, making him feel a member of the right club; glamour and good food he had discovered with Delphine; intellectual stimulation with Arabella, who also hailed from the same *Kinderstube* as the Germans called it, someone who had shared the same background, while with Ilonka he had had sex, what they called seamy sex . . . A composite of perfection which no woman on her own could achieve. What had she, Maggie, represented for Jeremy, she wondered. How dreadful if she had been just the perfect diplomatic wife following meekly in his wake. Hopefully, Esmeralda was right. Jeremy had also found Maggie fun.

That night, she had another dream. This time she was in Venice walking alongside the Grand Canal when she saw Jeremy lying in a gondola in his new lilac and grey striped pyjamas. One elegant hand was trailing in the water. "Jeremy," she shouted. "Jeremy!"

He turned to look at her. "It's time for me to go," he said, looking at his watch with a characteristic gesture: Jeremy was long-sighted and held his wrist far from his face, slightly tilted to avoid the reflection on the glass.

"But why, Jeremy?" Maggie called out in her sleep. "Why?"

"I loved you very much, my dear," said Jeremy and Maggie saw to her dismay that the gondola was beginning to sink. Water started lapping around Jeremy's bare toes and washing overboard.

"Goodbye," said Jeremy.

"Wait," Maggie screamed, "wait . . ." The water was gurgling around Jeremy's neck.

"There is something you ought to know," were her husband's last words. The waters of the canal closed over Jeremy and she saw the gondola sink to the dark bottom, the pale oval of his face still visible below the surface. All that was left of her husband were concentric rings spreading out over the surface of the water.

Next day in the car, the Pandora Matrimonial Investigations Agency became reality. It was Zoltan's idea that initially at least, the offices should be Jeremy's old flat in Ebury Street. "It is a smart address and it's furnished in a comfortable, elegant way." Then, if the venture took off, they could look for new premises. Zoltan, it was agreed, would be their foot soldier, shadowing the errant husbands and if need be insinuating himself into offices and apartments. Simona knew what the average charges were for services of this kind, having worked for Rome's most famous investigative agency. As her prices were somewhat out of date and this, after all, was London, they promptly raised them by twenty-five per cent. Simona would be in charge of the accounting. Maggie would receive clients in Jeremy's sitting room wearing one of her Paris ensembles.

"And I will open the door," said Esmeralda, "welcome our clients and bring refreshments."

"And we will all be partners in Pandora's Matrimonial Investigations Agency," said Maggie.

The four partners sat in a row in front of the desk in a solicitor's office which they had found in the yellow pages. London was one city where Zoltan had no friends. The solicitor looked uncertainly over his spectacles at the little group, his poised ballpoint pen wiggling in hesitation. "Won't there be a problem with the gentleman who is Hungarian?" he asked.

Zoltan threw back his shoulders. "Hungary is now officially a member of the European Union," he said proudly.

Afterwards, at the pub, they toasted their new venture with champagne.

"Viva Maggee!" said Simona.

"Viva Pandora," said Esmeralda.

"To a great partnership!" said Maggie.

They went to work that same afternoon. Maggie decided to put an advertisement in *Harpers & Queen* and *Tatler*. As an afterthought, she also put one in *Horse & Hound*. You never knew what people would get up to after too much stirrup cup with all those haystacks around.

"Pandora's Matrimonial Investigations Agency," read the ad. "Utmost Discretion. Our fee will be returned if suspicions prove unwarranted."

Maggie had insisted on the last sentence. "People will be encouraged to come to us," she explained. "We are feeding on their hopes that their fears are unfounded and that their husbands have been faithful all along."

They found someone to make a discreet brass plaque which Zoltan screwed onto the door jamb next to the bell.

At Zoltan's suggestion, Maggie bought potted plants to enhance some of the emptier corners of the room. Offices always had plants in them, he said. She chose suitable music to put on the hi-fi. Restful and conducive to confidences, she thought, and eventually decided on Schumann. Mozart was altogether too lively and Rachmaninoff would make them cry, while she did not want her clients, like Lucy Honeychurch in *A Room with a View*, to be exposed to "too much Beethoven". Esmeralda prepared far too many little open sandwiches and deep-fried titbits which, no clients having arrived, they ended up eating for lunch.

At the end of the fourth day after the sign had been hung out and the advertisement published in the glossy magazines, the partners received their first client. The office was instantly galvanized. Esmeralda answered the door in the black satin dress and starched white apron she had worn in the embassy. Zoltan was sitting in the hall stroking his moustache with his long fingernail looking every inch the sleuth. He had taken to wearing gel in his hair, which he parted down the middle like a Chicago gangster in the thirties. Maggie was seated behind Jeremy's desk in the soft light of the table lamp, her legs neatly crossed with a diagonal slant, trying as hard as she could to look like Nancy Mitford.

The client was a tall woman in her fifties dressed in uncompromising tweeds. She had read the advertisement, she said, in *Horse & Hound*. She was sure, she told Maggie, that she had nothing to worry about and that was why she was there. "After all," she laughed, "you offer a money-back guarantee." It was just that lately her husband had been behaving strangely. He had never taken much care of his appearance, but now he had become quite the dandy. He had started wearing an objectionable brand of cologne. He kept telling her that he had to go away for a day or two to look at a horse, but they hadn't bought a new horse for years. He was always looking into space and never seemed to be listening when she asked him questions. And then she had found this — she produced an orange chiffon scarf — in his pocket. Had she asked her husband whose it was? asked Maggie. Yes, she had, the client said, and he had said he had found it entangled in the hedgerow and had put it in his pocket because he thought it might belong to a member of the hunt.

"I see," said Maggie. She pulled out a sheet of Jeremy's blue stationery and started writing. Name? Address? Age? How many years married? What else could she ask, she wondered. Had the husband any previous convictions?

The client, whose name was Marjorie, looked surprised. No, in thirty years of marriage she had never had cause to complain. Perhaps they should start printing out forms, thought Maggie. Esmeralda arrived with tea served in bone-china cups and some dainty sandwiches on a tray. Zoltan was summoned.

He bent low over Marjorie's hand and brushed it moistly with his lips. "Kiss the hand," he said.

As mollified as she had been by the ladylike Maggie and by Esmeralda's tea-cups, Marjorie now looked visibly startled. "Kovacs Zoltan at your service," he said blithely, clicking his heels.

It was agreed that he would leave for Sussex tomorrow with his assistant. There would of course be a deposit to be paid right away, something Maggie left with a regal wave to what she described as "the accounts department". Simona emerged from the dining room laughing beneath her blonde fringe in black leather pants and a skimpy T-shirt which revealed a few inches of plump midriff. Marjorie looked at her doubtfully as she signed her cheque and Simona gave her a receipt from the block they had had specially printed.

"We have an international clientele," Maggie said by way of explanation as Esmeralda helped Marjorie into her duffle coat.

"*Arrivederci*," she said cheerfully.

There was a certain amount of jubilation among the four partners as soon as the door closed behind Marjorie. Pandora and her Matrimonial Investigations had been officially launched. They finished off Esmeralda's sandwiches and Maggie sent Zoltan round the corner to the off-licence for a couple of bottles of Prosecco. He and Simona would go by car to Sussex, he declared, brushing away Maggie's doubts. "I have been practising."

They left next morning in Maggie's car, Zoltan wearing large dark glasses although, as he said with his accustomed gloom, the day promised to be wet and rainy. Maggie had persuaded Simona to wear neutral clothes and a hat covering her straw-coloured hair, so that she would pass unobserved, she explained without conviction. Zoltan had been issued with a brand-new British mobile phone which stuck out of the breast pocket of his checked jacket. Esmeralda and Maggie waved goodbye from the kerb. There were no more clients that morning.

At five o'clock that afternoon the telephone rang. Zoltan had evidently decided to speak with an American accent, like a character out of Dashiel Hammett.

"At fourteen twenty hours I followed the party from his home. He was driving a red Ford Focus." Zoltan quoted the licence plate. "He drove for forty minutes into the town of Brighton."

"That's pronounced Bryton, not Brigton," said Maggie. Zoltan paid no attention.

"In Brigton, the party checked into the Hotel Esplanade," he went on, "and approximately thirty minutes later, at fifteen hours forty-five, he exited from the hotel dressed as a lady."

"Dressed as a *what?*" asked Maggie aghast.

"As a lady, Modome."

"What happened next?"

"I followed the party on foot to a bar in a less elegant part of town. I followed him down into the basement, but it was a private club and they would not let me in. But I saw through the open door that there were a number of women sitting at the bar who seemed to be wearing wigs and did not look like women at all."

"You mean transvestites?"

"I believe that is the term, yes," said Zoltan. "I have taken photographs of the party before and after his transformation."

How on earth was she going to give this information to Marjorie? Maggie agonized. She dialled the number she had written on Jeremy's blue notepaper and rehearsed her speech as the number rang for a long time.

"Hello," said Marjorie's brisk voice. There was a deafening noise of barking dogs.

"Marjorie?" Maggie ventured. "It's Pandora."

"Oh, hello. Have you any news for me?"

"I'm afraid I cannot discuss the matter over the telephone. Could you come back to London so that we can talk about it in person?"

"Yes, I could I suppose. But is he or isn't he?"

"Let us say that it is an unusual situation," said Maggie.

Meanwhile, Pandora's Matrimonial Investigations Agency had acquired a new client. She was a mousy young girl who worked round the corner at the baker's shop for which Esmeralda had made the aprons.

"I'm not sure if I can afford this," she said, looking nervously around at the subdued elegance of Jeremy's flat. Esmeralda, who was intent on carrying in a cup of coffee and some digestive biscuits, started winking grotesquely behind her back.

"Well, I'm sure we can work something out," said Maggie soothingly. "We have a special tariff for people in the neighbourhood."

Louise was going out with a young man who worked in the estate agent's down the street, she explained. They had been seeing each other — Jeremy had always snorted when people used that expression, Maggie remembered — for two and a half years now. To be precise, it would be two years and one month and ten days. They had met on Valentine's Day, she said. Ben was always very attentive and they met at the pub every evening after work, but at weekends he went home to his mother's house in Richmond, he said, and he had never offered to introduce her to his family. Louise was beginning to think that he didn't take her seriously.

Maggie wrote down the details on another piece of stationery. "We'll look into it for you," she promised Louise, "as soon as our detective comes back from a mission in Sussex." Esmeralda patted her hand and told her not to worry. Louise looked relieved and took her leave. "Dona Margarida, we have two clients!" she said as soon as the door clicked shut.

Marjorie arrived from the country next day, flushed and clearly apprehensive. This time Esmeralda settled her onto one of the sofas and expertly mixed a gin and tonic for their client. Gently, Maggie told her the gist of Zoltan's investigation. She showed her the photographs which had come out remarkably well. She was not prepared for the storminess of Marjorie's reaction. She sobbed, she stamped her feet, she shouted abuse until, exhausted, she leaned back and closed her eyes in something approaching a catatonic state. Esmeralda topped up her drink.

"What I would suggest," said Maggie, "is that you talk it over with your husband. He is clearly going through some sort of mid-life crisis. Maybe he needs some psychiatric help?"

Marjorie's eyes flew open. "Psychiatric help, my foot!" she said. "He needs a kick in the arse!"

As Marjorie took her leave, slamming the door, and Simona totted up their first earnings in her books, Maggie began to wonder whether their first client could be considered a success or not. She had little time to dwell on the subject, however, as that day Pandora's agency welcomed another two new clients.

In fact Maggie was to discover that the city of London was full of aggrieved wives and angry mistresses, and in the two months since their inauguration the agency had never once had to return the deposit based on unfounded suspicions. Only with little Louise they were lucky. Ben really did go home to see his mother in Richmond at weekends, but the old lady had Alzheimer's and was being looked after by Ben's older sister. He had perhaps not felt ready to confess this to Louise. For several weeks after this revelation, croissants hot from the bakery were delivered daily to Pandora's Matrimonial Investigations Agency.

With many of her clients, Maggie became a friend and counsellor. She had become an expert, after all, in creating a new persona from the outside in and she shared this knowledge with a whole succession of unhappy women anxious to win back erring mates or to snare a new one. On Saturdays when the agency was closed, she took them shopping, concentrating in particular on the lingerie section of the big department stores. She took them to a hairdresser who was almost as skilful as the young man in Paris near the Place de la Concorde. Extreme cases she accompanied to a beauty salon for a facial and mask. Her most outstanding success was undoubtedly Evangeline.

Evangeline was a long-legged American girl from Boston married to a banker in the city. The daughter of a minister, it had never occurred to Evangeline that husbands could be unfaithful, and discovering that her British husband had a liaison had been a terrible shock.

Maggie took her firmly in hand. Evangeline's underwear, she discovered, was rigorously white cotton and she favoured sports bras so that her magnificent bosom would not bounce when she went jogging. Like all Americans, she abhorred any kind of hair on her body and used an electric razor daily on her legs and everywhere else. Maggie explained that this would only make her bristly and she took Evangeline to be pampered and primped in a beauty salon, before whisking her around the more exclusive lingerie departments of the capital. She must stop wearing trainers and tracksuits to go shopping in the morning, Maggie told her sternly. After all, Coco Chanel had said that one should always try to look one's best as you never knew when you might bump into your destiny.

Evangeline meekly joined a Cordon Bleu cookery class and Maggie even accompanied her to a cricket match. She also made Evangeline read the entire *A Dance to the Music of Time*, and regularly quizzed her on current events and the meaning of the universe. Floris drops, fragrant with tuberose, were sprinkled on little terracotta rings which were placed on top of what Maggie insisted should be pink bulbs in the table lamps in Evangeline's Chelsea flat. The trainers and tracksuits were banished altogether as jogging was abandoned in favour of yoga, and Evangeline relaxed at home in silky Indian trousers. Cashmere sweaters hugged the magnificent bosom which teetered over the top of a frilly balcony bra, and Maggie proposed bangles to jingle playfully every time Evangeline waved her square American hands. Maggie became Evangeline's Pygmalion. Everything she would have liked to have done to create the composite perfection of Jeremy's ideal she enforced on the compliant Evangeline. As a fortuitous afterthought she went out and bought her a book on the amatory arts of the Orient.

Meanwhile Pandora's Matrimonial Investigations Agency was an unqualified success. They no longer needed to advertise, as news of their exploits spread by word of mouth. Zoltan was complaining that he was overworked and delegated some of the cases to Simona who, not without difficulty, was learning to be less garish and merge nondescriptly into the crowd.

One afternoon, just after Easter, Maggie was sitting at her desk when Esmeralda came in furtively closing the door behind her.

"Dona Margarida," she said in a stage whisper, "we have a man!" She returned, ushering in a man in a tweed jacket and corduroy trousers, his hair standing up on end as he had evidently just removed his hat. He looked over his shoulder in panic, but the door had closed firmly behind him. He brushed his short strong fingers through his hair, which remained resolutely awry. He looked altogether crumpled and untidy, his tie askew, his blue denim shirt trying to escape from his trouser belt.

"Oh, *mon Dieu*," he said. "This cannot be true. *C'est une erreur*. I have made a mistake." He strode over to Maggie and took her hand, bringing his lips to within an inch of her fingertips. "I never thought I would find you again." It was Luc de Bosquières.

"Please sit down." Maggie smiled at Luc, unutterably happy to see him. "And tell me why this is a mistake."

"Ah, Schumann," he said, cocking his ear as he perched on the edge of his chair. "I have never been to an agency like this before. It is not what I expected. I certainly didn't think I would find you here." He started looking over his shoulder again at the door through which he had come. "I really don't want to take up any more of your time. I . . ."

At this point the door opened and Esmeralda came in carrying a bottle of Jeremy's Bordeaux on a tray with two long-stemmed glasses. "Oh, Château Palmer," said their guest, visibly mollified, "and 1961. *C'est magnifique!*"

"Let's drink to the mistake," said Maggie.

"So this is the mystery behind it all. The import-export. You are Pandora!" said Luc, his face breaking into smiles as he savoured his wine and feasted his eyes on Maggie in her new role.

"How is Attila?" asked Maggie.

Luc's face lit up. "Oh, Attila has been a big success," he said. "He and my prize sow have had twenty-one children already." He swirled the wine around in the glass and sniffed it noisily. "I met Evangeline at dinner last night," he said, "and she recommended I come and see you. Of course, I had no idea it would be you."

Maggie smiled at him encouragingly. "Now that you are here," she said, "why don't you tell me what the problem is?"

"I have come about my wife," said Luc, glass in hand, starting to lean back in his chair. "But it seems so strange telling you about it. Evangeline told me you were the best, the very best . . ." he said doubtfully.

"You told me you had been married for over twenty years?" asked Maggie. She had proper forms now and sat stiffly, trying to be professional, her pen poised.

"Twenty-three years," said Luc de Bosquières.

"And you think," Maggie couldn't think of any other way of putting it, "that your wife is unfaithful?"

"My wife is English," said her client, "but we live in France. As I told you, I have a little chateau in the Dordogne."

Again, Maggie tried to imagine what a little chateau looked like.

"But we also have an apartment here in London," he said, "and that has perhaps been a mistake." Another mistake? "Because you know, my wife, she missed England and her friends and she always spent a lot of time in London. Lately she has been spending nearly all her time here."

274

"But that in itself . . ." said Maggie soothingly.

"Well," Luc de Bosquières looked embarrassed. "She no longer wants to make love to me. *Merde, c'est vachement difficile.* It's so difficult to talk to you about all this. You of all people."

"But that could mean many things," suggested Maggie. Luc looked at her, astonished. Surely she understood that only another man could dissuade his wife from pursuing their conjugal bliss?

"And then there have been telephone calls. A man's voice. He hangs up when I answer."

"I see," said Maggie. "Well, look, you know, you may have nothing to worry about. I can send Zoltan around to investigate. What is your address?" Luc dictated an address in Knightsbridge.

"Is your wife in residence now?" asked Maggie.

"Yes, and so am I, but I can move into a hotel while the investigation takes place. I'll just tell my wife that I am going back to the Dordogne to oversee the grafting." He took a large sip of Bordeaux. "I never thought I would come here and do something like this." He looked so miserable, Maggie felt like reaching out and stroking his arm but resisted. "You see," said Luc de Bosquières, "I am someone who loves with all my heart. I believe in sharing everything with the woman I love. I have no secrets from her and I trusted her unreservedly. There are no half measures. For me there is no other way. Perhaps I am old-fashioned, *naïf?*" he said, looking at Maggie imploringly.

275

"Oh, no, you're not," said Maggie warmly, "not at all. I am like that too. That is the only way to love somebody . . ."

Her client looked up from his glass in surprise. "So you agree?"

"Oh, absolutely," Maggie said earnestly, a note of passion creeping into her voice. "I myself only ever loved one man and I trusted him completely. There is no other way."

"Your husband?" asked Luc.

"Yes. I was married for twenty-five years," said Maggie and, to her horror, she burst into tears.

Luc de Bosquières sprang to his feet. "Oh Pandora," he exclaimed, pulling a crumpled handkerchief from out of his tweed pocket. "Oh, *je vous supplie*," he said, pressing her shoulder with his strong hand.

Esmeralda made her entrance carrying a tray of what looked like freshly baked vol-au-vents. "Dona Margarida," she cried, thrusting the tray into their client's hands and taking a trembling Maggie into her arms. Luc de Bosquières stood there holding the tray in front of him, completely at a loss, until Maggie finally got a grip on herself.

"I'm so sorry," she said, "I'm never like this usually." She smiled up at him through her tears. He looked so hapless standing there with the tray held awkwardly in his hands that she found herself laughing. After a while, Esmeralda and Luc joined in. Their laughter must have been loud because Zoltan peered around the door to see what all the noise was about. "Oh," said Maggie, "Zoltan, look who's here!" Zoltan vigorously shook

Luc's hand. Esmeralda took the tray and passed around the vol-au-vents. They stood in a circle, their mouths full.

Maggie was the first to swallow and resume the conversation. "We will get to work right away," she said, "but you didn't tell me your wife's name?" She sat down and picked up her pen.

"My wife's name is Lavinia," said Luc de Bosquières.

It did not take Zoltan long to establish that everything in the de Bosquières' *ménage* was not as it should be. As soon as Luc was out of the house, his wife received a guest, a muscular young man with a swarthy complexion who looked about thirty-five. Zoltan followed him back to his flat in Earl's Court and then to his office in a merchant bank in the City next morning. Simona chatted him up at the pub where he had lunch. He hinted at a liaison with an older English woman but did not give her the impression he was averse to more than one fling at a time. Photographs were taken and an appointment made with Luc de Bosquières.

Zoltan was at his most professional. "The party returned home at nineteen hours. Half an hour later, a young Italian banker called Enrico Morozzi rang her doorbell and she admitted him. Cooking smells emanated from the apartment and then everything went dark. Enrico Morozzi returned to his flat in Earl's Court at two in the morning."

Luc was shown a photograph of Enrico Morozzi outside Lavinia's front door. Even Maggie, who loved Italians, had to admit he looked a little vulgar.

"*Quel mauvais goût!*" said Luc dismally. He was shown photographs of the pair dining in a little Italian restaurant in Soho. They were holding hands and the expression on Lavinia's face was unequivocal in its eloquence. Maggie stared at the photograph for a long time. She was not looking at Lavinia's expression; she was staring at her hair: Lavinia de Bosquières' long wavy hair was emphatically red.

Esmeralda and Maggie helped Luc into his coat sympathetically. Simona stood with his cheque in her hands and Zoltan bowed with the solemn face he had used for visiting dignitaries. They all escorted him to the door.

"I'm so sorry," said Maggie looking after him as he went downstairs.

He ran back and took her hand. "You have been so kind, Pandora," he said. "It was obviously destiny that I should meet you again. *Au revoir!*"

After office hours, Zoltan and Simona announced that they were going to the cinema. Esmeralda retired early. She said she had sewing to do, but her loud snores could be heard through the kitchen door. Maggie curled up on the sofa with a cup of tea and watched a sitcom on television. The doorbell rang. Maggie slipped on her shoes and went over to the door. "Who's there?" she asked anxiously.

"Pandora, it's me, Luc." He stood on the threshold, a bottle of Veuve Cliquot under his arm and a huge bunch of flowers in his hands. "Oh, you're still here. Thank God," he said.

He had confronted his wife. He had asked for a divorce. She had not offered any resistance. His marriage was at an end. He could not face going back straight away to his hotel. He wanted to thank her for her help, for setting him free. It was a terrible imposition, he knew, but did she mind if he spent an hour with her before he went back to his hotel room? She had been so kind . . .

Later Maggie could not explain it to herself how it was that Luc had never made it back to his hotel room. They had gone over to the sofa and he had opened the bottle of champagne. He had sat there squarely, his short fingers splayed out over his muscular thighs, and told her the story of his marriage to Lavinia.

She had been so English, he said, delicate as bone china with her white skin and this mane of dark red hair like a pre-Raphaelite painting. She had made him think of a mermaid calling to him from the waves with her soft musical voice, and he had felt so privileged to carry back this prize to his little chateau in the Dordogne. He himself, he explained to Maggie, was like a bear, so clumsy, so *maladroit*, he had always been afraid to harm this elfin creature when he crushed her to his heart. They had had a son, who was just like his mother. He sometimes felt they looked down on him, a country boy who loved working in the vines, visiting his pigs, walking with his dogs, drinking *un coup de rouge* with the locals in the village. His family went back nine centuries but they had always been rooted in the rich earth of the Dordogne. He was *rustique, quoi*, he knew

279

he was unsophisticated. Maybe it was his fault that his wife had found him so lacking in social graces, so *insortable*.

Maggie felt her heart going out once more to this wounded bear, so earthy and lovable, so honest, so spontaneous. Together they drank the bottle of champagne and she felt a warm aura surrounding them both as they sat there on the sofa.

He raised his glass. "You are such a beautiful woman," he said, and once again he reached to kiss her hand.

Later, Maggie couldn't remember what had happened in between, but she found herself sitting on the quilted chintz bedspread with this wounded bear by her side. She dimly realized that the situation had got out of control but, befuddled as she was by champagne and by this all-embracing warmth, it didn't seem to matter. Luc took her in his arms.

"You know," Maggie murmured, "I've rather forgotten about making love."

"*Mon amour*," said a voice in her ear, "it's like riding a *bicyclette*. You never forget."

Next morning, Maggie woke up to find herself alone in bed. She lay there reviewing the events of the night before and found herself blushing at the pleasurable memories this evoked. Her body felt bruised, her cheeks rough from Luc's abrasive embraces. She realized that it was late and Esmeralda had not yet brought her tea. The telephone rang. "Hello," said Maggie. "Who is it?"

"It's me, Evangeline," said a rapturous voice. "I just wanted you to know. St John and I have made up. He's leaving his mistress. He says he wants to make it up to me. And, I have to tell you, we made love last night and I have never had such a wonderful time in my life."

"Neither have I," said Maggie as she hung up and reached for her dressing gown.

She emerged rather sheepishly from her bedroom to find her fellow partners in Pandora's Matrimonial Investigations Agency all very much awake. Esmeralda was being waltzed around the floor by Luc who was looking even more rumpled than usual. Zoltan was smoking a cigarette and looking studiously unconcerned. Simona was jumping up and down, giving the thumbs-up sign behind Luc's back. "I am in love," Luc declared to the assembled company. "I want to marry you all!"

Luc booked himself on the first flight back to France to go and consult with his lawyer. He and Lavinia had been married in Paris, so their marriage would have to be dissolved according to French law. He promised them all he would be back as soon as he could and ran back up the stairs three times to kiss Maggie goodbye. Everybody was in a jubilant mood. Esmeralda sang in the kitchen, Zoltan forecast sunny weather and Simona was triumphant. "Viva Maggee!" she hooted at regular intervals.

The clients who brought their matrimonial woes to Pandora's office that morning were visibly puzzled by the atmosphere of euphoria that reigned on the premises. Maggie smiled idiotically at the procession of wronged wives that filed through Jeremy's drawing room, forgetting them as soon as they left. Esmeralda served *bacalhau* for lunch. The only person who didn't lose his head was Zoltan.

Luc called every day from the Dordogne. Lavinia was there, packing up her things, he said. Thank goodness he had Maggie because it was so heartbreaking to divide the memorabilia of a lifetime. Which book belonged to him, which CD to Lavinia? Hers were the towels with her initials on them, his was the antique shoe scraper that they kept by the front door. She had made no objection, however, to his keeping their whole collection of classical music and his well-stocked cellar of vintage wines. His lawyer was working on the case. He would obviously pay Lavinia whatever she wanted and she could have the apartment in London. He was having problems with his son. Although the boy was grown up and studying at Aix en Provence he was not at all happy with the state of affairs. Luc had not wanted to go into too much detail, but the boy seemed to be taking his mother's side. Luc was coming back soon, he said, as he missed them all. And Pandora, he told her over and over again, he loved with all his heart.

He would be arriving at 2.45 in the afternoon, he said, on the Air France flight from Paris. Maggie stood at the barrier waiting as the doors opened automatically and people spilled out pulling their luggage on wheels. There were mothers and children met by adoring grandparents, lovers clasping each other in the joy of reunion, businessmen walking wordlessly over to the drivers who stood in a row like the chorus at the opera holding up names stencilled onto boards. Every time the door slid open, Maggie felt her heart lift. She realized that she wanted with an almost unbearable longing to see Luc's thickset figure stride through the doors. After a while, the flow of arriving passengers trickled to an end and the door remained resolutely shut. He wasn't coming back. Of course he wasn't coming, he had changed his mind. It had all been too good to be true. Men always said they loved you, but they usually didn't mean it, Maggie knew; she had interviewed a large cross section of women in the preceding months. Maggie found herself weeping silently in utter disappointment, a feeling more wretched than anything she had ever known.

Suddenly, the doors slid open and Luc was standing there, his arms spread wide in a dramatic gesture. "*Mon amour!*" he shouted at the top of his voice.

Maggie had not been inactive while Luc was away. She had decided to rent a new flat somewhere on neutral territory, somewhere that would remind neither of them of their past lives and past loves. They would set out on a new life in Notting Hill. The rest of the family would continue to live in Ebury Street where Pandora's Matrimonial Investigations Agency would go on exactly as before.

She took Luc by taxi to their new home. She had furnished it with modern Italian furniture in a minimalist style. It was a complete break from everything she had known before, from the bourgeois comfort of Ledbury and the chandeliers of embassy residences and the staid conventional style of Jeremy's flat. Luc was enthusiastic. He lay down on the low Chinese lacquer bed and stretched luxuriously. "Oh, Pandora," he murmured, "please come into my arms." He had a hole in his sock, Maggie couldn't help noticing as she nestled in his embrace. From now on she would look after him.

After they had made love, they lay side by side looking up at their new ceiling. How true it was, thought Maggie with a sigh of contentment, that everything sexual was always referred to as French.

Luc reached out and drew her to him. "I'm so glad you are here," he said. "It has been very hard, putting an end to a life like this."

"I know," said Maggie quietly. "Did you tell Lavinia about me?"

"Yes, of course I did."

"Did you tell her my name?"

"Yes. She said she knew the name, but had never heard of anyone in the family called Pandora."

"That's hardly surprising," said Maggie.

"But for me you'll always be Pandora," said Luc.

"Didn't she ask what kind of person I am?" Maggie insisted.

"No, but I told her anyway. How beautiful you are, how sensual, how charming, how warm and kind, how loyal and steadfast, ma douce Pandora."

"Is that all? She must be dying to meet me," said Maggie drily.

284

Luc turned to look at her, dimly aware that he was being teased.

"She didn't ask any questions?"

"She wanted to know where you grew up and what school you went to. You know the English. They always want to know what school you went to."

Maggie thought back to the dark red pleated skirt and cardigan, the uniform of Malvern School for Girls. She had been on the hockey team. How cold it had been on the hockey field, how cold in the long flagged corridors where they had marched in single file, how cold in the classrooms where they had vied for a seat next to the radiator. How cold the school mistresses, withering on the bough of life. How silly it was to say that schooldays were the best in your life. Maggie realized that she was truly happy now for the very first time.

They would get married as soon as the divorce went through, Luc told her. A little private ceremony with Esmeralda and Zoltan and Simona as witnesses. He hoped his son would come too. "You must meet Jerome. I am sure the two of you will get on once you know each other. You are both English, after all." They would live part of the year in London so that Maggie could keep an eye on the agency and he could sell his wine, and the rest of the time they would be together in his little chateau. Maggie was going to love it in the Dordogne, he told her, striding up and down their new sitting room. She would love the old house and his dogs and his pigs. She would see Attila again and his growing family. They would harvest the grapes together and join the vine workers on the estate at long tables set out in the courtyard, to celebrate the new vintage.

"We'll eat *tripes à la mode de Caen*," said Luc, quite carried away.

"Tripe," wavered Maggie, a shadow momentarily passing across what had hitherto been a cloudless horizon.

"And we'll dance the java," Luc went on. He looked suddenly doubtful. "Do you know how to dance *le java?*"

"No," said Maggie, "but I do know how to tango."

Her family could join them whenever they wanted.

Maggie realized that he was not referring to Jim and Sue and the girls, but her family in Ebury Street. She was fully aware that Esmeralda and Zoltan and Simona saw her in a new light now that she had a man by her side. Why was it, she wondered, that women were considered more interesting if they had a mate? As a widow and cuckolded wife she had cut a sorry figure, she realized now. Zoltan treated her with renewed respect and Simona had got in the habit of winking at her and making a chopping diagonal motion with her hand, an Italian gesture signifying: "You sly dog, you, what have you been getting up to?" Esmeralda, meanwhile, was busy at her sewing machine, turning out linen sheets and monogrammed towels, determined, as Maggie's mother had been all those years ago, that she would not cross the threshold of the little chateau empty-handed.

286

★ ★ ★

Sometimes, she and Luc came over to Ebury Street for dinner. He insisted on helping Esmeralda in the kitchen, cutting up the onions and stirring the pans. After a while, however, he gently managed to reverse their roles. He was the chef, his square frame enveloped in a large apron that did not stay clean for very long, while a doting Esmeralda was demoted to the cutting board. Luc was a gentleman in the true sense of the word, Maggie reflected, as he managed this manoeuvre without in any way jarring on Esmeralda's Portuguese pride.

At home in their new apartment, after only one of Maggie's Sunday roasts, it was always Luc who cooked. To the volatile strains of Mozart issuing from the complex stereo system which had been his contribution to their love nest, Luc prepared delicious meals that Maggie's mother would have found inordinately "rich". Maggie had a pang of sadness when she thought of how proud her mother would have been: her daughter a French *comtesse*! How she would have lorded it over the ladies at the Women's Institute about Maggie's chateau, which would never have been described as small.

"Weep not for little Leonie!" Sue had teased her over the telephone from Ledbury, "abducted by a French marquis."

"He's a count, not a marquis," protested Maggie.

"Though loss of honour was a wrench, just think how it's improved her French."

"He speaks very good English, I'd like you to know," she informed her sister crisply.

One day Maggie came back from the office to find that Luc had installed a large easel in the corner of the room where the light was best. "You must start painting again," he said. "You are a true artist!" Maggie painted a powerful portrait of Luc which owed much to Lucien Freud, and which Jeremy would no doubt have found irremediably OTT. It was a far cry from the prim pen-and-ink likeness of her late husband, now languishing in storage in a London basement.

Luc flew back and forth to France often in the months that followed. He had business to attend to at home and his lawyer needed to consult with him on a frequent basis. Maggie became quite a regular at the barrier at the airport waiting for his flight to arrive. Luc was unfailingly the last off the aeroplane.

"Guess what?" he asked Maggie as he enveloped her in a bear-like embrace during one such reunion. "Jerome is arriving next week. He is coming to stay with his mother and he wants to meet you."

Jerome's flight was delayed. Luc and Maggie wandered around the airport killing time, looking at boutiques and novelty shops. Luc bought a copy of Le Monde. "You know," he said, "it is a pity you and I couldn't have a child."

Maggie felt the familiar ache that the subject of children never failed to provoke. "Yes," she said, "it is."

288

"He would have been a real Frenchman," said Luc confidently. "You will see, Jerome is a lovely boy, but he is very, very *anglais*."

In Maggie's imagination little Edward would have been rather English too, with his school cap and blazer and his knobbly little knees under the hem of his grey shorts, but these were things that were not worth arguing about.

They stood at the barrier watching the doors opening and shutting, disgorging the passengers from Paris. The moment the young man walked through the glass doors, Maggie knew with incontrovertible certainty that it was Jerome. He smiled as he walked towards them and, with soft fingers tapering to pink oval nails, raised Maggie's hand to his chin. She stared at the perfect parting above the high forehead of his young head bent over her hand. "You're late," said Luc patting him on the back.

Jerome looked at his watch, tilting it at an angle to avoid the reflection on the glass in a gesture that Maggie recognized only too well. He gave a little laugh out of the corner of his mouth. "Well, I hope I was worth waiting for."

"Oh, definitely," said Maggie.

She followed father and son out of the airport terminal, watching them patting and punching each other, the awkward way men have of showing affection, and her heart felt ready to burst.

And as she sat between the two men on the seat of the taxi driving into London, nursing a secret that she was condemned never to share with a living soul, Maggie reflected that, after all, Jeremy had had the last word.

ISIS publish a wide range of books in large print, from fiction to biography. Any suggestions for books you would like to see in large print or audio are always welcome. Please send to the Editorial Department at:

ISIS Publishing Limited
7 Centremead
Osney Mead
Oxford OX2 0ES

A full list of titles is available free of charge from:

Ulverscroft Large Print Books Limited

(UK)
The Green
Bradgate Road, Anstey
Leicester LE7 7FU
Tel: (0116) 236 4325

(Australia)
P.O. Box 314
St Leonards
NSW 1590
Tel: (02) 9436 2622

(USA)
P.O. Box 1230
West Seneca
N.Y. 14224-1230
Tel: (716) 674 4270

(Canada)
P.O. Box 80038
Burlington
Ontario L7L 6B1
Tel: (905) 637 8734

(New Zealand)
P.O. Box 456
Feilding
Tel: (06) 323 6828

Details of **ISIS** complete and unabridged audio books are also available from these offices. Alternatively, contact your local library for details of their collection of **ISIS** large print and unabridged audio books.